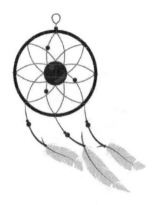

JOY'S SONG

A Bluecreek Ranch Christian Novel

By

Ruth Kyser

To my grandchildren,
and all those who will come after me.
With love.

Have not I commanded thee?
Be strong and of a good courage;
be not afraid, neither be thou dismayed:
for the Lord thy God is with thee withersoever thou goest.
Joshua 1:9

AUTHOR'S NOTES:

Several years ago I wrote the *True Cover* series. At the time, many readers asked if there was the possibility of a sequel somewhere down the road. Well, I've learned early on in my writing to never say 'no' to a question like that. Instead, I simply said it would depend if the Lord ever gave me another storyline I thought would fit.

Well, He did.

This time the story is from the point of view of FBI Agent Bill Parker, Sam Morgan's former employee and friend. It was fun to revisit the Morgan family and the beloved Bluecreek Ranch. Who knows? Sometime in the future, there may be another book (thus the subtitle for this book—*A Bluecreek Ranch Christian Novel*.)

If you haven't read any of the *True Cover* series books yet, I would suggest you at least read the first book in the series – *True Cover*. If you *have* read all three books in the series, then you will be totally up-to-date with the Morgan family when you begin *Joy's Song*.

Many thanks to my dear friend Michèle Lemière, who bravely took on the job of 'first reader.' Her sharp eyes and wise counsel is always appreciated, and I thank the Lord daily for her faithful Christian friendship. Without her help, *Joy's Song* would not be the book it is.

Again, many thanks to all my readers. Your constant encouragement and communication keeps me enthused about this crazy occupation called 'writing.' God bless you all!

All praise to the Father, the Son, and the Holy Spirit.

In Christ's love,
Ruth Kyser

JOY'S SONG

A Bluecreek Ranch Christian Novel

CHAPTER 1

It was the first time FBI Agent Bill Parker had ever arrived at the airport in Montana and not had someone waiting there to welcome him. But then, he hadn't let anyone know he was coming.

Bill supposed he should have taken the time to call his old friend, Sam Morgan, before he left Washington, D.C. He could have. But he hadn't wanted to answer all the questions he knew the former FBI agent would have for him as to why he was coming to Montana now.

Out of the blue.

When it came right down to it, Bill wasn't sure why he'd hopped on the plane with this destination in mind. He'd just known he needed to get out of D.C., and spending some time visiting his friends on a remote ranch in Montana had seemed like a good idea at the time.

Now that he'd arrived, he was starting to have second thoughts.

After collecting his luggage from the baggage area, Bill made his way through the busy terminal to the exit doors. Hopefully, he'd be able to find a cab that could take him to the bus station, then catch a bus that would take him to the town of Denning. That was as close as Bill was going to get to the Morgan family ranch without contacting someone at the ranch to come and get him.

But he'd worry about how he planned to get from Denning out to the ranch later. When he was ready to talk to someone.

It was the latter part of August, and as soon as he exited the airport terminal doors, the sun's heat slapped Bill in the face. Fortunately, an air-conditioned cab was parked and waiting for a fare just outside the doors. Bill threw his large duffle bag in the back seat and got in, then told the driver to take him to the bus station.

As the driver took off through the traffic congestion around the airport, Bill leaned back against the seat and released a weary sigh. He hadn't slept a wink on the plane and was currently running on fumes.

Maybe he'd get a room in Denning for at least one night before he attempted to get to the ranch. It might be best if he had his wits about him before he had to explain his sudden appearance to his old boss. Because there *would* be questions.

Samuel Clemens Morgan, and the owner of Bluecreek Ranch, was a former FBI Special Agent, and Bill's past boss. Sam had taught Bill everything he knew about law enforcement and the FBI, and Bill had nothing but respect for the man. Even though Sam had left the Bureau ten years earlier, Bill still looked to him as a mentor and would always consider him a good friend.

Which was why, when it came time to leave Washington, D.C. and get his head on straight, Bill knew he needed to come to Bluecreek Ranch, Sam's home in Montana. Sam and his wife Julie, would welcome him with open arms. They had always treated him more like a family member than a former employee.

But Bill also knew his old boss well enough to know that Sam was going to question why Bill had suddenly appeared in Montana and wasn't back in D.C. doing the job he'd been hired to do. Well, that was an excellent question. Too bad Bill didn't have a good answer. But he knew he'd have to work on coming up with a plausible explanation before he had to face Sam. And he knew whatever he told Sam, it would need to be the truth.

He'd never lied to Sam Morgan in the past, and he certainly wasn't going to start now.

It didn't take the cab driver long to navigate the city streets to the bus station. Bill paid the man, grabbed his bag, and entered the station where he barely had time to buy a one-way ticket to Denning. After purchasing the ticket, Bill hurried to get on the bus before the doors closed and the bus pulled out of the station.

Finally, settling into his seat, Bill released a sigh of relief. He'd made it in time. In about an hour, the bus should arrive in Denning, and then he'd have to figure out his next move. Maybe he'd get a room for the night at the local bed and breakfast in town. Tomorrow would be soon enough to decide what came next.

In the meantime, hopefully, he could catch a little shuteye, because he sure could use it.

♪ ♪ ♪

Isaac Newton Mosher, better known to his friends as Zeke, tossed the last of the supplies for the ranch into the back seat of the SUV, then tugged his hat down to block out the rays from the morning's sun. It felt like it was gonna be another scorcher.

He dug the crumbled piece of paper his boss had given him at breakfast out of his jeans pocket and read through the list one last time, making sure he hadn't forgotten anything. If he drove all the way back to Bluecreek Ranch only to discover he hadn't purchased all the supplies, Zeke would be furious with himself, and his boss wouldn't be any too happy either. His eyes slowly scanned the list, and he finally gave a satisfied nod. It looked like his mission was complete.

Stuffing the note back in his pocket, Zeke raised his head and glanced across the street, wondering if he had time to stop at the diner for a cup of coffee before he headed back home. It would give him a chance to check on Jack Byrd's niece, Joy. He'd given her a ride into town that morning, but seeing her working in the diner would give him an opportunity to see how she reacted to being around other people—and to make sure she was really doing as well as she kept telling everyone at the ranch she was. Because she was Jack's niece, that made her almost family. And family took care of family.

Usually, Joy would have driven her own car to work, but that morning, her car hadn't started. Since Zeke had been coming into town for supplies anyway, he'd offered to bring her in. Which reminded him, he needed to check out her car as soon as he got back to the ranch. Hopefully, whatever was wrong with it would be an easy fix. Zeke knew Joy didn't have any extra money for car repairs. And even though any number of people at the ranch—including Joy's Uncle Jack and Aunt Mary—would be more than happy to help Joy out financially, Zeke also knew that wasn't going to happen. Young Joy was every bit as stubborn and independent as her Aunt Mary Byrd was.

Zeke had just decided to go grab that cup of coffee when a tall, blond-haired man appeared across the street in his line of vision. The man was strolling down the sidewalk from the direction of the *Henry House,* the local bed and breakfast. About that time, the other man glanced up and spotted Zeke.

It *was* Bill Parker.

What's he doing in Denning?

"Hey, Bill!"

Upon hearing Zeke's yell, the other man grinned and raised his right hand in greeting. Zeke glanced both ways for traffic before trotting across the street to join him. After the two men shook hands, Zeke took a few seconds to study the other man. Bill looked much the same as the last time he'd

4

seen him—shortly after the twins' birth. That had been almost two years ago.

Bill Parker sure had made himself scarce at the ranch lately. But then, Zeke supposed he was a busy man, working for the FBI as he did.

"How ya doin', Bill? And what in the world are you doin' in Denning? Does the boss know you're in town?"

Zeke stopped talking when he realized he'd just asked the poor man three questions in a row. How did he expect Bill to have time to answer any of his questions if he just kept asking him more?

"Hey, it's great to see you too, Zeke. Naw. Sam didn't know I was coming."

Zeke noticed the redness creeping up the other man's neck and wondered what he'd asked that had the other man so flustered. He didn't know Bill exceptionally well, but he did know him well enough to know the former Marine and current FBI agent, didn't generally get rattled easily.

"Well, I was just going over to the diner and grab a cup of coffee before I head back out to the ranch. Wanna join me? I'll buy."

Bill gave him a smile and a nod, and the two of them made their way down the sidewalk to the front door of the small diner named *Peggy's Place*—a play on words as the owner's name was Peggy Place. A little bell over the door tinkled as they entered, and Zeke's eyes quickly scanned the room, nodding at several people he knew. Making his way through the crowded restaurant to a back corner table, he knew Bill was tagging along behind him.

"Let's sit here," Zeke said as he pulled a chair out and took a seat, then motioned for Bill to sit across the table from him.

They had no more than got settled when Joy Whitefox crept up to the table. Zeke noticed Bill's eyes grow wide as they fell on the little gal, and Zeke struggled to hold back his smile. There was no doubt about it; Joy was a cute gal. With her raven black hair and high cheekbones, snapping brown eyes, and gentle smile, she caught second glances from most every male in the county. But Zeke also knew how shy and easily spooked she was, so he sincerely hoped his friend didn't start teasing the gal and send her into tears. Zeke had seen it happen before, and he didn't want either of his friends to have to go through that embarrassment.

"Coffee for both of you?"

Joy kept her eyes glued on Zeke, even though he was sure she was well aware there was another man sitting at the table. That was her way of dealing with uncomfortable situations, though, so he wasn't going to make a big deal out of it.

Zeke gave her a quick smile and a nod. "Yes, please. And how about a couple of slices of that cherry pie I saw up there in the cooler?"

Joy's eyes briefly darted over to Bill, then landed back on Zeke, and with a timid smile, she gave him a nod and turned and left their table.

"Who was that?"

Bill's deep voice held more interest than Zeke wanted to hear.

"*That* is Jackson Byrd's niece, so I'd tread softly if I were you."

The other man must have caught the warning in Zeke's voice as he turned his gaze from watching the girl walk away back to lock on Zeke's eyes, a surprised look on his face.

"She's Jack's niece?"

"Yeah. Well, actually she's Mary's niece, but you understand how it is."

"Hmmm."

Zeke wasn't sure what that meant but decided to let the subject drop. It wasn't like Bill didn't know Jackson Byrd and how protective the man could be. And Zeke knew for a fact that Bill Parker was engaged to a beautiful woman back in D.C., so there really wasn't anything to worry about just because Bill was curious about the gal.

Besides, Zeke had more interesting things he wanted to discuss with the man sitting across the table from him. Like what he was doing in Montana.

Before he had an opportunity to start asking Bill any questions, though, Joy sidled back to their table with a tray with two mugs of coffee and two plates loaded with large slices of cherry pie—topped with large dollops of whipped cream. Zeke thanked her, and after she left with her eyes lingering on Bill a little longer than Zeke would have liked, he turned back to the other man.

"So, you gonna tell me what you're doing in Montana? And furthermore, why nobody here knows you're here?"

He watched as Bill chewed and swallowed a hefty bite of his pie, and waited patiently for the other man to answer his question. He was positive that if Sam and Julie Morgan, his boss and his wife, had known Bill was in town—or even that he was coming to Montana—everyone at the ranch would have been aware of it. Especially Zeke's wife, Jessica—Bill Parker's former partner at the FBI.

"I didn't know I was coming until I got here."

Zeke replayed Bill's words in his head and stared at the man across the table from him for a moment or two before responding.

"What in tarnation does that mean?"

He heard Bill's heavy sigh before the other man raised his head, his eyes locking on Zeke's.

"I needed to get out of D.C. for a while, okay? Things there weren't…going the way I thought they would, so I took a leave of absence from the Bureau for a bit. Thought I'd come out here and get things sorted out in my head."

"Hmm. 'Things,' huh?"

Bill sighed again, then shook his head as if he were tired—even though it was only nine-thirty in the morning.

"Not ready to talk about it, Zeke, my man."

Zeke fell silent for a few seconds, then picked up his fork and attacked his own piece of pie. He could live with that answer. For now. He knew what it was like to have

7

something eat away at your mind and heart until you were barely able to function. And by the haunted look on his friend's face, something was definitely eating away at him.

"Well, when you're ready to talk, buddy, just remember I'm here to listen."

He was rewarded by Bill glancing up at him, the corners of his lips raised into a small smile.

"Thanks, Zeke."

♫ ♫ ♫

Bill finished his piece of pie, just then realizing how hungry he'd been. That morning he had eaten a little of the breakfast buffet provided by the place he was staying, but he hadn't had much of an appetite at the time. Running into Zeke Mosher from the Bluecreek Ranch had suddenly anchored him again, and he'd found the taste of the pie and coffee Zeke had offered to buy for him had hit the spot.

He almost felt human again.

Zeke Mosher was a good friend. Bill had met him years ago when he'd come to the ranch to visit the Morgans. Zeke's dark bronze skin, short-cropped black curly hair, and black mustache, along with his dark brown eyes, spoke of his African-American heritage. But he was quite simply, a cowboy—through and through. The fact that he'd won the heart of Jessica Thorne, Bill's former partner, and dear friend, had always made Bill feel as if Zeke were more like a brother than a friend. And Zeke had always treated him as such.

Bill also knew Zeke had to be curious about what had brought him to Montana. He could almost read the questions in the man's eyes—especially the unasked questions. But Bill wasn't ready to dump his story on anyone yet. The wound was still open, and the pain too fresh.

Without meaning to, Bill allowed his eyes to scan the now-busy diner until they landed on the cute little waitress who had brought them the pie and coffee. So that was Jackson and Mary Byrd's niece, huh? She sure was gorgeous, but she acted like a lost little fawn—poised and ready to run at the least hint of danger. There was a story behind that look, Bill was certain. He hadn't been an FBI Special Agent for as long as he'd been without learning to read the signs of trauma.

His attention was drawn back to the man on the other side of the table when Zeke spoke again.

"So, I suppose you need a ride out to the ranch?"

Bill grinned. "Ever since the bus dropped me off last night, I've been trying to figure out how I was gonna get there without walking." He chuckled. "And I don't think I'm up to walking that far."

Zeke's deep laughter warmed Bill's heart. Zeke Mosher was a good Christian man and had battled long and hard to win the heart of Jessica Thorne. The two of them had their share of heartaches and pain during their courtship, and there had been a time when Bill had wondered if they'd ever make it together. But now the two of them were married with two small ones in their lives—twins born just two years earlier. Bill had a hard time envisioning the street-smart Jess he remembered from the FBI as a mother to two toddlers, but if he was going to be at the ranch for a while, he guessed he'd get to see her in action soon enough.

"So, how'd you get to Denning?"

"Came in on the bus late last night and got a room at the *Henry House*." Bill smiled as he remembered his late arrival into town. He'd been so tired, he hadn't really cared where he'd laid his head. Fortunately, the inn where he'd stayed was really comfortable.

"I was hoping someone would eventually wander in from Bluecreek, and I could hitch a ride. I really didn't want to call out there and ask for somebody to make a special trip to town to come and get me. I know you are all busy with work to do."

Zeke shook his head. "You know better than that, Bill." He picked up the bill from where it sat next to his now-empty plate and grabbed his ever-present Stetson from the tabletop where he'd placed it when they'd first come into the diner.

"All you had to do was call."

Bill grinned at him. "Don't have to now. You're here."

He clapped his hand on the other man's right shoulder, feeling the hard muscle beneath. Zeke Mosher was the foreman at the Bluecreek Ranch and had been for many years. It was easy for Bill to tell by the muscles underneath his denim shirt that the man knew all about hard work. Bill had seen him throw a rope around a calf and wrestle him to the ground like the animal was a puppy dog. The man amazed him.

Zeke chuckled as he finished paying the bill at the counter and plopped his hat on his head. Bill followed him out the door and across the street toward where a dark blue SUV was parked.

"Well, hop in and buckle-up, buttercup. We'll stop at the *Henry House* long enough for you to grab your stuff and pay your bill. Then we need to hit the road before they all think I've been kidnapped or run off with the money they gave me to buy the supplies."

Bill laughed along with the other man as he got in and snapped on his seat belt. He hadn't been sure at first about coming to Montana, but now he was beginning to think he'd made a wise decision.

Being around friends was sure to help. He hoped.

CHAPTER 2

Bill watched the scenery fly by as Zeke drove the SUV down the flat country roads outside of Denning. Zeke was chatting to him—sharing something about some new piece of farming equipment the ranch had recently purchased. But Bill wasn't really listening. He knew he should, but he couldn't get his mind to stop replaying his last few days in D.C.

The previous Friday evening, he had a date with Zoey Beckett, his fiancée. That night, Bill had no clue what was coming. He'd gone home after work and changed from his usual suit and tie into more casual dress clothes, preparing to take Zoey out to a movie and dinner. They'd had the date planned for a week. With their busy work schedules, they only seemed to find time to get together on weekends, so Bill looked forward all week to those times they could spend together.

But that night, he had hoped to talk seriously with Zoey so they could finally agree on a date for their wedding. He was tired of all the delays and waiting. They'd known each other for over three years and been engaged for almost two of those years. Bill was more than ready to make her his wife.

The first time he'd seen Zoey, Bill had been instantly attracted to her. But at the time, it hadn't been advisable for the two of them to get involved since she had been a part of

Bill's Field Team, and he had been her direct supervisor. Bill had always made it standard practice to never get romantically involved with someone he worked with. It caused distractions. And in his line of work, distractions got somebody killed.

Fortunately, Zoey had soon transferred to the Cyber Crime Division, so Bill hadn't had to break his rule about not dating a co-worker. She had evidently felt the same attraction to him that he had to her, because the first time he'd asked her out on a date, she'd immediately agreed. For the past three years they'd dated exclusively, and even though it had been two years since he'd asked her to marry him and she'd said yes, they'd never been able to settle on a date to make the event happen.

Bill had decided that the time had come to take action. He was tired of waiting.

But when he'd arrived at Zoey's apartment on the agreed-to time, it had been to discover she wasn't ready to go yet. He'd expected her to apologize and tell him she'd just arrived home, and it would only take her a few minutes to get ready.

Instead, she'd asked him to sit down, and she'd told him they needed to talk.

That was when Bill's whole life had changed. Zoey had quietly and calmly informed him that she had decided they needed some time apart. She'd decided she wasn't ready to get married. She was well aware Bill had been hoping to set a date, and she didn't want to string him along any further, so it was best if they split up.

Feeling as if his life was spiraling out of control, Bill had tried to console Zoey and assured her that it was okay. He wasn't in a big rush. If she needed more time, he'd wait. But she had been adamant. As he'd watch her pull off her engagement ring and reach out to hand it to him, Bill had felt the earth shift.

She was serious. Zoey had decided she didn't want to marry him.

Ever.

After that, he hadn't really remembered all she had said to him. He knew Zoey had told him she'd made a mistake, accepting his proposal. That they weren't meant to be together, and she'd known it. And that she was sorry.

All Bill could hear was a loud roaring in his ears that made him feel like he was underwater, struggling to breathe.

One thought kept running through his brain, though. Zoey was breaking up with him, so it must have been his fault. What had he done? Even though she kept telling him it wasn't because of anything he'd said or done, Bill hadn't believed her. He must have done something to make her change her mind, and if he could discover what that something was, perhaps it wasn't too late to salvage their relationship.

He could change whatever it was he'd done. And then maybe she'd come back to him.

Even though deep in his heart, Bill knew now that was a foolish plan, it had still been hard for him to believe it was over between them. He had loved her—he was looking forward to spending the rest of his life with her. Having a family someday.

And now. Now, she was no longer a part of his life, and somehow, he had to forget her.

Since they still worked for the same organization, and in the same building, it was a very awkward situation for him, though. Chances were good, Bill was going to continue to run into her, if not daily, at least weekly. And every time he did, it would be like having a knife stabbed into his chest all over again.

No, Bill didn't want to live that way.

So, after a couple of weeks of trying to avoid Zoey and attempting to mend his broken heart, Bill had finally decided he needed to do something. That was when he'd gone to his boss, Director Mark Roberts, and told him he needed to take some time off. Bill had simply told the Director that something was going on in his life that he needed to deal with if he was going to be able to continue to be an effective Agent. Director Roberts had finally agreed, and Bill had turned his Field Team over to another agent.

Then he'd packed his bags and left D.C. behind.

And somehow or another had found his way to Montana.

He glanced through the front windshield as Zeke turned down a dirt lane between two tall wooden posts with a familiar sign hanging above. The sign announced they had arrived at Bluecreek Ranch, the Morgan family ranch, and seconds later, the vehicle rumbled across the cattle guard Bill remembered from his previous visits.

Five more minutes of driving through open pasture land, and Bill could finally see the ranch buildings up ahead. Zeke pulled the vehicle up in front of the huge two-story farmhouse and parked. Then glanced over at Bill and gave him a toothy smile.

"Well, now you're gonna have to face the boss man and his questions." His deep chuckle filled the cab of the vehicle as he pushed open the driver's side door. "Good luck with that, man."

Bill frowned as he yanked open his own car door. Zeke was right. Bill could put off answering Zeke's questions, but he wasn't going to be able to stall when it came to answering Samuel Clemens Morgan's questions about what had brought Bill to Montana. Sam knew him too well, and Bill had known Sam long enough to be aware that eventually, he would have to tell Sam the whole story. That was the only thing that would stop the inquiries. When he'd still been at the Bureau, Sam Morgan had been known as one of the best interrogators they had.

Zeke grabbed Bill's bag off the back seat of the vehicle and handed it to him, gave him a little salute, then got back in and rolled down his window, his arm resting on the side of the SUV.

"Gotta take these supplies out to the barn to Jack. See ya later, Parker. Welcome back to Bluecreek."

14

Bill gave him a salute in answer, then a grin. "Thanks for the ride, Zeke-man. Talk to ya later."

Zeke backed the vehicle up enough to turn it around, and Bill watched him drive out back of the house toward where the large horse barn and other outbuildings sat. Bill knew there was also a bunkhouse located out there, along with several other buildings.

He was also aware there was a cabin located not far from the house where Jackson and Mary Byrd lived. Jack was the wrangler and blacksmith for Bluecreek Ranch, and Mary worked at the main house as the housekeeper, doing the majority of the cooking and helping Julie Morgan with running the household. The Byrds were more family than employees, though. Sam had told Bill often how he and Jack had practically grown up together as brothers.

Bill also knew that somewhere out on the ranch was a newer little house Zeke had built for him and Jessica to call home. Bill had yet to see that house, and he was looking forward to it.

Yup. It had been way too long since he'd visited.

Bill turned at the sound of a door opening behind him. Julie Morgan stood in the open front doorway, a look of surprise on her face. Then that expression was replaced with a huge smile, and Bill quickly braced himself for the impact of Julie grabbing him in a hug. She wasn't a very big woman, but could sure pack a wallop when she ran at you.

"Bill! It *is* really you!"

Julie pulled back and grinned up at him, pushing a stray wisp of her light brown hair out of her eyes. She looked around as if in confusion.

"When did you get here? *How* did you get here?"

Bill finally released the laughter he'd been holding back. Ever since they'd first met, he'd thought of Julie as a loving big sister, and she had always fascinated him. She was so full of life and joy—even though her life certainly hadn't been an easy one. And he knew that probably better than most people. She had never let it steal her joy from her, though.

"Zeke gave me a ride out from town. He just dropped me off and then drove back to the barn to unload supplies."

She grinned up at him. "So, Zeke's the only one who knows you're here?"

He chuckled. "Well, yeah—other than you, that is."

"Well, come on in the house, and we'll get you settled in. It's about lunchtime, and Mary and I were just gonna feed the kids, so your timing's perfect."

She glanced over at him as she headed up the steps into the house with him following.

"I still can't believe you're here. Sam's going to be thrilled to see you."

Her eyes got big as if she'd just remembered something. "Oh, and Jess too!"

She grinned again. "We'll have Zeke, and Jess, and their boys come over to the main house for tonight's meal so you all can catch up."

Bill just nodded and tugged his duffle bag higher on his shoulder as he tried to keep up with the woman walking beside him. He knew from past experiences that when Julie Morgan got that look in her eyes, that it was best if you didn't get in her way.

But hopefully, having Zeke and his family around at supper tonight would hold off Sam's questions a little longer. Maybe by then, Bill would be ready to answer them.

♫ ♫ ♫

After stowing his gear in the downstairs guest bedroom just off the front entry hall as Julie had directed him to do, Bill made his way down the hallway and through the great room at the back of the house that served as the main living area. The other times he'd stayed at the ranch, Bill had slept in one of the four bedrooms upstairs. But now that Sam and

Julie had kids, he figured they'd redone this downstairs room to use as a guest room, and it appeared quite comfortable.

As he walked through the great room, Bill glanced around him. The room had always fascinated him, boasting a tall vaulted ceiling with vast wooden beams running its length. Tall windows that looked out toward the barnyard filled one wall near where a long trestle table sat. A massive stone fireplace took up the majority of one end of the room, and an arched opening acted as a divider between it and the large kitchen.

He would have stopped and looked around more, but was presently headed for the back door. Bill figured he'd wander out to the barn and see if he could find out where Zeke had disappeared to earlier. Or maybe he'd run into Jack Byrd out there somewhere.

Hopefully, Sam would still be out on the ranch working someplace. Not that he didn't want to see his old friend. Bill just wasn't anxious to have to face the man yet.

Bill could hear the sound of Julie's and Mary's voices coming from the kitchen, along with the higher-pitched voices of Sam's and Julie's two children. Samantha was their eleven-year-old daughter and looked like her beautiful mother. C.J. was their five-year-old son and was named after his grandfather—Clayton Frederick Morgan Junior. C.J. for short. He was, according to anyone who had known him back then, the spitting image of Samuel Morgan at that age. Bill adored both of the Morgan children and hoped to have the time to get to know them better while he was visiting.

As Bill made his way through the room, he saw Julie peeking through the open doorway between the kitchen and great room. As soon as she saw him, she gave him a smile and a brief wave as he motioned to her that he was headed outside. He'd visit with Mary and the kids a little later. Right then, he craved some fresh air.

His hand on the doorknob, Bill stood for a moment and eyed the row of Stetson hats on hooks near the back door, then shook his head and opened the door and went outside. Just because he was visiting a ranch in Montana, that didn't mean he was a cowboy. He'd manage just fine without a hat on his head.

Stepping down the stairs leading to the back yard, Bill paused a moment and let his eyes take in the view in front of him. The big barn lay to the left of the house, with pastureland spreading for miles beyond it. Next to the barn were fenced-in paddocks, where several horses were milling around, their tails flicking around—probably chasing away the ever-present flies.

Bill knew from the past times he'd visited Bluecreek that most of the horses would currently be out on the range, ridden by the menfolk to do whatever they did on the ranch. He didn't understand much about ranch life but knew from what Sam had told him over the years that Bluecreek was a working ranch, and most of the time, the hands rode horses to go out and tend the livestock, mend fences, etc. The ranch did have several four-wheelers they occasionally used, but many of the places they needed to go were more easily accessed on the back of a horse. Since he'd never been a rancher, Bill figured he'd just have to take Sam's word for that.

As Bill took a deep breath of air, he felt his body relax. Even the air smelled different in Montana. There was an earthier odor to it, which he assumed was because of all the cattle, horses, hay, and all the things that went with horses and cattle. But it was an easier air to breathe—without the obnoxious smell of car exhaust and too many people crammed into a city.

It wasn't all bad being back in Montana.

He strolled across the yard in the direction of the barn, noting the hot sun was still beating down, which made him wonder if he should have grabbed one of those crazy cowboy hats, after all, to protect his head from the brutal sun. It certainly hadn't cooled off any.

Once Bill reached the partially open big wooden doors of the barn, he paused a second or two before entering and allowed his eyes to adjust to the darker interior. When Bill did step inside, the smell of hay, leather, and horses hit him full-force. He was glad no one was around to see him wrinkle his nose at the odors. But what did they expect? After all, he *was* a city boy, and clearly out of his comfort zone.

He could hear the sound of muted voices coming from the rear of the barn where Bill remembered Jack Byrd had a forge set up to do his blacksmithing. Hearing the sound of metal hitting metal, Bill headed in that direction. Hopefully, Jack could take a little time off from his work to chat for a bit. Bill had always enjoyed talking to the Native American man. The big guy could be more than just a little intimidating when he wanted to be. Bill had met a lot of scary men in his line of work, but there was something different about Jack Byrd that had always kept Bill on his toes whenever he was around him. Jack was a good man, Bill knew. But he didn't think he'd ever back down from protecting those he cared about, which wasn't all bad as far as Bill was concerned.

The sound of Jack's hammer ringing on iron resonated through the barn then stopped entirely. Based on the voices he'd heard when he'd first entered the barn, Bill had to assume Jack was talking to someone instead of working. That was good. Then he wouldn't feel so bad about interrupting him.

Sure enough, when he reached the rear of the vast building, it was to find Zeke and Jack, sitting on bales of hay and chatting, their muted deep voices echoing quietly through the building. Zeke saw Bill first and gave Jack a little punch in the arm. Then they both stood to meet Bill, hands outstretched.

"I heard you were back in Montana," Jack said, his deep voice steady as he firmly shook Bill's hand, his dark eyes studying his face. Bill was always amazed at the strength he felt in those calloused hands of Jack's. The man had to be Sam's age or older, but you wouldn't know it when you shook his hand.

Jackson Byrd was a man who had a great deal of Bill's respect. Sam had shared a little of Jack's early life on the reservation, but Bill knew there was probably much more to the story of how he and his wife Mary had ended up at Bluecreek Ranch. He'd never felt brave enough to ask questions about it from the man himself, though. Jack was a tall, dark-skinned, muscular looking man. Not a speck of gray hair had colored his jet-black hair, and his square chin and long noble nose spoke of his heritage.

Bill also remembered that Jack was a well-known tracker in the area and was often called into the search for a missing child or an adult who had wandered off the path. He'd seen the man in action himself years earlier when Julie had been kidnapped by a crazy man out to kill Sam Morgan and his kin. Jack had been instrumental in tracking the man directly to his hide-out, and they'd been able to capture him and save Julie without even firing a shot.

"I was just tellin' Jack I ran into you in town and dragged you back to the ranch with me," Zeke gave him a wink. "Not sure what we're gonna do with you now that we got you here, though. If I recall, you aren't a fan of spending much time on the back of a horse."

Bill chuckled, strangely touched at the camaraderie he felt from these two men—men very different from him— men he hadn't seen or talked to in several years. Yet they greeted him almost like he was family.

"You would be correct in that memory, Zeke. I spent enough time on a horse the last time I was here to last me a lifetime. But while I *am* here, I'm sure Sam will come up with something to keep me busy."

The other two men laughed along with him, and Bill took a seat on a bale of straw across from where they sat, hoping Zeke and Jack would go back to whatever they were discussing when he'd arrived. Bill wanted to get a feel for what was happening on the ranch, and he'd learned a long time ago, the best way to find out what was going on was simply to listen.

"Sam doesn't know you're here yet?" Jack turned his dark eyes on Bill, studying him as if trying to discern why an FBI Agent had shown up unannounced on the ranch.

"Nope. Thought I'd surprise him and Julie."

"Any particular reason *why* you're here?" Jack's eyes still studied him carefully.

And Zeke was now staring at Bill too as if waiting to see what his answer would be.

Bill grinned, hoping a little humor would lighten up the atmosphere. Good heavens. He hoped they didn't think he'd come here on official FBI business.

"Just here for a visit, boys—nothing at all to do with the FBI, I promise." He dropped his head for a few seconds to stare at his running shoes, remembering he'd have to dig out the boots he'd bought the last time he was here.

"I just needed to get out of Dodge for a while, and figured it was time I come to see everyone here before Zeke's twins are all grown up and heading off to college."

That earned a few chuckles, and before Bill knew it, the other two men were back to chatting about what was happening on the ranch. They told Bill about the new tractor Sam had bought earlier that summer, and Zeke and Jack shared worries about a couple of mares that were due to foal any day.

Bill just sat on the bale and let the calmness of the barn sweep over him. Here, there was no job to do—no bad guys to take down—no paperwork to complete, and no phones incessantly ringing. He could just unwind and enjoy the cool, refreshing breeze blowing through the open doors of the barn and contemplate what he was going to do now that he'd arrived.

Good question. Too bad he didn't have an answer.

CHAPTER 3

Sam Morgan stood in the barn and finished brushing down his horse Rusty, made sure the animal had plenty of water and oats available and gave a wave to the other men as he exited the barn. He knew the other men would head to their bunkhouse after they finished tending to their own horses. It was standard practice that every man took care of his own horse. Jack kept the tack in good order, kept the horses shoed, and otherwise in good health, but it was each man's responsibility to unsaddle, groom, and take care of his own animal at the end of the workday. That was the way Sam's father had run the ranch, and his grandfather and great-grandfather before him. Sam wasn't about to change something that worked.

As he exited the barn, Sam released a weary sigh. He was sure glad it was Friday night. It had been a long, hot, tiring week, and even though there would still be work to do tomorrow, hopefully, it would be a more leisurely day.

Sam tugged off his Stetson and pounded it against his dirty jeans, hoping to remove at least some of the dust before he went into the house. Mary and Julie wouldn't appreciate him tracking half of the ranch in through the back door.

Stopping to hang his hat on one of the hooks just inside the door, Sam paused for a moment to inhale the smell of good food that emanated from the kitchen. Then the sound of a deep voice from that part of the house caused him to perk up his ears.

He recognized that voice.

Instead of going directly upstairs for a hot shower as he'd intended, Sam bee-lined to the kitchen where he was met at the open doorway by his lovely wife, Julie.

"I thought I heard the back door."

She stretched up on her tip-toes to give him a kiss, then smiled as she turned toward the man sitting at the end of the kitchen counter on a stool. Samantha and C.J., Sam's and Julie's children, sat one on either side of him.

"Look who showed up this afternoon," Julie continued as she looped her arm through Sam's arm and led him further into the kitchen.

Bill Parker stood, and his blue eyes met Sam's while he reached out to shake Sam's hand. Sam chuckled and grabbed hold of the offered hand, then pulled the man in closer for a quick back-slapping 'man-hug.'

"Special Agent Bill Parker! What are you doing here, man?"

Sam gazed into the eyes of his former team member—one of the finest men he'd ever had the privilege of working with. Bill hadn't been to the ranch for a few years, and Sam was more than shocked to find him sitting in his kitchen now. He hadn't had any idea Bill was coming for a visit.

The younger man had the grace to blush a little before giving Sam one of his trademark grins.

"I had some vacation time coming to me, and I figured I'd better come to visit you folks before these kids of yours are all grown up."

He reached out to place a hand briefly on the head of Sam's five-year-old son who, in turn, glanced up at the big man next to him, his grin wide. It was easy for Sam to see that even in the short time Bill had been there that he'd gained the admiration of young C.J.

Sam continued to stare at Bill, his mind evaluating everything the other man had said so far. Sam had already noticed the weary look on the other man's face and the haunted look in his usually bright eyes. Bill could talk all he wanted about this visit being a vacation, but Sam was reasonably certain there was something else going on in his former co-worker's life that had led him to Montana.

"Well, we're glad you're here, Bill."

He glanced over to see Mary Byrd, Jack Byrd's wife, quietly watching the interplay—a gentle smile on her face.

"I trust the ladies have made you feel welcome and found someplace for you to bunk?"

Julie nudged him in the ribs as if to remind him she was standing right next to him. Like he needed to be reminded. Thoughts of his lovely wife were never far from Sam's mind, and he was more aware of where she was than anyone else in the world.

"We put Bill in the downstairs bedroom—if that meets with your approval, Mr. Morgan," she said in her quiet voice, giving him a smile and Bill a wink.

"That sounds like a good plan." Sam glanced down at his dusty boots and sighed.

"Give me a chance to go shower and change, Billy-Boy, and then we can do some catching up." He reached out to lightly punch the other man in the arm.

"But it sure is great to see you!"

♫ ♫ ♫

Bill watched Sam Morgan exit the kitchen, then returned to his seat on the kitchen stool and released a quick sigh of relief. He'd been worrying ever since his arrival how Sam would react to him showing up unannounced at his

25

ranch. Oh, he'd known Sam would welcome him—that wasn't an issue. He just didn't know what Sam would think about his coming for this little visit—claiming to be using some of his unused vacation time. Sam knew him about as well as anyone in the world, and would likely see through his pretense.

Yeah. There would be more discussion between the two of them later, Bill was sure about that.

He turned from watching Sam walk out of the kitchen to find both Mary's and Julie's eyes on him as if they'd understood the significance of Sam's parting words.

"Sam looks good," he finally said to break the silence of the room.

Julie gave him a smile. "He's happy here, working on the ranch. Originally, I wasn't sure how he'd adapt to leaving law enforcement, but he seems quite content."

She chuckled, and the sound brought a smile to Bill's face as she added, "There's never a dull moment on the ranch, so it's not like there's time to get bored around here."

Mary Byrd spoke up then. "I'm sure Sam will love having another pair of hands around, Bill. There's always more work to do on Bluecreek then men to do it."

Bill laughed. "Yeah, well. If you remember, Mary, I'm not a cowhand. I can ride a horse, but that's just about it. You won't find me out on the ranch roping any steers."

He watched Julie push her daughter Samantha's dark brown hair behind her ear to get it out of the youngster's face. The two young people had been sitting quietly at the kitchen counter, eating cookies fresh out of the oven and drinking glasses of milk, watching the adults, and quietly listening to their conversations. He'd never seen two more well-mannered children. They didn't interrupt, they didn't make noise, but their eyes and ears were taking in everything the adults were saying. Sam and Julie had done a fantastic job of raising their two kids so far.

Moments later, Bill heard the sound of more people coming through the back door. Bill stood and headed toward the great room, knowing that area was where everyone would congregate. He also knew they'd be seated around the long trestle table—at least until after the evening meal was eaten. The ranch hands always ate their evening meals over at the bunkhouse, but the family members ate their evening meals together.

Jack Byrd had arrived, along with Zeke Mosher and Jessica, his wife—Bill's former partner. Zeke and Jess each grasped the hands of one of the two little toddlers with them, and Bill had to smile at the sight of Jess acting her part as a mother so well. The two little tykes were cute—sturdy little bodies topped by black, tightly-curly hair that signified their African-American heritage from both their parents. And there was no question as to who their father was. The little guys looked just like Zeke—even had their father's toothy grin.

As soon as Jess saw Bill, she relinquished the hand of the one twin to her husband, then rushed across the room to grab Bill in a bone-crushing hug.

"Zeke called me when he got back from town and said you were here! I couldn't believe it!"

Bill returned Jess's hug, then released her, and stepped back to get a better look at her.

"You look pretty good for having two rug rats to raise, Jess," he said. He felt his face crack in a huge grin when he saw her eyes narrow, and a look crossed her face that told him to be careful what he said next. He remembered that look well.

Jess *did* look good. Married life and being a mom obviously agreed with her, and he couldn't remember seeing her look more contented. Of course, probably ol' Zeke had something to do with that. Bill was pleased his two dear friends had found each other—and through each other, found happiness. Their early days together hadn't been easy, he knew—remembering a time when Zeke had come to D.C., looking for Jess, who had disappeared from his life right before they were supposed to get married. They'd finally discovered Jess called off the wedding and left Montana to infiltrate a gang to try and save the sister to her old partner, who had been killed early on in her career. Jess and the young woman had finally gotten away from the gang, but Bill knew it had taken Zeke sometime before he was ready to trust her again with his heart. They'd come through their adversities, though, and their marriage now appeared to be a strong one.

However, Bill had recently come to the conclusion that blissful married life was not something that was going to happen for him.

As the two little guys, each one hanging onto one of their father's hands, got vocal, Jess turned and picked up the closest one.

"Have you met our little angels yet?" She gave Zeke a wink before turning back to smile broadly at Bill.

"I haven't. Although Zeke sang their praises all the way from town."

Zeke picked up the remaining toddler and moved closer to where Jess stood in front of Bill.

"This little guy is Charles Isaac Mosher—better known as Charlie. And Daddy's holding Benjamin Isaac Mosher, usually called Ben, unless he's in trouble—which happens frequently." Bill had to hold back a grin as he saw Jess roll her eyes in that way he remembered from when they worked together. "Then he gets to hear his full three-part name. These two keep Momma *very* busy." She gave Bill a huge grin. "But I love every minute of it."

Bill reached out to take hold of the hand of each little guy, one at a time, shyly offered for a handshake, their dark eyes studying him as if trying to figure out if he was a good guy or somebody they should be afraid of. When Bill had finished shaking the little hands, he was relatively sure his hand was covered in drool and some unknown sticky substance and tried to unobtrusively wipe it on his jeans.

"They're very handsome, Jess. How did that happen? Must be they got all their good looks from you, huh?" He gave Zeke a wide grin.

"Hey!" Zeke reached over with his free hand and gave Bill a playful punch in the arm. "I think they look more like me than Jess."

Jess laughed at both of them. "I agree with Zeke on this one, Bill. Our boys are the spitting image of their Daddy—which I think is a good thing since he is one handsome man."

Bill was saved from having to come up with a comeback to Jess's observation as right then, Mary and Julie came into the room from the kitchen and motioned for everyone to take seats at the long table. Bill found himself seated between Jack Byrd and Zeke, with Julie and Mary sitting directly across from him. Sam was sitting at the head of the table—a few chairs away, so that meant that at least during the meal, Bill would be excused from being interrogated by the man. The other side of Zeke sat Jess, with the two little guys in highchairs. Next to Julie sat daughter Samantha and next to her, sat young C.J.

That was when Bill realized who was missing.

"Hey, where are Clay and Lottie? I just realized they're not here."

After losing his first wife and Sam's mother Laurie, years earlier, Clay Morgan, Sam's father, had married his second wife, Lottie, three years earlier. Bill realized with a pang that Zoey had been with him for that visit as they'd come for Clay's and Lottie's wedding. A little twinge appeared in the vicinity of his heart at the remembrance that back then, he'd been so incredibly optimistic about his own future with Zoey.

Well, that was history, and he might as well forget about it.

Bill's attention was pulled back to the present by the sound of Zeke's chuckle.

"If you can believe it, they're on a cruise. Lottie's been able to get old Clay to travel more than I can ever remember. It seems like they're always gallivanting off someplace else."

Julie smiled across the table at Bill. "They're due back home tomorrow, Bill. You'll get to see them, I promise."

Then it grew quiet around the table as Sam stood from his chair to ask the blessing, and Bill bowed his head and closed his eyes in preparation.

"Father God, we come to You in thanks for another day—filled with family, good friends, and hard work. Bless this food You have once again provided for us—and bless the hands that prepared it. And we especially thank you for the presence of our friend Bill, who has surprised us with a visit. We ask all these things in Jesus's name, Amen."

A chorus of 'amens' echoed around the table, and hands started passing the platters filled with food. Bill took a dinner roll before reaching for the bowl of fruit salad headed his way. He placed an ample spoonful of the salad on his plate and passed it along, then reached for the next dish coming from the person seated beside him. One thing about eating at the Morgan table, you never went away hungry.

The conversation around the table ranged from the most recent purchase of a new bull for the herd to Mary's and Julie's plans for the next day that included canning vegetables from the garden.

During a lull in the conversation, Julie posed a question directly to Bill that brought everyone's attention to him.

"Do you know how long you're going to be able to stay, Bill? Hopefully, this is more than just a quick visit like it's been in the past."

Bill raised his head to find everyone's eyes locked on him as if waiting for his answer. He slowly finished chewing his bite of food and swallowed. He'd really hoped no one would start asking him questions during dinner.

"Uh, I'm not sure. I think I should be able to stay a couple of weeks, at least. If that's all right."

"Good." Sam's deep voice came down the table as Bill turned to look toward where he sat. Bill knew Sam's gray eyes were studying him. Even at this distance, Bill could feel the force of his perusal. "You know you're welcome to stay as long as you want, Bill. And that way, we should have a chance to get caught up. Right?"

Bill gave Sam what felt like a half-hearted grin. "Sure. That'll be great."

He was saved from further questions from Sam as Jess started asking Bill about people she used to know at the Bureau, so Bill spent the rest of the meal catching her up on shared acquaintances.

By the time dessert was served—warm chocolate brownies covered with scoops of ice cream—Bill was feeling a little less stressed about his upcoming talk with Sam. He didn't know when it was going to happen, but he felt reasonably sure Sam wasn't going to postpone it.

After everyone finished their meal, they all helped carry the dirty dishes and what few leftovers there were to the kitchen. Bill watched as Zeke scooped the twins out of their highchairs and carried them into the great room, then sat on the sofa with one on each side of him and started to read a book out loud. C.J. curled up in the corner of the sofa near the cowboy to also listen to the tale. The sight of Jess's husband surrounded by the three boys brought a smile to Bill's face. That was what life should look like.

It wasn't long, and Mary, Julie, Jess, and with Samantha helping, shooed the menfolk out of the kitchen—stating they'd finish the cleanup.

Jack announced he was leaving anyway as he had to run into town to get his niece Joy, who was getting off work. Bill knew from what Zeke had told him earlier that he and Jack had been able to fix the problem with Joy's car—it had just been a loose battery cable. An easy fix. But, of course, someone still needed to give the young woman a ride back to the ranch tonight.

Released from more kitchen duty, Bill headed back toward the great room and plopped down in one of the comfortable chairs near the fireplace. He planned to spend a little downtime relaxing after eating all that delicious food. It had been quite a while since he'd eaten such a large meal, but Mary Byrd was one good cook. It was a wonder, Jack, her husband, wasn't overweight. But the man was as slim and trim as he'd been the first time Bill had met him, years earlier. Hard work tended to do that to you.

Bill had no more than leaned back against the rear of the chair when Sam strolled into the room and stood directly in front of Bill. He tried to ignore the other man by shuttering his eyes closed, but Bill quickly realized he wasn't fooling anybody. It was only seconds later when Sam cleared his throat and spoke directly to him.

"Time for our talk, Bill. Why don't you follow me to the office where we can have a little more privacy and won't disturb everyone else?"

Sam's chin moved a bit in the direction of Zeke reading to the boys on the sofa, and Bill heaved a sigh of surrender before giving him a nod.

It looked like his reprieve was over.

CHAPTER 4

Joy Whitefox, whose official first name in the Crow/*Absároke* tribe was *Daasitche Uuxdaake*—meaning *Happy Fawn*—saw her Uncle Jack's dark blue pickup truck pull into the diner's lot and park in front of the building.

"Goodnight, Peggy," she hollered, so the older woman who was Joy's boss would know she was leaving.

She heard a muffled 'goodnight' from the back room as she grabbed the backpack off the counter that she always brought with her to work, then exited the diner. As Joy slid into the front seat of her uncle's truck, the lights were already going off inside the restaurant, and she could see Peggy locking the front door.

Peggy Place had been a real friend to Joy since she'd hired her a year earlier. When Joy had first walked into the small diner, hunting for employment, Peggy had at first appeared coarse and uncaring. But after working with the woman a few weeks, Joy had quickly learned that Peggy had a soft side. And once the other woman had learned what had happened to Joy to cause her to leave her home on the reservation, she had quickly taken Joy under her wing.

"Thanks for coming to get me, Uncle Jack."

Her uncle turned toward her, and in the light of the parking lot, Joy saw the love reflected on his face.

"No problem. By the way, Zeke and I got your car fixed."

Joy released a sigh of relief. At least when she had to come back to work in the morning, she wouldn't have to bum a ride off someone else. She hated having to ask for help—even if Uncle Jack was family.

"So...how much did it cost?" She hated to ask. What little she was making as a waitress wasn't nearly enough if she ever wanted to get out of Montana.

"Nothing."

When Joy turned and gave her uncle a frown, he just smiled back at her and chuckled.

"I'm telling you the truth. It didn't cost a cent. There was a loose connection at the battery. We tightened everything up and cleaned the posts, and the car started right up—first try."

He smiled as he added, "I'll pick up a new battery cable the next time I'm in town and the car part store's open."

"Thanks, Uncle Jack."

It was quiet in the cab of the truck for a time as the wheels rolled down the highway, taking them deeper into the night. Now that she was finally off her feet, Joy allowed her tired body to relax. It would be so easy to drift off to sleep, but she didn't want to sleep now. When she got back to the ranch, she still had things to do.

"By the way, who was that guy I saw with Zeke Mosher earlier today? Some big guy with really short blond hair. They came into the diner for coffee and pie."

Her Uncle Jack's loud laughter took Joy by surprise.

"'Some big guy,' huh?" His laughter became a deep chuckle. "Little one, *all* guys are bigger than you."

Joy grinned back at him, loving the sound of her uncle's laughter. She couldn't argue his statement, though. She *was* a short person and had struggled for years with functioning in a world made for taller people.

"Okay. I admit you've got a point there. But regardless, who was he? I've never seen the guy around before—yet he and Zeke acted like best friends."

Her uncle glanced over at her briefly before turning his eyes back to the road.

"Yeah, well, they've known each other for a long time, so they're pretty close. The man's name is Bill Parker. Jess Mosher used to work with him before she and Zeke got married. So, did Sam. Back then, Sam was Bill's and Jess's boss."

Joy's mind spun as she took in all the information her Uncle Jack was throwing at her. If this Bill Parker had worked with Jessica Mosher and Sam Morgan in the past, then that meant this Bill guy must work for the FBI too.

"Oh."

Knowing that about the man, Joy suddenly didn't want to ask any more questions about him. If he worked for the FBI, he sounded like a scary dude, and Joy didn't want or need any more scary dudes in her life.

"Bill Parker's one of the good guys, Joy. You have no need to fear him."

Always surprised when her Uncle Jack picked up on her emotions without her ever saying a word, Joy gave a little nod in the dark. Once upon a time, she'd thought someone else had been a good guy, and that hadn't worked out so well.

She heard her uncle's sigh from the other side of the cab, and it held frustration—whether at her or the circumstances, she couldn't tell. She hated that her aunt and uncle worried about her. She wanted so badly to be a brave person—willing to go out into the world and forget everything that had happened to her. She was working on it, but then moments like this would remind her she still had a long way to go.

"Bill's gonna be staying at the ranch for a few weeks, Joy, and you have no reason to hide from him. Just go about things as normal. Live your life like you have been. It will be fine. I promise. And if you happen to run into him sometime, talk to him. He's a fine man. He would never do anything to hurt you. He puts people that hurt other people into prison."

Joy chewed on her lower lip and tried to still the fear attempting to overtake her.

"Okay. I'll try."

But having a stranger at Bluecreek Ranch was going to upset the quiet, safe life Joy had finally built for herself. It had taken her more than a year to get to where she was emotionally. Now with a stranger living on the ranch, it felt as if she were starting all over again.

♫ ♫ ♫

Sam pushed open the door to his office located off the front hall of the house and motioned for Bill to enter the room ahead of him. Bill really wanted to turn around and go someplace else.

Anyplace else would do. Even the barn with the horses.

Once through the door, Bill dawdled a bit, taking the time to glance around him. This was the first time he'd ever been invited into the 'inner sanctum' of the business part of the ranch.

"Nice office, Sam."

Sam gave a little nod as he stood just inside the door, his eyes watching Bill's every move.

"I don't spend as much time in this room as I used to since Julie took over most of the ranch's bookwork." He gave Bill a little smile. "I still think of it as my dad's office, you know, even though he's turned the operation of the ranch over to me."

Bill saw Sam's eyes drift toward the large desk. "I can't see that desk chair without seeing my dad sitting in it behind the desk."

He sighed. "Of course, Pop is still around the ranch and helps out—when he's home. But he doesn't really spend any time in here anymore—even though I've offered to let him be a part of running the show." He chuckled. "I think he and Lottie are having too much fun for him to want to run a ranch anymore."

Nodding, Bill looked around more at the room. Sam's office was a nice-sized room with overflowing bookshelves that ran along two walls. The previously-mentioned sizeable wooden desk sat at one end of the room, and a leather sofa and two leather chairs sat along the outside wall where a wall of windows looked out over the ranch.

As they moved further into the room, Sam pointed in the direction of those chairs.

"Pull up a chair, Bill, and relax."

Bill watched Sam take a seat in one of the chairs and prop his feet up on the matching ottoman in front of it. He plopped down in the chair next to Sam's, wondering if Sam really expected him to feel relaxed in this room. It was obviously Sam's domain.

"So, you came for a little visit."

Sam Morgan's steely gray eyes were locked on Bill's face, and he immediately felt the intensity of them. How could he have forgotten why Sam was so good at his job as an FBI Special Agent? If Bill lived to be a hundred, he'd never be the agent Sam Morgan had been back when he was at the Bureau.

"Yup."

"Using a little of that accumulated vacation time you've been saving, huh?"

Bill gave a little nod in agreement. "Uh, huh."

Maybe at this point, silence was the best mode of action, Bill decided. The less information he volunteered to Sam, the less trouble he'd be in. Hopefully.

It was quiet between the two men for a few seconds, and Bill had a sinking sensation that he'd best enjoy the silence while it lasted. He knew from past experience that Sam was nowhere near done with him.

"So, how's Zoey doing?"

He hadn't seen that question coming and suddenly felt as if he'd been hit in the chest with a sledgehammer. Bill raised his head to find Sam watching him. When Bill didn't say anything right away, Sam just nodded and leaned back in his chair.

"Hmm. So that's how it is, huh?"

Bill swallowed hard, determined to not lose it in front of his mentor. He kept reminding himself that he was fine. He wasn't great, but he was still breathing. And he'd get over losing Zoey. He knew he would. Someday. Maybe.

"She decided she didn't want to marry me," Bill finally ground out the words between clenched teeth as he tried to hold back his emotions. He all but snorted in his frustration.

"Three years of my life, I've spent planning my future—our future—around her. And then she just up and tells me she doesn't want to be engaged to me anymore. That she's decided she isn't ready for marriage—to me, or anyone else. But certainly not to me."

Bill shook his head, fresh pain rushing through him as he replayed his last conversation with Zoey Beckett. He still couldn't believe she'd said those things to him. He'd thought she loved him. Well, he'd certainly been wrong about that.

Sam leaned forward, dropping his eyes from Bill as if he couldn't stand to look at him. Well, Bill felt that way about himself. What was wrong with him that the woman he'd loved for so long would just dump him?

"I'm sorry, Bill."

He kept waiting for Sam to go on—to tell him it was for the best; that Zoey hadn't been the right woman for him after all; that God had someone better planned for his future. He just needed to be patient and wait. Bill had spent hours telling himself those same things, but it hadn't helped lessen the pain any.

But Sam didn't say anything other than those three little words.

I'm sorry, Bill.

Somehow that meant more to him than any platitudes Sam might have offered. Bill had told his story. Sam had listened. And Bill knew from those three simple words, that Sam understood his pain.

After a few more moments of silence, Bill heaved out a weary sigh, feeling as if he could finally breathe. He'd told Sam everything, so he didn't have to pretend anymore. Sam knew him well enough to understand how hurt the incident had left him.

"I'm not just here on vacation, Sam. I took a leave of absence from the Bureau. I couldn't stand to be there in the same building with her right now."

Bill shook his head. "I'm not sure I can ever stand it. Every time I run into her or someone she works with, it's like a knife being pushed into my gut all over again."

Sam nodded, and Bill glanced at his face long enough to read the compassion there. Not judgment, not disappointment. Just sadness.

"I can see where that could be a problem. So, do you know what you're gonna do about it?"

Bill shook his head. He felt so lost—so unsure how to proceed with the rest of his life. He needed help from somebody.

Maybe that was why he'd come to Montana—hoping his friend and mentor would know what Bill needed to do to make everything in his life okay again.

"Can we pray together about it, Bill?"

The other man reached out and touched Bill briefly on the arm before sitting up straighter.

"I'd like to pray for you."

Bill finally nodded, blinking hard to hold back the moisture that kept building up behind his eyes at his friend's kind words. This was ridiculous. He was an FBI Agent and a former Marine. What was the matter with him?

He wasn't sure prayer was going to change anything. It sure didn't feel like his recent prayers had been reaching God. But if Sam wanted to pray for him, maybe God would listen to his friend.

The two of them bowed their heads, and Bill closed his eyes, taking the time to wipe the moisture from around them since he knew Sam's eyes were closed. Then Sam's deep voice broke through his misery, and Bill focused on the words of the other man going heavenward on his behalf.

"Father God, my brother Bill is hurting tonight. We don't know why this has happened in his life right now, but we know You are aware of it all. We turn his future completely over to You and ask that You give him peace about whatever he faces ahead. Guide him and direct him. Give him a clear head as to how to move forward so he can live his life in Your will—whatever and wherever that may be. We thank You for hearing us and answering our prayer. We ask all this in Jesus's name, Amen."

When he finished the prayer, Sam stood, and Bill quickly followed suit, thankful that the ordeal of spilling his guts to one of his best friends was over. There wasn't any magical answer from heaven, but at least he'd told Sam. Someone else knew what he was going through, so he didn't feel so alone anymore.

He felt Sam's large hand on his shoulder.

"Is it okay if I share this with Julie?" He quickly shook his head. "I can promise you that if I tell her to keep it just between us, it will go no farther."

Bill nodded. "I know Julie well enough to know that, Sam. Sure." He gave him a small smile.

Sam sighed. "And she'll be praying for you too, you know. I'm sure right now it doesn't feel that way, but you *will* get through this, Bill. And I'm glad you felt you could come to the ranch. I want you to always feel you can come here."

That statement made Bill's heart feel a little lighter. Perhaps coming to Montana hadn't been a mistake after all.

CHAPTER 5

The next morning, Bill was up before daylight. After getting dressed, he tiptoed out the front door of the farmhouse. He didn't know if the womenfolk were already in the kitchen or not, but he doubted it since it was a Saturday morning. He remembered from previous visits that weekends were more laid-back on the ranch than the rest of the time. And unlike during the week, on Saturdays and Sundays, the ranch hands ate all their meals at the bunkhouse, so only the family would be around the main house.

Because it was so early, Bill tried to be as quiet as possible—not only because he didn't want to disturb any of the family—but also because he wanted some time alone. After he'd had first awakened, Bill had felt the need to get out of the house and get some fresh air. His bedroom was comfortable but rather small, and it was making him feel a tad claustrophobic.

Bill padded across the huge covered porch that wrapped around three sides of the old farmhouse and paused at the rail, taking a deep breath of the morning air. He stepped down the stairs and stopped at the bottom to take a moment to gaze across the landscape. The sun was just coming up in the eastern sky, and a wispy mist was drifting across the area beyond the barn and paddock area. Bill stood in amazement as the immensity of the wide-open spaces around him registered in his brain.

How could anyone live out in this part of the country and not feel tiny?

Based on the previously scorching day, Bill knew it was probably going to be another hot one. But as it was still fairly dark, the morning air still felt fresh and comfortable, and he gulped in mouthfuls of it as if he couldn't breathe in enough. He'd never been a real morning person, but if he had this to wake up to every morning, he might have to change his mind.

Running his fingers through his short-cropped hair, Bill strolled across the still-dark yard, not sure where he was headed. The need for solitude swept over him, and the sight of the big sky above him with a few stars still visible made him feel small. He knew God was out there somewhere, ready to help him if he needed, but Bill wasn't sure he wanted to talk to God yet. Even after Sam's heartfelt prayer for him the day before, Bill was still feeling a bit of resentment toward God. After all, He could have changed Zoey's mind about dumping Bill. Wouldn't a loving God have done that?

No, Bill was having a little trouble right then feeling the love.

When he reached the wooden fence surrounding the horse paddock, Bill came to a halt. Leaning his arms against the top rail of the fence, he closed his eyes and tried not to think about the pain in his heart. A part of him knew it was probably best that Zoey had broken off their engagement. It was best that things ended before their relationship had gone further, and they'd actually set a date for the wedding. But he still felt as if his feet had been knocked out from under him. It was going to take him some time to heal.

And hopefully, he'd eventually be able to accept what God had allowed to happen. Right then, though, Bill was still struggling. He just hoped and prayed God would be patient with him and wait.

That thought had no more than registered in his brain when his ears caught the muffled noise of a horse galloping. Bill raised his head and peered through the lightening mist to see a lone rider coming across the pasture and into the far side of the corral. It looked like a smaller fellow, and he was riding a beautiful dark gray-colored horse. Bill didn't know enough about horses to recognize anything other than the fact that the rider appeared to know what they were doing as they vaulted out of the saddle, grabbed hold of the horse's bridle, and led the horse toward the door at the far end of the barn. Then the cowboy hat was removed, and Bill was able to clearly see the long dark-colored hair flowing around the rider's shoulders.

That was no cowboy! That was a *cowgirl*.

Bill's assumption about it being one of the ranch hands, possibly coming back from checking on the herd, quickly evaporated. Part of him was curious to do a little investigating to find out who it was, but perhaps it would be wiser to ask Sam who she was later. He couldn't imagine the ranch having a female ranch hand, but he supposed it was possible.

Regardless, Bill was hungry and more than ready for breakfast. As if in agreement with that idea, his stomach gave a loud rumble. He gave a little snort and turned back toward the house.

Then after breakfast, it was time for Bill to find something to do to keep from going crazy. Sam hadn't told Bill he needed to work while he was there, but Bill knew there were always chores that needed doing. And he needed things to do.

And what Bill didn't know how to do, he could always learn. So, that would work out just dandy.

♫ ♫ ♫

Joy rushed toward the cabin where she was staying with her Aunt Mary and Uncle Jack. She had exactly an hour to shower, change into her usual work uniform of jeans and a white blouse, grab some breakfast, and then it would be time to make the drive into Denning to the diner and another day of work.

Some mornings she wondered why she took the time for a ride before work. But once she was out in the morning mists, riding her horse across the open pastureland and feeling the wind blowing through her hair, she knew why she took the time. There was something almost mystical about the time spent on the back of a horse. It was as if Joy and the animal were one, running through the tall grasses. There was a feeling of freedom on the back of her horse that she never felt anyplace else.

It was worth it—even if it did mean she had to hurry to get ready.

She knew her aunt and uncle were more than likely already at the main house, so when she entered the small cabin where they lived and found it empty, she wasn't surprised. Ten minutes later, Joy was brushing out her damp hair and braiding it into one long braid down her back. All traces of horse smell and the dust from her early morning ride were gone, and she was ready to face the world for another day.

One last look at herself in the mirror, and Joy was out the door and walking the well-worn path to the Morgan house. It only took her five minutes, and she was in the backdoor of the house and being greeted by her uncle and Mr. Sam Morgan himself. Joy gave them a shy 'good morning' before she made her way across the great room to the kitchen, where she found her Aunt Mary and Julie Morgan already busy at work. Julie's eleven-year-old daughter Samantha, was also bustling around the kitchen, doing her Aunt Mary's will.

"There you are, sweetheart." Her Aunt Mary gave her a quick, one-armed hug before turning back to the stove where she was pushing hash brown potatoes around in a large skillet.

"You're just in time to help Samantha and her mom put the rest of the food on the table."

Joy gave a quick nod and took the offered platter of biscuits from Julie and followed her as she carried a plate of pancakes, sausage, and bacon. Julie's daughter, Samantha, followed with a large pitcher of orange juice.

Placing the plate of biscuits on the table, Joy turned when she heard an unfamiliar voice echoing across the great room. What Joy saw stopped her in her tracks. It was that big FBI guy she'd seen talking to Zeke Mosher at *Peggy's Place* the previous day. He was the man her Uncle Jack had told her about on the ride home the previous evening—the one visiting from Washington, D.C.

Bill Parker. According to her Uncle Jack, that was his name.

She swallowed hard and forced herself not to bolt from the room. Seeing a strange man in her midst never failed to affect her. Even after working at the diner for over a year, whenever a new face appeared in town, Joy wanted to hide in the back storeroom instead of asking what they wanted to order. Just recently, she'd finally been able to overcome some of her fears. She would just have to do it again. This man was the Morgans' guest, and he was here because of them. She more than likely wouldn't have much to do with him anyway, so all she needed to do was quickly eat her breakfast, then she could be on her way to work.

Julie lightly touched her arm in greeting, and Joy swung around to focus on her.

"Joy, I don't think you've met our guest yet, have you?"

Julie Morgan's blue eyes were gentle as she quietly asked Joy her question. Sam's wife was so kind, so sweet. It was almost as if she could tell Joy was scared, and she probably could. Joy felt as if her whole body must be quaking in fear.

Instead of answering, Joy just gave her head a little shake—suddenly feeling like an idiot. Why couldn't she get over this terror of meeting new people—especially men?

Again, Julie touched her arm and led her around the table where the blond-haired man stood, smiling, and shaking hands with her Uncle Jack.

"Bill, I'd like you to meet Joy Whitefox. She's Mary's niece and is staying on the ranch with Mary and Jack for a while."

Joy raised her eyes and looked at the tall man in front of her. The first thing she noticed was the color of his eyes—deep blue like a Montana summer sky. And as they locked on hers, the only thing Joy could think of was how he looked perfectly harmless. Then she remembered how looks could be deceiving.

"Joy, this is Bill Parker. Our dear friend from Washington, D.C. He used to work with Sam and Jess when they were still at the Bureau. He's here at the ranch for a visit."

Joy swallowed hard and slowly raised her hand when he reached out to shake hers. His hand was warm and large, and Joy felt for a second or two as if by taking her hand, he'd reached out and touched her in her pain. Feeling a little unsettled, she pulled her small hand from his and took a step back, dropping her eyes from his for a brief moment before looking back up at him.

"Nice to meet you, Mr. Parker."

His smile grew wider, and she noticed that when he smiled big, he had two faint dimples that appeared on both sides of his cheeks. Not big dimples like Sam Morgan had, but they were there nonetheless.

"Bill, please. Nobody calls me Mr. Parker—other than my dentist."

Fortunately, Joy was saved from any more small talk by her Aunt Mary, who shooed them all over to the table. After everyone found a seat, Sam stood and gave the blessing on the food, then platters and bowls began to be passed around.

Joy didn't take much food and quietly ate what she did put on her plate. After a few minutes had passed, she glanced at her wristwatch and groaned. She needed to leave right then if she were going to get to work on time.

She turned to her aunt sitting next to her.

"Thanks for breakfast, Aunt Mary, but I've gotta run if I don't want to be late."

Her Aunt Mary pulled her into a quick sideways hug before allowing her to stand from the table.

"Excuse me," Joy murmured to no one in particular before turning and hurrying toward the back door. She was usually much more polite than that, especially to the Morgans. But the sight of Bill Parker's blue eyes watching her every move had upset her comfort level this morning.

It was a good thing she had to go to work. The last thing she needed was to spend the whole day on the ranch with him there.

CHAPTER 6

Later that morning, after Sam and a couple of the other ranch hands had saddled their horses and rode out to check on the herd, Bill made his way across the yard toward the barn. Zeke was headed to the airport to pick up Clay and Lottie Morgan, and for a moment, Bill wondered if he should have offered to go with him—just for something to do.

Bill was sincerely hoping Jack had some chores that needed to be done. Bill had spent about as much time in the house as he could. Listening to Julie and Mary and the two young people's chatter while they worked in the kitchen, canning vegetables, was beginning to get on his nerves.

Bill made his way through the vast expanse of the barn toward the rear where he could hear the sound of hammer meeting metal. He assumed the man was at his forge doing blacksmithing work. He knew from what Sam had told him in the past that Jack was responsible for all the farrier work done on the ranch.

Not wanting to interrupt the man's work, Bill hung back and watched as Jack hammered a piece of steel clamped by a set of tongs he held in his left hand. Each stroke of the hammer in his right hand resonated throughout the barn, and Bill was in awe of the power Jack must have in those arms of his to swing that hammer with such force and so often. Which was a good reminder that he never wanted to get in a fist-fight or a wrestling match with Jack Byrd. Because Bill knew he'd lose.

Finally, Jack held up the finished horseshoe and looked it over carefully, then dropped it into a bucket near his feet where it hit the water with a hiss. He turned to place his hammer on the workbench behind him and finally noticed Bill standing there.

Jack arched his eyebrow as if in question, and Bill pushed himself away from the wooden post he'd been leaning against.

"Morning, Jack."

"Morning, Bill."

He watched as the other man pulled off his thick leather gloves and tossed them onto the workbench where he'd just placed his hammer.

"Anything I can do for you?"

Bill chuckled. "Yeah, you can save me from having to spend the entire day in the house with the women-folk canning. Surely you've got something out here even a city-slicker like me can do."

Jack's laughter rang throughout the barn almost as loudly as his hammer had earlier.

"Pull up a bale, City-Boy, and we'll consider the options."

Bill followed the older man over to some rectangular bales of straw and plopped down on one of them. Now that he'd asked Jack for something to do, he was beginning to get a little nervous, with thoughts of past hazing he'd undergone as a probie at the Bureau sweeping through his mind. Hopefully, Jack wouldn't be too hard on him.

"So, tell me why you're really here in Montana, Bill?"

Swinging his head around to gaze at the other man, Bill felt a moment of indecision. Should he tell Jack Byrd the whole wretched story of his love life? Nah. That wasn't what Jack wanted to know. He was just curious.

"I mean, coming to a place like Bluecreek isn't most city folks' idea of a vacation, Parker."

Bill chuckled. "You got that right."

He sighed. "No, I just needed some time out of the city, and I've meant to come visit Sam and Julie—and of course, see Zeke and Jess and their little family—and hadn't gotten around to it before this."

"Hmm," was the only response from the other man as he continued to gaze at Bill as if he was positive that wasn't the complete story. Well, it wasn't, but Bill wasn't up to sharing everything with this very imposing wrangler. He was sure Jack Byrd was a good listener, but Bill's heart was still too sore, and his emotions too tender to speak about it with a man he didn't really know all that well. It had been difficult enough to tell his sob story to Sam.

It was silent between the two of them for a few seconds, and Bill finally felt it necessary to say something to get the focus of the conversation off of him.

"How long have you been working here on the ranch, Jack? I don't think I've ever heard the story of how you came to be here."

The big man swung his head around and looked over at Bill, and his dark eyes lit up.

"Shortly after we married, Mary and I came to work for Reese Morgan—that's Sam's grandpa. A whole lotta years ago."

Bill saw a small smile creep across Jack's face.

"One of the best decisions we ever made was to come here when we left the reservation. I've never been sorry. I firmly believe God led us here, and the Morgans have always been good to us. We consider them family."

What had it been like, Bill wondered, for young Jack Byrd to grow up as a Native American Indian? Had he had a happy childhood? Had it been a tough life?

"If I can ask, what was it like for you—growing up on the reservation?"

The smile instantly left Jack's face, and Bill flinched, wondering for a moment if Jack would even answer his question. He probably shouldn't have pried into the other man's life, but he *was* curious.

"There were many good things about living with the people on the reservation and being raised in the way of the Crow. I was taught the language at an early age, how to hunt, and how to live off the land. We didn't have much, but the family managed to get by, and my mother made the simple house we lived in a home. Of course, that was fifty years ago. And many things have changed."

He frowned as he stared downward, and Bill saw him flex his large hands as he looked down at them before raising his eyes back to Bill.

"I hurt for the young people of today—having to make wise decisions about how and what to do with their lives. There are so many evil things to drive them away from the old ways—it's becoming harder and harder for them to live a good life. And not all of them have been raised with the Truth of the Gospel."

The other man dropped his head for a few seconds before raising it again, and his eyes locked on Bill's face.

"That is why Mary and I brought her niece here to the ranch to live with us."

Bill nodded. "You're talking about Joy."

He saw Jack's nod and read the sadness in his dark eyes.

"The reservation was not a good place for Joy to be anymore. It's not safe for her."

Not safe.

Somehow, Bill knew there was a whole story behind those two words. He really wanted to ask more about it, but Jack put his hands on his knees and pushed himself up from the bale of straw. Evidently, the conversation was over.

"So, what can you do on a ranch, Mr. Parker?"

Bill chuckled.

Good question.

"You probably don't know anything about blacksmithing."

Shaking his head, Bill stood next to the other man, feeling smaller and younger than he had in years.

"Nope."

"How about roping cattle, baling hay, or mending fences?"

"Nope."

Jack gave him a toothy grin.

"I bet I know one job you can handle." He put his large hand on Bill's shoulder, and Bill felt the weight of it there.

"You afraid to get a little dirty, City-Boy?" His deep voice was full of humor as he continued to smile over at Bill.

Bill grinned back, sure that he was setting himself up for something he probably wasn't going to enjoy. At all.

"Nope."

"Good. Follow me."

♬ ♪ ♫

Two and a half hours later, Bill was starting to think he'd make a huge mistake by going to the barn and asking Jack if there was anything he could do to help. During those hours, he'd mucked out horse stalls and spread down new straw bedding, carried buckets of water and feed, and fought off more flies than he'd ever known even existed. Just when Bill thought he'd finished a job, Jack would find another one for him to do.

Bill had always prided himself on staying in shape. He usually did a series of push-ups and sit-ups every morning after rising and went to the gym at least twice a week to work out. This was a different kind of work, though, and Bill had a great deal of respect for the guys who did this job daily. Cowboys certainly weren't wusses.

Finally, when Bill thought his arms were about to fall off, Jack poked his head around the door to the stall Bill had just finished cleaning out.

"Lunchtime."

Bill looked down at his filthy pant legs and boots and groaned. He couldn't go into Julie's house looking and smelling like this and expect to get fed. And there was no sense cleaning up just to eat as he was sure after lunch, Jack would have more disgusting jobs for him to do.

The other man just gave him a toothy grin.

"Mary and Julie took the kids into town to some function going on at the library and won't be back until later. We'll go to my place for lunch. Mary left stuff for sandwiches."

Heaving a sigh of relief at that news, Bill left his shovel propped up against the wall of the empty stall and followed Jack out of the barn. Jack stopped near the horse trough and turned on a faucet, then took the hose hanging there and scrubbed his hands with a bar of soap resting on a little ledge on the outside of the fence, then rinsed off his boots before offering it to Bill.

"Mary isn't nearly as fussy as Julie, but she still doesn't take kindly to having horse manure on her kitchen floor."

Bill gave the other man a grin, grabbed the offered garden hose and scrubbed his own hands, also cleaning as much of the stuff off his boots as he could, and then followed Jack as he strode purposefully across the barnyard toward where Bill knew the Byrd cabin was located.

As they approached it, Bill took the opportunity to really look at the one-story cabin. The first time Bill had visited the ranch, Sam had told him the story of the structure—that it was actually the first cabin Sam's great-grandparents had built and lived in when they'd come west and homesteaded the land back in 1915. That meant the cabin was over a hundred years old.

Unbelievable.

He could tell the old cabin had been remodeled several different times. There were updated windows, a new metal roof, and the front porch posts, rails, and floorboards looked fairly new. But the central part of the structure itself still seemed to be the original.

It fascinated Bill to think how a hundred years or so earlier, a man had cut down trees—without the ease of a modern chainsaw—hewed them, notched them, and then stacked them until it became the structure he was now looking at. Even more surprising was the fact that over a hundred years later, that same structure would not only still be standing, but was being lived in.

He followed Jack up the two steps onto the covered porch and through the heavy wooden door into a small living area. Jack stopped long enough at the entrance to toe off his boots and leave them on a mat just outside the front door, and Bill quickly followed suit. He couldn't do much about the muck on the legs of his jeans, but at least he wouldn't be tromping all over Mary's clean house in his dirty boots. He'd just have to be careful not to brush up against any of the nicer furniture.

"Come in and make yourself at home," Jack motioned toward the kitchen area where a round oak table and ladder-back chairs sat.

Bill followed Jack into the kitchen and pulled out one of the chairs and took a seat.

"What can I do to help?"

"Rest. I got it."

Jack pulled a loaf of bread out of the cupboard and put it on the table, followed by several packages of sliced meat, a jar of pickles, a bag of sliced cheese, lettuce, a plate of sliced tomatoes, a plastic bag of sliced onions, and several kinds of condiments. He then pulled silverware, glasses, and a couple of dishes out of a cupboard and added it to the other items on the table.

"I'll let you fix your own; that way, it will be the way you want it."

Nodding, Bill pulled one of the plates over in front of him and went to work making a sandwich. He was hungry, and after seeing all the food spread in front of him, he realized how long it had been since breakfast. No wonder the cowboys on the ranch ate such big meals. They worked it all off during the day.

While he built his own sandwich, he watched in awe as Jack piled everything imaginable onto his. When he finished, the sandwich stood so tall Bill wasn't sure how the man intended to eat it.

No worries, though. After Jack had said a short prayer of thanks for the food, he wasted no time taking a huge bite of the sandwich on his plate. Bill went to work on his own, practically inhaling it in his hunger. Mucking out the barn had made him famished. He couldn't remember a time when he'd been so hungry—even after working without a lunch or two in his lifetime.

"I appreciate you helping out this morning, Bill."

Bill nodded as he chewed another bite of food and swallowed.

"No problem."

Jack gave him a grin. "Don't suppose you'd want to do that every day though, huh?"

Chuckling, Bill shook his head. "Not particularly."

The older man's grin grew even bigger. Nothing was said by either of them for a few more minutes as they focused on their own sandwiches. When their lunches were gone, Bill took a swig of the iced tea Jack had poured for him and leaned back in his chair, feeling a little more energized. He would never again think that work on the ranch wasn't tough, physical work. Not that he ever had. But Bill had first-hand experience now and was left with nothing but respect for Sam and Zeke and the rest of the men who did that kind of work every day. It made his job back in D.C. look like a cushy desk job—even if he *was* out on the streets hunting down criminals most of the time.

Thinking of bad guys made Bill recall Jack's words earlier when he'd spoken of the need for his niece to leave the reservation.

Not safe.

"Why did you say the reservation isn't a safe place for Joy?"

Jack grimaced and shook his head, then leaned back in his own chair with his arms folded across his chest.

"I shouldn't have said anything. Forgot for a minute who I was talking to."

Bill just kept staring at Jack, hoping the man would divulge more information without him having to get pushy. Something told him Jack Byrd would be a hard egg to crack during an interrogation, but since he'd already opened up the conversation, maybe Bill wouldn't have to keep pushing him for more information.

Finally, the other man heaved what sounded like a resigned sigh and unfolded his arms.

"Almost two years ago, Joy was attacked, beaten, and raped."

"What?"

Bill sat up straight in his chair, feeling a sense of helplessness at Jack's words. What crazy maniac had hurt that sweet, shy gal? Whoever he was, they'd better have caught the guy. A surge of anger swept through him that surprised him in its intensity. If Bill ever got his hands on the man, he'd beat him to a pulp for hurting someone like Joy.

Jack held up his hand. "They got the guy. He's currently in prison serving his sentence."

Blowing out a breath and to release some of his pent-up anger, Bill sat back and tried to relax.

"Hopefully, the scumbag got put away for a long, long time."

The frown that appeared on Jack's face didn't bode well for that hope.

"He was found guilty on two counts. Aggravated Assault, which is a felony, with the additional charge of Stalking. He got one year of imprisonment with a $1,000 fine for the first count, and another year and another $1,000 fine for the second count."

"What?" Bill shook his head in disbelief. "That means the jerk will be getting out of jail after only two years? That's not right, Jack! They should have locked him up and thrown away the key. Ten years wouldn't be enough!"

Jack nodded, his lips compressed tightly together.

"Trust me, I wasn't any happier about it than you are, but there was nothing anyone could do about it."

"Which means he'll be getting out of jail when?"

"A little over three months from now—the end of the year."

Releasing a sigh of disgust, Bill gazed at the man across the table from him, his mind spinning as he thought about all Jack had told him.

"Which is why you're so concerned about Joy's safety. The attack happened on the reservation?"

Jack nodded. "Yes, and even though it is a safe enough place most of the time, after the attack, it became less safe for her. There were some there who blamed Joy for what happened—sure it was her fault for leading the man on. Which was the farthest thing from the truth."

The other man shook his head in disgust. "That was why Mary and I made the decision to bring Joy to the ranch to live with us. Sam and Julie agreed."

"Is she doing better here?"

There was a brief nod from Jack, but nothing more was said.

Bill felt a sense of frustration he hadn't felt in years— ever since his partner Jess had infiltrated a gang of gun and drug dealers to try and help out a friend, and Bill hadn't known if she was even alive or not. That incident had ended okay, but who knew how this situation with Joy and the man who had attacked her would end?

And if anyone deserved to have a happily-ever-after, it was Joy Whitefox.

CHAPTER 7

Joy carefully stepped down the ladder leading from her loft bedroom in her Aunt Mary's cabin, her purse slung over her shoulder, and her Bible in her hand. She wasn't going to make it to the church in time for Sunday school, but at least she'd get there for the morning worship service—even though she might be later than usual. She'd been so tired the night before, she'd crashed as soon as she'd arrived home from work. Saturdays were always the busiest days at the diner. And the longest. Thank goodness, the restaurant wasn't open on Sundays.

After chugging down a glass of orange juice and one of the cinnamon rolls her aunt had left for her on the kitchen counter with a note to be sure to eat something for breakfast, Joy grabbed her keys and headed out the door.

She'd just pulled away from the cabin and drove the short distance to the dirt lane that went by the Morgan's when she saw Bill Parker coming down the steps of their front porch. He was much more dressed up than she'd seen him in the past—wearing dark blue pants and a light blue button-down shirt and a black tie.

He must have heard her old car coming down the drive because he stopped and raised his head when he reached the bottom of the steps. Joy put her foot on the brake, and rolled down the driver's side window, leaning out to make sure he could hear her.

"You headed to church?"

Bill gave her a crooked grin. "Yeah, well. I thought I was, but it appears I overslept this morning, and they all left without me. I was just coming outside to try and figure out how I was going to get there…"

She couldn't hold back her smile. He was a big, tough guy alright, but obviously didn't have a clue how to survive living in the country. Just how did he think he was going to get to church anyway? Saddle up old Chester and ride him all the way? Or did he plan to steal the keys for the rusty pickup truck Sam Morgan kept in the back of the cowshed?

"Hop in, Cowboy. Something tells me you need someone to keep you out of trouble."

Joy watched Bill scurry around the front of her vehicle. He tugged open the passenger-side door and folded his long body into the passenger seat, holding his Bible on his lap as he clicked on his seat belt. Once he was settled, Joy put the car in drive and headed down the well-worn dirt trail toward the main road, wondering what she was thinking, offering to give this man a ride to church?

At that thought, a moment of panic rushed through her, and for a second or two, it felt as if her heart was going to thump right out of her chest. She took a couple of deep breaths and slowly released them, forcing her mind and body to relax. It had been quite awhile since she'd had a panic attacked like that, and Joy chewed on her lower lip and recited all the reasons this wasn't one of the craziest things she'd ever done.

Giving the man a ride to church wasn't a crazy idea. It was the right thing to do for a guest of Sam and Julie Morgan's. After all, Bill Parker was an FBI Agent. She should feel totally safe with him. Her Uncle Jack had told her so. And Sam Morgan and Jessica Mosher both adored the man, so he must be a good guy. He was no threat to her in any way.

"Thanks for the ride, Joy." His deep chuckle filled the small car. "Not sure how I would have gotten there if you hadn't shown up when you did."

She glanced across the car toward him, once again noting how he filled the front seat with his presence. Because she was so petite, everyone else always looked so much larger. But there was no doubt about it, Bill Parker was a big man. And today, his fair-skinned face looked a little pinker than normal. Was he actually embarrassed at having gotten left behind?

"Well, I suppose you could have always jumped Fred Morgan's old Ford pickup in the back shed and driven it," she finally said. Just thinking about him trying to get the old truck running forced her lips into a grin, and she felt her body begin to relax a bit.

Bill chuckled. "Sure—and hoped and prayed there was enough life in the engine and gas in the tank to get me to town."

She turned her eyes from the road long enough to give him a quick smile, suddenly feeling unsettled by his swift wink as he added, "And I suppose I could have saddled one of those horses out in the paddock and ridden to town—although I'm not sure how well I'd do at that. Although I have gotten really good at cleaning out their stalls—thanks to your Uncle Jack."

Joy smiled at his comment, then turned and studied his profile again for a few seconds before turning her eyes back to the road ahead.

"You're not much of a cowboy, are you, Agent Parker?"

His deep chuckle unexpectedly warmed Joy's heart. Bill Parker wasn't like any man she'd known in the past—other than perhaps her Uncle Jack—who she trusted with her life. Bill Parker didn't put on a show or try to be anything but who he was. And her Uncle Jack had been right; he seemed genuinely nice.

"Never pretended to be one, Miss Whitefox." He turned toward her and gave her another wink. "I suppose I could learn, though, with the right teacher."

Joy gazed back at the road and swallowed at the surprising pleasure that swept through her at the look on his face and the teasing sound of his voice. Then she steeled herself to ignore the way he made her pulse jump. He was the first man since the attack who had ever made that happen without the presence of fear causing it, and she wasn't sure she liked the feeling. She needed to be careful around the man. Just because Bill Parker was nice, didn't mean he was safe.

Fortunately, they'd reached the edge of the town of Denning, where the church was located, and Joy quickly pulled her small car into the parking lot and found a place to park.

"We're here," she spouted, then felt silly for stating the obvious.

"Thanks for the ride, Joy." She couldn't help but notice the sincerity in his voice as he gave her a nod and a smile.

Still feeling unsettled, Joy got out of the car and quickly grabbed her purse and Bible from the back seat and glanced over long enough to see the gentle smile on Bill's face as he unsnapped his seatbelt and opened the car door.

"You're welcome...Cowboy," she finally answered, knowing even as she added on the final part, that Bill Parker was anything but a cowboy. But somehow that didn't bother her like she'd thought it would. And it tickled her to be able to tease him about it.

He gave her a toothy grin, and the two of them headed for the church doors, Joy struggling to keep her own face stern at the unexpected pleasure she felt at having the big man walking by her side.

♫ ♫ ♫

Bill held open the church door for Joy, then followed her into a small entryway off the main sanctuary doors. An usher was just inside the entrance to meet them—an older gray-haired man that greeted Joy by name before he shook Bill's hand.

"I don't think we've met yet, sir, but welcome."

Taking the offered bulletin from the man, Bill nodded.

"Thanks. I'm Bill Parker, a friend of Sam and Julie Morgan."

"Well, we're certainly glad you're here with us this morning."

Giving the man another nod, he hurried to catch up with Joy, who had already entered the sanctuary. She glanced back long enough to see he had followed her in, then paused in the center aisle as if undecided where to go.

"I usually sit near the front with Uncle Jack and Aunt Mary, but you can sit with the Morgan family—or wherever you want to," she said to him in what he thought sounded like a nervous whisper.

Bill looked around long enough to notice several sets of eyes watching them. He didn't want to cause any awkwardness for her, so he decided to sit in the obvious place.

"I'll go sit with Sam and Julie then. Thanks again for the ride, Joy," he whispered back to her.

Sam evidently saw Bill coming and moved over in the pew so there would be room enough for him to have a seat. Julie peered around her husband long enough to give Bill a smile. He could see C.J. and Samantha sitting on the other side of Julie. Clay and Lottie Morgan sat further down the row.

"We thought you were still sleeping, Bill. I didn't know you wanted to come this morning. Sorry," Sam's deep voice was only a murmur.

"No worries." Bill gave his friend a quick smile and turned his attention to the front where the service was ready to start.

It was a traditional church service, filled with both old hymns and more contemporary songs. The sermon, preached by the pastor Bill remembered meeting several years earlier—Pastor Beaumont—was a great speaker. His message that morning was from the book of Proverbs and was about trusting God with everything.

"'Trust in the Lord with all thine heart; and lean not unto thine own understanding. In all thy ways acknowledge him, and he shall direct thy paths.'"

Pastor Beaumont looked out over the congregation, his eyes almost seeming to land on Bill as if that verse was specifically for him. Well, Bill knew he did need to work on trusting God more. He'd been trying to do it all on his own, and that hadn't worked out so well. Perhaps he *did* need to allow God to tell him what to do and where to go. Bill knew he needed something to change in his life. His choice for a future wife sure had blown up in his face.

With that thought in mind, and while half-listening to the pastor, Bill found his eyes drawn to where he could see the back of Joy Whitefox's head two pews from the front. Her shining, black hair hung around her shoulders, almost like a cape. She was so beautiful, every time he looked at her, he found himself trying not to stare. He didn't want to do or say anything to make her more afraid of him than she obviously already was.

Bill had found her to be exceptionally friendly toward him by offering to give him a ride—especially since he knew it had to have been uncomfortable for her to do so. And speaking of trust, after everything she'd been through, Joy had every reason in the world to not trust men—any men.

Which made him even more surprised that she'd given him a ride to church.

♫ ♫ ♫

After shaking Pastor Beaumont's hand, Joy followed her aunt and uncle through the open double entry doors of the church onto the sidewalk. The first thing she noticed was the lack of sunshine. The day was warm, but clouds had moved in during the service, so at least the sun's heat wasn't beating down on them like it had been the day before.

Sam and Julie Morgan came through the doors behind them, Sam's hand holding the hand of his five-year-old son, C.J. Their daughter Samantha trailed after them, chatting with another girl who looked to be about her age.

As soon as Julie spotted Jack, Mary, and Joy, she turned toward where they stood and headed straight for Aunt Mary.

"You're all coming back to the house for lunch, right?"

Her Aunt Mary glanced over at her husband, then turned back to Julie, and hesitantly nodded. "If you're sure you want us, Julie. With Zeke's family and Bill being there too, I didn't know for sure if your offer from earlier in the week still stood." She chuckled. "I certainly don't expect you to feed us with all the other mouths in your house to feed, Julie."

Joy watched Julie shake her head. "Don't you try and weasel out of my invitation, Mary Byrd. You know there's always room for you and your family at the Morgan table."

Once she got a positive response to her invitation, Julie gave Mary a quick hug and a wave, then hurried to catch up to the rest of her family, who was walking toward their vehicle in the parking lot.

Joy saw her Aunt Mary shrug before she gave her husband a little smile. "Looks like I don't have to fix lunch today after all."

Uncle Jack chuckled as he stuck out his arm for his wife to take hold of. "Like you won't be out there in the kitchen helping Julie anyway. You forget who you're talking to, woman?"

Smiling at the teasing, yet tender tone of her uncle's gruff voice as he looked at his wife with evident love, Joy turned and watched Bill Parker as he joined the Morgans in the parking lot. It looked like he was planning to ride home with them, so apparently, he wouldn't need a ride back to the ranch with her. Joy wasn't sure why, but that caused her a moment of disappointment.

All Joy knew was, the man confused her. Mostly because he wasn't anything like she'd thought he'd be—although she wasn't sure what she'd expected. The only other FBI agents she had ever known were Sam Morgan and Jessica Mosher. As far as she could tell, they weren't any different from any of the other people she'd known in her lifetime.

Well, other than for the fact that sometimes Sam Morgan could be extremely intimidating. At least, Joy felt that way. The man always seemed to know what you were thinking, and his gray eyes missed nothing. His wife Julie was a sweetheart, though. And Joy knew her uncle and aunt adored the Morgan family, so she guessed she didn't have anything to fear from either of them.

And Jess Mosher was a wonderful woman—a kind friend, and a terrific mom. Joy was enthralled with the mental strength that practically exuded from Zeke Mosher's wife. She wanted to be that brave and strong when she grew up.

But this newest FBI agent's appearance at the Bluecreek Ranch had upset the calm that Joy had recently felt. She wasn't afraid of Bill Parker. Uncle Jack had assured her she had nothing to fear from the man. No, there was something else about him. When his blue eyes landed on her, it felt as if he could see parts of her that Joy preferred to stay hidden. The inner terrors of what she'd experienced almost two years earlier had never left her, and it was as if Bill Parker knew that and somehow felt her pain too.

As she hurried to her car to follow her aunt and uncle back to the ranch, Joy shook her head. She was thinking about the man way too much. Bill Parker was nothing to her and would be leaving the ranch in another week or so to return to his life in the city.

In the meantime, she just needed to try and steer clear him.

♪ ♪ ♪

Bill sat in one of the wooden rocking chairs on the front porch of the Morgan farmhouse and propped his feet up on the porch rail. He had a full stomach, and the warmth of the afternoon was making him sleepy. A nap sure did sound good, but he knew if he slept now, he wouldn't sleep well that night. And he'd been struggling lately getting a good night's sleep anyway. That was probably why he'd overslept that morning and almost missed church.

The squeak of the screened door behind him announced someone else was coming out to join him. A few seconds later, the long, lean frame of Samuel Clemens Morgan plopped down in the rocking chair next to Bill's. Sam released a sigh, and Bill allowed his lips to turn up into a little grin. Sounded like the boss man was feeling much the same as Bill did—stuffed and relaxed.

The women had chased the menfolk out of the kitchen shortly after lunch. Clay and Lottie Morgan had left the house to go for a horseback ride around the ranch. The Byrds and Joy, and the Moshers and their little guys had returned to their cabins. Samantha had gone up to her room to read and study, and C.J. had retreated to his bedroom to supposedly take a nap, and Bill and Sam had escaped to the front porch.

"Sorry about taking off for church this morning without you, buddy. When we couldn't raise you, Julie said just to let you sleep. We figured you needed the rest."

"No problem. I got there okay."

He felt Sam's eyes land on him briefly before the other man turned his head back to gaze out over the yard.

"For the record, Samantha did knock on your door a couple of times to find out if you were going."

Bill nodded. "I figured as much. I must have been sleeping really hard not to have heard her."

The sound of Sam's sigh drifted through the afternoon air. "And it looks like you made it all right on your own."

Turning to glance over at his former mentor, Bill wondered what Sam was really saying. Was he angry that Bill had caught a ride to church with Joy?

"Thankfully, Joy was around to give me a ride." He found himself grinning as he recalled her suggesting he could saddle a horse and ride into town. Like that would ever happen.

"I'm just surprised she felt comfortable enough with you to offer a ride."

Sam shifted in his chair and turned toward Bill.

"Has anyone told you the reason Joy is living here on the ranch, Bill?"

Bill pulled his booted feet off the porch rail and sat up, turning to face the other man. Now they were getting down to the reason for all of Sam's questions. He'd been wondering where the discussion was leading.

"Jack told me."

The other man's eyes locked on his, his eyebrows going up.

"That surprises me. Jack doesn't like to discuss family business with outsiders."

Flinching a little at Sam calling him an outsider, Bill stared at the porch floor a moment. Well, Sam was right, of course, Bill wasn't a part of the ranch. And he could see that about Jack Byrd. He'd always felt the man was extremely private.

"He probably wouldn't have told me anything if I hadn't asked him." Bill cleared his throat. It was probably best if he gave Sam the whole story.

"Friday, I was working with Jack in the barn, and he mentioned in passing that Joy was living here on the ranch

70

with them because it wasn't safe for her anymore on the reservation."

Sam narrowed his eyes and nodded. "And Bill Parker, the FBI Agent, started asking questions." The other man gave him a crooked smile. "You can't get away from who you are, can you?"

Bill chuckled. "Guess not." Then the smile left his face.

"I was furious when Jack told me what happened to her and that the jerk that did it only got a couple of years of jail time."

Sam's sigh drifted across the porch. And this time, it sounded weary.

"Yeah. I think the Tribal Code needs to be updated a bit as far as I'm concerned, but there's nothing to be done about it now."

Bill heard the frustration in his friend's voice as he added, "Ernie Wolffe should have been put away for a long, long time for what he did to Joy. That poor girl was a basket case when Jack and Mary brought her here to recover."

It was silent between the two of them for a few moments before Sam posed another question.

"So, how did Joy act around you on the drive into town?"

Bill thought about Sam's question. How had Joy acted? He didn't feel as if she'd been terribly nervous or afraid of him. But then again, maybe she was good at hiding her true feelings.

"She seemed friendly enough. Gave me a rough time about getting left behind." Bill chuckled as he remembered her smile and teasing voice. "She even called me 'Cowboy' a couple of times."

Sam snickered. "Now, there's a nickname that will never stick, Parker."

Bill laughed. "Yeah. Shows she really doesn't know much about me."

"Well, at least she appears to be coming out of her shell a little bit. The first few months she was here, you couldn't get her to even look you in the face—let alone speak to you. She still acts like she's terrified whenever she's around me."

Thinking about his friend's words, Bill stared out across the yard, not really seeing the leaves on the trees blowing in the hot breeze, or the blades of the windmill slowly turning in the wind. He was thinking about Joy Whitefox and how one man's evil actions against her had changed her life forever.

"I'll be praying for her, Sam. You can count on that."

Bill didn't bother praying for himself anymore, but he could bring himself to pray for the sweet little gal that had been through more than anyone should have to go through.

Sam gave him a somber nod. "Thanks. I think she can use all of the prayers she can get."

CHAPTER 8

The next morning, following an early breakfast with Clay and Sam Morgan, Jack, Zeke, and the rest of the ranch hands, Bill made his way across the ranch on a four-wheeler Jack had let him borrow—after a brief amount of ribbing first, of course.

"You sure you wouldn't rather travel by horseback, Bill?"

Bill had quickly shaken his head at the man, easily reading the teasing in his snapping dark eyes.

"Not this time, Jack. Maybe next time."

So, Bill was currently bouncing along on the narrow dirt trail that Jack had told him would eventually lead him to the Mosher house. Zeke had mentioned that morning that Jess was expecting him to come for a visit, and Bill had decided there wasn't any reason to keep putting it off. He did want to spend some time with his old partner and get a chance to see her twin boys again. But Bill also knew the former FBI agent would take advantage of the opportunity to ask Bill what had really brought him to Montana, so he was steeling himself for another interrogation.

I'm here for a visit. You got a problem with that, Jess?

He shook his head as he pushed his foot down harder on the gas pedal of the four-wheeler to get a little more zip out of the machine as he came to the bottom of a small hill.

There's no way Jess is going to accept that as an answer, Parker, and you know it. A typical visit would have been for a few days, and I would have already been chomping at the bit to get back to work.

Just the fact that Bill had stated he was here for a couple of weeks would surely have set off an alarm in Jess's brain. Yup, he'd best be prepared for more questions. And this was Jess—not Sam. Whereas Sam was a guy and would let Bill tell him only what he wanted and be content, Jessica Thorne Mosher wasn't going to be happy until she had all the details out of Bill. Just thinking about it was enough to make Bill groan in frustration.

The other side of the rise, Bill spotted the Mosher house in the distance. It sat on a small hill, surrounded by several trees. It wasn't a large house, but Bill did notice the fancy rail that ran around the outside of the porch and the decorative newel posts on the steps' handrails. Somebody had put a lot of time into the design of the house, and he instantly wondered if Zeke had built it himself. If so, the man had done an excellent job.

He had just turned the four-wheeler into the short drive when he spied Jess along with two little toddlers in the back yard. It looked like Jess was hanging laundry on a clothesline, all the time trying to keep track of her youngsters. Bill couldn't hold back his grin as he shut off the vehicle and got off. Looked like the cavalry had arrived just in time. He'd been looking forward to spending time with the two Mosher boys ever since his arrival in Montana.

Right then, Jess turned around and spotted him.

"Bill!"

She dropped the wet towel in her hand back into the laundry basket at her feet and headed in his direction, then turned back and grabbed one of her boys who had decided it was a good time to crawl in the same basket.

"Charlie, get out of there! Come greet your Uncle Bill. Benjamin Isaac, get over here, and quit harassing that poor cat!"

Bill chuckled and grabbed up the closest of the two twin boys—he thought he had Charlie—and gave him a little toss in the air before plopping him on his shoulders. The little guy promptly took hold of Bill's ears as if to anchor himself—even though Bill had a firm grasp of the small body.

The other twin Jess had called Benjamin, promptly deserted the cat who took off across the yard like a shot. That youngster then ran over and tackled Bill in the leg, hanging on for dear life. Bill laughed and gave his former partner a look of what he hoped appeared to be a cry for help.

"Are the boys always this friendly to strangers?"

Jess laughed and shook her head, then grabbed the toddler stuck to Bill's pant leg and hoisted him up on her hip.

"No. But for some unknown reason, I think the boys have decided they like you."

She gave Bill a wink and motioned toward the back door of the house.

"Come on in, and I'll see if we can find something to keep these two rug rats occupied for a couple of minutes so we can talk."

Bill followed Jess through the back door into a spotless kitchen, ducking down as he entered to keep the little guy on his shoulders. Once inside, Bill swung Charlie down and held him in front of him in his arms as if he was a chair. Charlie's giggle echoed through the room, and Bill's heart felt lighter than it had in months.

Jess, with Ben still riding her hip, motioned for Bill to follow her through the kitchen and into the living room that ran across the front of the house. It was easy to tell this house was occupied by children by the variety of toys scattered across the carpeted floor.

"Sorry about the mess." Jess plopped Ben down on the floor in the middle of the disarray, then grabbed Charlie from Bill's arms, and set him on the floor next to his brother. Then she released a sigh and gave Bill a wide smile.

"What a nice surprise to have you show up this morning."

Bill chuckled as he took a seat on a comfortable-looking sofa sitting under a window that looked out over the front yard.

"I wasn't sure you'd have time for a visit. Looks like you've got your hands full with these two."

Jess grimaced. "You have no idea, Parker." She pursed her lips and gave him a steady look for a few seconds.

"Do you think you can keep an eye on these two long enough for me to go out and finish hanging up the wet laundry?" She frowned. "I hate to ask…"

Bill waved his hand through the air as if to dismiss her fears.

"Go on, Jess. I'll be fine with them."

She stood there in front of him with a doubtful look on her face, then back at the two boys happily playing with their toys on the floor.

"Are you sure?"

He nodded. "Yup. Go." He pointed in the direction of the back door. "Get your stuff done, and we'll be here when you finish."

Finally, Jess gave him a little smile and turned and left the room. After Bill heard the sound of the back door closing, he turned his attention to the two little black-haired guys sitting on the floor in front of his feet. It shouldn't be too tricky taking care of two toddlers for a few minutes, should it?

♫ ♫ ♫

Fifteen minutes later, Bill had decided he'd gotten the better job of the two adults. Jess could stay outside and hang up wet laundry as long as she wanted, and he'd gladly stay in the house and play with her sons.

Charlie and Ben were such cute little guys—their dark eyes reminded him of their mother's. But their big smiles were all Isaac Newton Mosher's and melted a part of Bill's heart he'd never even known was there.

They talked to him—sort of—chatting as they told him about their toys. Bill got down on the floor, and the three of them built towers with the wooden blocks, then the boys took turns knocking them down—screeching with glee as the blocks tumbled to the floor around them.

Then Charlie toddled over to a bookshelf in the corner and came back with a couple of kids' books and dropped them in Bill's lap.

"Wead to me?" the little guy said, his eyes filled with hope.

Ben quickly caught up the cry of his sibling, and when Jess came back in the house, Bill was sitting on the sofa with the boys on his lap, reading out loud to them. He couldn't believe how well-behaved they were as he read the words on the page to them and pointed out the colorful pictures. He was sure they'd had these same books read to them dozens of times, yet they acted as if this were the first time.

He heard the back door open and a few moments later, he glanced up to find Jess standing in the doorway between the kitchen and the living room, watching the three of them. When Bill came to a stop in the book and gave her a questioning look, she simply smiled.

"Do you think you can keep them occupied a little longer so I can fix their lunches? Then I'll even fix you lunch if you'd like."

Bill gave her a grin. Lunch with his old partner sounded good.

"No problem, Mommy. Charlie and Ben and I are reading books."

"Weading!" Ben stated firmly as he tugged on Bill's arm as if to remind him it was time to get back to the book in his hand.

Jess's laughter could be heard from the kitchen as Bill bent his head and went back to reading to the boys about a fire engine that could talk. By the time Bill had finished reading three more books to them, their mother was back to tell them lunch was ready.

Bill carried Charlie and Ben into the kitchen, one in each arm, and put them in the high chairs Jess had ready for them. It didn't take the boys long to dig into the meal of chicken fingers, French fries, and grapes that their mom had prepared for them, along with milk in some individual little plastic cups Jess called sippy-cups.

While Jess turned back to the refrigerator to pull out more ingredients to make lunches for the two adults, Bill leaned against the kitchen counter and watched her. She looked good. Sure, she'd put on a few pounds since having the twins, but that was a good thing. Bill had always thought Jess was too thin. Today, her black wavy hair was pulled back in a ponytail, and she was wearing a T-shirt and worn jeans. She'd evidently kicked off her shoes when she'd come back in the house as she was now barefoot.

"You look good, Jess."

She glanced up and gave him a crooked grin as she pulled the makings of sandwiches together on the countertop.

"Thanks, Parker. You look alright too. Life in D.C. must still agree with you."

Bill flinched a little at her words, wishing for a moment that he could tell her they were true.

"I'm doing okay, I guess."

Her dark eyes studied his face for a few seconds, and Bill was sure she was going to ask him what that meant. But then she was distracted by one of the boys complaining about wanting more milk to drink.

Having her sidetracked was fine with Bill. He'd seen the questions in his former partner's dark brown eyes and knew she was going to ask them the first chance she got. He was expecting it and actually hoped having an opportunity to talk to Jess would help. Maybe she had some answers for him in regards to what he was supposed to do next with his life.

Because right then, he was feeling as adrift as a boat on the open sea.

CHAPTER 9

Jessica Mosher tiptoed out of the twins' bedroom and carefully closed the door. Thankfully, her two sons were out cold, and as she left the room, they never let out a peep. As quickly as they had fallen asleep, it was apparent playing with their Uncle Bill had tired them out sufficiently that they should nap for a while.

She was still smiling as she entered the living room to find the very man she'd been thinking of sitting on the sofa, staring at the toys still scattered across the floor as if in a trance. He glanced up as she walked in.

"Are they sleeping?"

Jess nodded. "Yes, thank goodness." She paused before sitting down and motioned toward the front door.

"Let's sit out on the front porch. It's usually cooler there as there's a nice breeze that sweeps down through the canyon."

She lifted her lips a little at the thought of a few minutes of relaxation. She motioned for Bill to go on ahead of her.

"Let me grab us each a glass of iced tea, and I'll join you in a minute."

In the kitchen, it didn't take Jess long to prepare the glasses of tea. Once she was on the porch, she handed one to Bill, who was seated in a rocking chair, then placed her glass and the baby monitor on a small table next to the rocker she sat in.

"Ahh. Finally, a few minutes to relax." She stretched her legs out in front of her and stared at her bare toes as she flexed them.

Bill chuckled. "They *are* a handful, aren't they?"

She smiled, feeling the love of a mother sweep over her. There had been a time not that many years ago when she'd been afraid she would never marry—never know the love a mother has for her children. God had truly blessed her when Isaac Mosher had come into her life.

"You have *no* idea. Going after murderers and counterfeiters is *so* much easier," she murmured, feeling her lips turn up into a smile.

They shared a laugh, and then it was silent between them for a few moments.

"But you're happy, right?" Bill's deep voice asked.

She released a sigh. That question was an easy one to answer.

"Extremely."

A feeling of contentment swept over Jess as she stared across the front yard. She was living a completely different life from the one she had lived when she worked for the Bureau, but she wouldn't trade her life now for anything.

Which made her wonder about the man sitting next to her. Jess glanced over a couple of times to get a glimpse of her former partner, trying to decide when and how to open up a conversation about why he was really in Montana. When he'd told everyone he was here for at least a couple of weeks, Jess had immediately known something was wrong. She'd never known Bill Parker to take more than a couple of days off at a time.

Ever.

Finally, she decided to jump in feet first.

"So, what are you *really* doing here, Bill?"

Bill's chair stopped rocking, and he immediately raised his eyes to look over at her.

"I came to see you and the boys."

She shook her head. "You know that's not what I mean, wise guy. Why are you *here*—in Montana—at the ranch?"

Jess held up her hand as if to stop him from answering. "I know. You came to visit us, and that's nice. But what are you running from back in D.C.? And what has your face looking like you've lost your best friend?"

♫ ♫ ♫

Bill felt like groaning as he heard Jess's words. He'd know this was coming and had been dreading it all morning. He released a sigh and leaned back in the chair, letting the back of his head rest against the rear of the chair he was seated in. The pain in the region of his heart had lessened some since he'd come to Montana, but now it returned with a vengeance.

"Zoey broke up with me."

Just saying the words out loud wrenched his heart.

"Oh, Bill." The quiet words of his friend further tugged at his control.

When Jess didn't say anything beyond those two words, Bill decided he might as well tell her everything. He knew her well enough to know she'd ask to know it all eventually anyway, so there wasn't any reason to stall.

"It was my fault, Jess. I pushed Zoey to set a date for our wedding, and it was obvious she wasn't ready."

Jess's feet hit the floor of the porch with a thump as she quickly sat up.

"After three years, Bill? She wasn't ready? Come on, you know it had to be more than that."

He glanced over to see Jess firmly shaking her head, a disgusted look on her face. He knew that look and was thankful Zoey wasn't present as he was sure Jess would have gone after her like a mother bear protecting her cubs. One thing about Jessica, she was a loyal friend.

But she was right. If Zoey hadn't been ready to get married after three years, then it was obvious they weren't supposed to get married at all. So why was he having such a hard time letting her go?

"Did you love her?"

Bill felt the familiar pain in his heart at the question. It was one he'd been asking himself a lot lately.

"I thought I did. I mean, you've met Zoey, Jess. She has this effervescent personality that draws you to her. How could I not be attracted to her?"

"But attraction is not true love, Bill."

True love.

Did that even exist—or was it just something songwriters and authors made up to make sales? Bill had always wondered.

"I never thought she was right for you, anyway."

Jess's words brought him back to the present, and he turned to look over at her.

"What do you mean?"

She gave him a crooked smile.

"Exactly what I said. Zoey Beckett is a strong-willed woman—more than capable of taking care of herself. She acts like one of those women who doesn't really need a man in her life, and that's not the kind of woman you need, Bill." She paused for a few seconds, and her smile gentled.

"You are a big, strong man, Bill Parker. But anyone who gets to know you, soon discovers that you have a big heart that's as soft as a marshmallow."

Bill couldn't hold back a snort as he shook his head. A marshmallow? Yeah, that was just what a man wanted to be known for.

Where was Jess getting all this stuff about having a soft heart? He was an FBI Agent, after all. Weren't you supposed to be a big tough guy if you worked for the FBI? Ready to take on the world and all its evil?

"Yeah, right. I'm like a marshmallow, huh? That's just great."

"I mean it. It *is* great. Just watching you play with my boys reminded me of how big a heart you have. And because of your big heart, you deserve to have a woman that understands who you really are."

She shook her head again, and a familiar stubborn look appeared on her face. "And I just don't think that woman is Zoey Beckett. I never did."

Then she added. "But somewhere out there is a woman that God has personally picked out for you to love, Bill. Someone who needs you and will love you back for the man you are. You'll find her, I guarantee it."

Bill turned to look back out across the expanse of the yard and thought about Jess's words. Maybe Jess was wrong. Perhaps he was meant to be alone. Perhaps God had other plans than marriage for Bill Parker. Maybe he was just supposed to dedicate his life to working at the Bureau and going after criminals for the rest of his life and forget about having a family of his own.

Then he thought about how much fun it had been playing on the floor with Zeke's and Jess's little boys, and he prayed God would someday give him a family too. He just knew it wouldn't be with Zoey Beckett.

It was silent between the two of them for a short time before Jess spoke, bringing Bill's thoughts back from reminiscing about a life he could never have with Zoey.

"I have to say, I'm surprised you're willing to be away from the Bureau for this long, though, Bill. You live and breathe your job. How it going with your team? Is everything okay in the squad room?"

He swung his gaze from the distant horizon to glance over at his former partner. Leave it to Jess to get to what was really bothering him. Sure, working in the same building with his former fiancée was going to be difficult, but he thought he could handle that. It hadn't been easy, but so far, he'd managed.

No. Jess was right. There was more to what was bothering him than just the breakup with Zoey. But he was surprised she'd picked up on it. Not even Sam The Man had noticed his discontent with that part of his life.

Bill sighed. "Sometimes I wonder if I should leave the Bureau. I mean, the job is long hours and dangerous work. You and I both know that, and I know somebody's got to do the job. But I just wonder if that's what I want to do the rest of my life."

He gave her a little smile. "Everyone I used to work with has moved on to other things and other places. You…Sam. So, I can't help but wonder if I'm supposed to move on too—especially after this breakup with Zoey."

He watched as Jess gently rocked her chair by pushing her nail-polished toes on the porch floor. She didn't respond right away, but that was expected. He knew she was digesting what he'd just told her. Bill was curious to see what her response would be. Jess had an uncanny ability to read people and get to the heart of them.

"So tell me, Bill Parker, when you were a little boy, what did you want to be when you grew up?"

Bill stopped rocking his chair and looked over at Jess. That hadn't been what he'd expected her to ask. At all.

"What?"

She gave him a crooked little grin. "You know—a fireman, policeman, maybe an astronaut and someday travel to the moon. Play pro football? What is your dream job, Agent Parker?"

He shook his head and smiled. Then he allowed his mind to drift back to his college days and the dreams he had back then—back before September 11, 2001, and back before he'd joined the Marines and gone off to fight a war.

"I always thought I'd like to be a Phys Ed teacher—maybe even teach history." He shook his head. "Sounds dumb, I know. And it wouldn't be possible now. After all, I've been out of college for a long time, and as they say, a lot of water has gone under that bridge."

Jess quit rocking and sat up in her chair, turning toward him.

"Not dumb at all. You finished your degree, right?"

He nodded. "Yeah..."

"So, all you need to do is complete whatever credit hours would be required for you to get your teaching certificate, right?"

Bill stared at his friend's expectant face, watching the wheels turn behind those chocolate brown eyes of hers. Then he released a grunt.

"I'm not exactly young anymore, Jess. It's kinda late in my life to start over."

She gave her head a firm shake. "Oh, Parker quit your moaning and groaning. A lot of people start second or even third careers well into their forties and fifties. You are *not* too old!"

Jess reached over and patted Bill on the back of his hand, resting on the arm of the rocker.

"Promise me you'll at least think about the possibilities. If it's something you really want to do, pray about it and see if it fits in with God's will for your life. Sometimes He tells us to stay, and sometimes He tells us to go. And if there's one thing I've learned, Bill, God can use our own restlessness and unhappiness in a situation to force us to move to where He really wants us to be."

He finally gave her a nod. "I think you're crazy to even suggest it, Jess. But I promise you I'll think about it."

♫ ♫ ♫

Joy finished mopping the floor of the diner and returned the mop and bucket to the janitorial closet where they stored it. She'd already wiped down all the tables, chairs, and booths earlier, and as she looked around the diner, she released a weary sigh. Her shift was finally over, and she could go home. And the best part was she had tomorrow and the next day off. She wasn't sure what she was going to do with her days off, although sleeping through one of them sounded pretty good right then.

"Thanks for helping close up, Joy," her boss Peggy said as she walked through the kitchen on her way to the office in the rear of the building.

The older woman gave Joy a weary smile. "You have a good time on your days off, and I'll see you Tuesday."

Giving her a nod, Joy grabbed her purse, backpack, and a bottle of water from the cooler and headed out the door to her car parked in the back lot. It was late, and she was tired. Thankfully, it had cooled down some after sunset, but it was still a balmy seventy degrees. The forecasted rain hadn't appeared yet. When it did, Joy was hoping and praying it would cool things down a bit. After a brutally hot summer, she was more than ready for autumn's cooler temperatures. Although she *wasn't* looking forward to winter and all the snow they'd receive.

She unlocked her car and got in, automatically locking the car doors after her, then put the key in the ignition to start the engine. Once started, she cranked up the air conditioner full blast and opened the bottle of water and swallowed a swig or two.

How Joy longed for the days before the attack when she would have felt safe. Back then, she would have rolled down her windows and not even worried about locking her car doors. Before it happened, Joy was probably naïve, but at least she hadn't felt the constant fear in her heart whenever she was alone.

Now, she dreaded time alone, and nights were the worst—even in the safety of her uncle's and aunt's cabin. Sometimes the nightmares brought back the terror of that night to the point Joy felt as if she were going crazy. Whenever the night terrors came, she'd turn on the light and pray and read scripture until she would feel God's peace enfold her, and then she could finally sleep.

She also prayed that someday, the constant fear would go away.

The drive home was quiet, and Joy liked it that way. She'd turned off the radio as all that was on that late in the evening was obnoxious music or radio talk shows. It was peaceful to sit in the darkened car and drive down a road with little or no traffic. It gave her time to talk to God with no distractions.

And whenever she began to feel that old fear sweep over her, she would grab hold of Bible verses that offered her comfort and courage. The verse from Psalms she'd most recently memorized ran through her mind.

In God have I put my trust: I will not be afraid what man can do unto me.

The familiar peace swept over her as she said the words over and over again out loud. God was still with her. She wasn't alone. She was never alone and didn't need to be afraid. She was loved by her Creator and would never be alone again.

CHAPTER 10

The week passed quickly with Bill working most every day next to Jack Byrd in the barn. Surprisingly, each day, he found himself becoming more and more comfortable around the horses—and Jack Byrd. The two of them talked more of their respective childhoods and their journeys to faith, with Jack surprising Bill with the depth of his knowledge of the Bible.

Jack told Bill the story of how he and Sam Morgan had met when Sam's grandmother, Clara Morgan, had helped run a Vacation Bible School on the reservation. It was there that Jack had come to the saving knowledge of the Gospel, and when he'd turned his heart and life over to God.

Bill sat enthralled while Jack told him about what his life had been like before he'd come to Christ, though.

"Shortly after I became a teenager, my father started drinking, and the man I had always looked up to as a child, became a drunken stranger. The first time he hit my mother and my little sister, I stepped in to stop him. He turned on me and knocked me halfway across the room. It was a miracle I didn't have any broken bones, but it didn't matter. He'd broken my spirit. I quickly came to hate my father, whether he was drinking or not."

Jack took a deep breath and released it. Bill almost wished then he hadn't asked Jack about his childhood as he could tell it was difficult for him to talk about—even after all these years.

"Then one summer, a group of people from the local church came to the reservation to hold a Vacation Bible School for the children of the Crow. Clara Morgan, Sam's grandmother, was one of those people, and she brought her grandson with her every day. Sam."

Jack smiled as he glanced over at Bill. It was easy for Bill to tell that the current relationship between Jack and Sam Morgan had begun that day.

"I went to the Bible School every day, and it was there I discovered the truth about love. No one had ever told me about Jesus before, or that He died on the cross for my sins so I could live a life of forgiveness. No one had ever explained to me before that God—my heavenly Father—loved me so much that He sent His Son down to earth to die for me, for my sins." Jack stopped to take a breath. "I made a decision that summer to follow Christ, to allow Him to come into my heart and make me the kind of man I should be. I also made a promise to myself that I would never be like my earthly father."

Bill took a deep breath and finally asked the one question Jack hadn't answered.

"So, what happened to your dad, Jack?"

Jack dropped his head for a moment, then raised it back up to stare into Bill's eyes.

"He eventually drank himself to death. He never accepted the knowledge that God loved him." Jack blinked a couple of times. "I sat by his deathbed during his last hours on this earth and told him I forgave him for the times he'd hit Mom, and Betty, and me. I told him Jesus died for his sins, and all he had to do to know His love was ask for forgiveness of his sins and God would accept him as His child. But he never did. I'm sorry to say, he died without God."

Bill shook his head, sad for the man who was quickly becoming a friend. It was silent between the two of them for a few moments before Jack turned to him.

"So, what's your story, Bill?"

Bill sighed, knowing it was only fair that he share the reason for his decision to accept Christ with the man sitting across from him. After all, Jack had bared his soul to Bill.

"It happened when I was stationed in Iraq. My best friend was killed by an RPG, a rocket-propelled grenade. He was a Christian."

Jack didn't say anything but simply nodded his head, almost as if he knew what was coming.

"Joe would do anything for anybody, all with a big smile on his face." Bill paused for a second or two as sweet memories of the young man he had known such a short time swept over him.

"I've often wondered if he sensed something was going to happen to him. The last few days, he read his Bible to me even more than usual and kept telling me I needed to get myself right with God; that none of us knew how many days we had left. But he didn't push it at me, you know?"

Jack gave him a nod, his dark eyes watching Bill closely.

"I just knew Joe was different. He had something I wanted; peace, for one thing. Peace to face whatever tomorrow brought us, even if it was death."

Bill released another sigh. "After Joe's death, I went to talk to the Chaplain at the urging of my CO. The Chaplain explained to me why Joe had that peace—which came from his faith in God. And he told me I could have that peace too. I've never been sorry I made the decision to give my life to Christ. Knowing my sins are forgiven and knowing where I'll go when I die has given me peace to face whatever happens. And knowing that He lives inside my heart and soul and is there to turn to no matter what—that is the best knowledge in the world. This life isn't easy. What I do for a living isn't easy—fighting evil in the world."

Jack didn't say anything for a few moments, and the two of them simply sat together, pondering the wonder of the salvation they both had found at the hands of God.

"Sam told me you were a good man, Bill Parker." He put his hand on Bill's shoulder, and this time it didn't feel so heavy, but more of a comfort. "He was right, my brother, and I will be praying for you as you continue to fight the evil of this world."

Bill gave the older man a smile—knowing that a line had been crossed and that Jack Byrd was no longer just an acquaintance or friend, but had accepted him as a brother.

♫ ♫ ♫

Before Bill knew it, it was another leisurely Saturday at Bluecreek Ranch. Well, as leisurely as it could be, Bill surmised. He knew the chores needed to be done, and the animals still needed to be fed and cared for. So, after breakfast, he headed to the barn and helped Sam and Jack feed the horses and make sure they had plenty of water. Strangely, Bill was starting to feel like he fit into the ranch life—although he knew he'd never make a cowboy.

Thankfully, it looked to be a cooler day than the previous week had been. There were enough clouds in the sky to deflect some of the sun's warmth, and a northwest breeze helped take off the brutal-ness of the previous day's heat.

He and the other two men had just finished the chores when a familiar figure strode purposefully across the barnyard toward the open barn door where the three of them had been standing and talking.

Joy.

Bill studied the petite figure as she walked in their direction. It always surprised him to see her and realize how little she was. Zoey wasn't very tall either, but Joy was just plain tiny. But she didn't appear to let her size slow her down any. He could remember watching her a few mornings earlier as she'd singlehandedly unsaddled and taken care of her horse after a morning ride. So, it was easy to tell she was stronger than she looked.

"Good morning, Joy," Sam was the first to speak, and even went so far as to step forward and pull the young woman into a quick sideways hug.

Bill noticed she stiffly accepted the hug, then appeared to adjust to the contact and partially hugged Sam in return.

"Morning, Sam, Uncle Jack." She turned her dark eyes on Bill, and he gave her a smile, hoping she'd return the favor. Instead, she gave him a brief nod.

"Good morning."

So, that was how it was gonna be. She wouldn't even call him by name.

"Good morning, Miss Whitefox." He gave his head a little dip as he greeted her.

Her eyes narrowed until she must have realized he wasn't teasing her or being disrespectful, then finally gave him a timid smile.

"You going out for a ride?"

She turned her eyes on her uncle at his question.

"Yup."

Jack nodded. "Just take care and avoid the herd. Don't want to do anything to spook them or stir them up. They've been a little cranky the past few days." He elbowed Bill in the ribs, causing him to grunt. "Like some other people I know around here."

Bill gave the man a look he hoped he could read. He wasn't in the mood for being harassed this early in the morning—from Jack or anyone else. He was well aware he'd been a bear to Jack all week as he helped him in the barn, but he couldn't help it. Ever since his visit and subsequent talk with Jess, he couldn't get a handle on what he was supposed to do next. And it was driving him crazy.

"Maybe the man needs to spend some time on the back of a horse. That always seems to help my disposition."

The heads of the other two men swiveled, their eyes moving from Joy and landing on Bill. He stared from them back to the young woman who had just made that unexpected statement.

"But then again, maybe the man doesn't know how to ride a horse," she added, a dangerous looking twinkle in her dark eyes as she tilted her head a little and stared up at him.

So, what was little Miss Whitefox up to this morning? Was she actually goading him into doing something she didn't think he could do? It was easy to read the dare in her dark eyes.

"I can ride." He frowned as he replayed that statement in his head. "Granted, I'm not a great equestrian by any stretch of the imagination, but I can ride."

She gave him a little nod, her dark eyes locked on his face.

"So?"

Bill glanced over at Sam and Jack just long enough to see the same look of surprise he was feeling on both of their faces. She was actually asking him—daring him—to go on a horseback ride with her.

"You want me to go for a ride…with you?"

Joy gave a tilt of her head and a little shift of her shoulders, the look on her face stoic. Now that she'd done so, she didn't look all that pleased about having asked him. Maybe he should just decline.

"Yeah. I mean, I could show you around the ranch some. You'll see it better on the back of a horse than you'd see it on the back of a four-wheeler." She gave a little snort as if riding one of those was sacrilegious. Hopefully, she didn't know he'd already used one of the four-wheelers to go see Jess and the boys.

"I think that's a good idea."

Bill looked over at her Uncle Jack in surprise as he stated his opinion—which shocked Bill almost as much as Joy's offer.

"Sure," Sam added with a nod. "She's right too, Bill. You can see the ranch much better on the back of a horse."

He gave Bill one of his dimply grins, and Bill realized he was outnumbered. No sense fighting it.

"Okay."

The smile that lit up Joy's face was more than a reward for finally agreeing to go with her—although he still didn't understand what was behind her offer. After what she'd been through, Joy shouldn't want to spend time alone with a man—any man. Especially a man she didn't know all that well yet. If her emotions were still as fragile as her Uncle Jack had led him to believe, Bill would definitely have to tread with care around her and not do or say anything to upset her.

"I'll saddle up Spirit for me," Joy turned to her uncle and stated. "You can saddle up Bess for him."

Bill snorted, then turned it into a cough. Bess sounded like a cow's name, certainly not a wild bronco's name. Perfect for him.

Between the three of them, they had the two horses saddled and ready to go in only a few minutes. Just as Bill readied to put his booted foot in the stirrup and mount Bess, Jack tossed him a cowboy hat.

"You'll need that, Cowboy." He gave Bill a crooked grin. "And don't let my little gal keep you on the back of that horse too many hours, or you won't be able to walk tomorrow, and I'd hate for you to have to limp into the church."

Jack and Sam were both chuckling as Bill got on the horse and took the reins in his hands, hoping he could remember how to make the horse do what he wanted. Trying to ignore the looks of the other two men, Bill nudged his horse forward to follow Joy on Spirit out of the barnyard.

Here goes nothing.

All he needed to do was keep his behind in the saddle and hope the mare knew what she was doing because he certainly didn't.

♪ ♪ ♪

Joy reined in Spirit long enough to allow Bill to catch up. He didn't look very comfortable on the back of old Bess, but hopefully, after a little time riding, he'd remember what to do. Sam had told her earlier in the week that Bill had spent time on the ranch before and could ride—although he certainly wasn't a pro at it. Sam had also added that Bill wasn't a fan of riding horses, which meant that his agreeing to go riding with her had to mean something. Perhaps he had just been embarrassed to admit he didn't want to go with her in front of her Uncle Jack and Sam.

Or maybe he was actually interested in spending time with her.

Although, why that should matter to Joy, she didn't know. She also didn't understand what had prompted her to ask him to go with her in the first place. She just knew there was something about the big blue eyes that looked out of Bill Parker's face that made her think he was a man she could trust. And her Uncle Jack had assured her she could, and spending some time alone on the back of a horse with a man might give her more courage for the next time she was near a man. After all, the two of them had already ridden to church alone in her car, and she'd managed to survive that.

No, it had been a good thing for Joy to ask him to come along on the ride.

They kept the horses to a walk for a time, then she kicked Spirit into a slow trot, struggling to keep the horse in control. Joy knew Spirit would fly into a full gallop and leave Bill in his dust if she didn't let the animal know who was boss. The gelding definitely lived up to his name. Looking to her left, Joy was happy to see Bill had likewise put Bess into a trot and was keeping up with her just fine.

She took him through the back pasture, opening gates from the back of her horse as they came to fences in their path. Even riding abreast, it wasn't conducive to talking to each other, so they were silent as they crossed the pastures and fields. Every now and then, she pulled Spirit to a stop long enough to point out something she thought Bill might be interested in, but most of the time, they just rode.

Half an hour into their ride, they came to a river—the Bluecreek—the river for which she knew the ranch had been named by Brady Morgan, Sam Morgan's great-grandfather. It was late in the summer, so there were no springtime or summer wildflowers. It was still a pretty place, though, and one of her most favorites places on the ranch.

Joy pulled Spirit to a halt and slid off his back, tugging on the reins and leading the horse over to a shady spot under a tree near the river. She turned long enough to see Bill was following her example and was leading Bess over too.

"They can get a drink here and graze awhile." She gave Bill a small smile. "And we can also get out of the sun for a bit."

She pulled a canteen off her saddle.

"I brought some water along." She grinned. "Even put a little ice in it, although I'm sure it's melted by now. But hopefully, it kept the water from getting too warm."

♫ ♫ ♫

Bill followed Joy through the tall, knee-high dry grass in the direction of a large tree at the river's edge. As she made her way through the grass, he noticed Joy kept her eyes on the ground, and Bill followed her example, always wary of snakes lurking. But there were only the usual grasshoppers jumping around as they made their way to the shade of the tree.

Once they reached the tree, Joy plopped down on the ground in the shade and took a swig of the water in the canteen. As Bill sat next to her, she passed it over to him.

"It's not ice-cold, but it's not bad," she said as she passed him the canteen.

He took a swig of the liquid, feeling substantially better just by having something to drink. As he gave the canteen back to Joy, he noticed she'd relaxed back against the trunk of the tree.

"So, what do you know about me?"

Joy's quiet voice pulled him back from his pondering the need to renew his gym membership, and wondering if there were someplace out of D.C. where he could ride a horse every now and then.

Glancing over at the young woman seated next to him, Bill thought about her question as he studied her face. She had the high cheekbones of her Aunt Mary and her aunt's jet black hair, which today was pulled back in a single braid that hung down her back.

"Well…" he hesitated, wondering how much he should tell her. "I know you're Mary Byrd's niece. I know you have Crow blood in you—just like your aunt and uncle."

She turned her dark eyes on him. "My father is half-Crow, and my mother was full Crow."

Bill tried to remember if Jack had mentioned that, but couldn't recall it if he had.

"Your mom—is she still alive?"

Joy shook her head.

"No. She died from breast cancer about five years ago."

"I'm sorry. That had to be hard."

She sighed. "I never saw her anyway."

Her lips turned down in a frown. "Mom deserted my dad and me when I was about eleven. She left the reservation and never came back."

Bill heard her sigh again.

"She could never understand my dad's obsession with their heritage. Mom was Crow but just wanted to have a normal life. I'm not sure Dad can do that."

"What do you mean?"

Joy glanced over at him once as if to measure how interested he was in her answer, then continued.

"It's like my dad wants to live in the past or something." He watched as she pushed a strand of silky-looking black hair out of her eyes.

"Don't get me wrong, I'm proud of my Crow heritage, but Dad...it's like that's all there is to him. Even though he's only half-Crow, he helps to organize the Crow Reunion on the res every year. And that's fine as I know he enjoys being involved in it. It's just..." She paused as if struggling to organize her thoughts. "It's almost like he wants to go back and live the way our ancestors did before the white man came. I mean, be real. Those days are over, and life has moved on. It's a different world, and we have to live in it."

She shook her head and released a little sigh. "It doesn't matter, I guess. Dad will have to live his life the way he sees fit, and I'm going to live mine."

"Do you miss living on the reservation?"

Bill watched as Joy's head swiveled, and her eyes locked on his. He could see so much in the dark pools of her eyes—so much hope, so much pain.

"No." She shifted her sitting position a little and looked away. "There is nothing for me there anymore."

He nodded as if he understood. And he did, somewhat. From what little her Uncle Jack had told him, Bill was aware the reservation wasn't someplace Joy needed to live. She was young and could start over someplace else—and that would be best for her, considering her circumstances.

It was silent between them for a few seconds before she spoke again.

"So, Special Agent Bill Parker, what else did Uncle Jack tell you about me?"

Bill was silent for a bit as he tried to decide how best to answer that question. Surely she didn't expect him to bring up what had happened to her.

"Jack said you were living with them now because that was best for you." He paused a second before he added, "He also told me what happened to you."

The jerk of her hand resting on her left leg was the only sign that what he'd said had upset her. She never turned to look at him, and Bill wondered for a moment if she were even breathing as she had become so still.

"I'm sorry. Jack probably wouldn't have told me the whole story if I hadn't pressed him to."

He saw her head slowly shake from one side to the other and worried that he'd hurt her by telling her what he knew. That hadn't been his intention at all, but she *had* asked, and he wasn't going to lie to her either. Bill had learned years ago that lies only led to more pain and misunderstanding.

Bill heard her take a deep breath and release it slowly, and the hand on her leg raised to her face where she covered her mouth. Finally, she relaxed and dropped the hand back to her lap.

"It's okay."

Her voice was so quiet, Bill almost didn't hear her. When she finally lifted her head and turned toward him, the resolve he saw on her face encouraged him to continue to talk to her about the subject. At least she hadn't gotten angry enough to jump on her horse and ride away. Which was vitally important, as Bill didn't have a clue how to get back to the main part of the ranch and the house and barns.

"Ernie acted real nice when I first started dating him. You know?"

Joy turned her big eyes on Bill, and he nodded, almost afraid to move as he realized she was actually going to tell him what had happened. That hadn't been his intent at all, but perhaps she needed to talk about it...with someone. And who better than someone who she wasn't close to...someone who wasn't family or a close friend?

"We only went out a few times. And at first, he treated me good. Took me out for dinners and to the movies."

She sighed. "Ernie had just returned to the reservation. He'd been gone for a couple of years, living in Bozeman, I think. Then he came back and moved back in with his mother."

Joy stopped talking for a second or two and simply stared at the river in front of them.

"I remembered him from school, and we girls always thought he was one of the most handsome men on the reservation. He was, you know, and he knew it."

She released a little snort, which shocked Bill and he almost chuckled, but then caught himself. He was afraid to make a move or a noise of any sort, for fear he'd remind her he was there and she'd stop talking.

"That night...the night it happened...we'd eaten out at a restaurant, and then he took me for a drive. There are places on the res that are very desolate, but beautiful. We went out near the buffalo range. I figured we were going to go somewhere and watch the sunset. Very romantic."

She turned her eyes on him for only a second before continuing. "Buffalo still roam the land on the reservation, you know, and even though they're kept in by fences, you can almost imagine what it must have been like two hundred years ago to live free."

Shaking her head, she released another breath. "Anyway, we drove out to an area that was a long way from anything. I should have never gone with him."

Her voice cracked on the last few words, but then she raised her head again.

"I fought him, you know. I fought with everything I had in me." Bill saw her swallow and wanted more than anything else in the world to pull her into his arms and comfort her, but he knew that wasn't what she needed right then. She just needed him to be there...and listen.

"Then he drove me back home like nothing had happened." She shook her head. "Of course, as soon as my dad saw me, he knew something awful had happened. My face was battered, and I had a black eye, and I was crying like crazy."

Bill saw her shudder.

"I don't remember a lot of what happened after that. Dad took me to the hospital, and then the police station. I can remember feeling like I wanted to die."

Tears were now running down Joy's face as she silently wept.

"Then Uncle Jack and Aunt Mary came. They told my dad that they thought it would be best if I came and stayed with them for a time. Of course, Ernie was arrested, and we had the trial and all that to get through. I had to sit in front of the Tribal Council and tell my side of the story. Fortunately, they believed me."

She shuddered again. "It was the most terrible time in my life, Bill."

It was silent between them for a few minutes. Once Bill realized she was done talking, he felt as if he had to say something to her. Anything to help ease her pain.

"For the record, I think the scumbag should have gotten a lot more than two years for what he did to you, Joy." He tried to keep his voice quiet and steady, but whenever he thought about what this sweet gal had been through, it made him want to scream.

Joy simply nodded as she kept looking at him. At least she wasn't crying anymore. Her tears had nearly undone him.

"I could have let it destroy me, you know."

He nodded. "I'm proud of you for not letting it do that, Joy."

She blinked a couple of times and then dropped her eyes from his. Then he heard her sigh, and she pulled her shoulders back as if in defiance. Seconds later, she hopped to her feet.

"Well, I think we've rested the horses long enough, Very Special Agent Bill Parker. Time to get you back in that saddle."

Bill chuckled and then stood and followed Joy back to the horses. Joy Whitefox might look like a tiny thing, but her heart was as strong as a buffalo, and her courage was as big as a lion's.

"Thank you for telling me your story, Joy. I know that wasn't easy."

She glanced over at him just once before putting her foot in the stirrup and getting on the back of Spirit.

"It wasn't. But I wanted you to know who I am. I will never allow anyone to hurt me like that again."

He nodded, then he also mounted his horse, thinking to himself that he had no doubt about who she was. Joy was one of the bravest, courageous women he'd ever known. And that was saying something.

As he got on the back of Bess, he sighed. He wasn't excited by the prospect of having to ride the horse all the way back to the ranch, but since there were no other options to get there, he supposed he could tolerate it a little longer.

The next morning, he was positive he was going to feel it in every bone and muscle of his body, but having the time alone with Joy and getting to know her a little better had been more than worth it.

CHAPTER 11

The following Monday morning, Bill ate an early breakfast with Clay and Sam Morgan, Jack Byrd, and the rest of the ranch hands. After the hearty meal, the rest of the men headed out for the day, which left at the house, Lottie Morgan, Julie, and Mary. A little earlier, Jack had left the ranch to take Samantha and C.J. into town for the church's Vacation Bible School program, which ran through the rest of the week. And, of course, Joy had gone to work.

Which left Bill wondering what he was going to do with the rest of his day.

Listening to the three women chattering away in the kitchen, Bill wandered around the great room, finally coming to a stop in front of the enormous stone fireplace. Above it hung a large framed map that drew his attention. Bill was standing there studying it when he heard the sound of soft footsteps behind him, and Julie stepped up to stand next to him.

"Bradford Morgan, Sam's great-grandfather, drew that map. It's a sketch of the original 320-acre tract he and Mattie homesteaded back in 1915."

He glanced over at her as she stared at the map as if in awe.

"Can you imagine what their lives must have been like back then…coming here and starting a new life with no one to help you? No family, and no idea what you were getting into?"

He shook his head as he continued to study the map. He couldn't imagine it. Bradford and Mattie Morgan had a lot of courage to do what they'd done.

"The ranch is a lot bigger than this now, though. Right?"

Julie turned to give him a smile. "Oh, yes. Over the years, when times were tough, and some of the other ranchers gave up and returned east, Brady was able to buy them out and add several more thousand acres to the ranch until it reached its current size."

He heard her sigh. "When I first married Sam, I was amazed at the family history that was behind this ranch." She gave him a sideways look. "As you know, I have no family of my own, so I embraced being part of a big family that had such deep roots in this area."

Bill nodded, remembering the woman Julie had been— before Sam Morgan had come into her life, and everything had changed for her.

"I'll never be happy about what happened back then, but I'm thankful the Lord gave me so much more to replace what I lost that day."

He gave her a nod, not knowing how to respond to that. Bill knew Julie's history, as few people did, so it was difficult for him to imagine being thankful for all the terrible things that had happened to her. Once upon a time, Julie had been another person, quietly living her life in a small town in Ohio, when the place she had worked at had been bombed. Julie had been the only survivor and the only one who could identify the bomber. So the FBI had sent a team to her hometown to investigate the bombing, placing Julie in protective custody after her own little house was blown up. She had barely made it out before that bomb had blown.

The FBI team, consisting of Sam Morgan, Jessica Thorne, and Bill Parker, had eventually caught the guy responsible, and Bill had even been the one to take down the member of the drug cartel after the jerk had found Julie and threatened her life. But because of circumstances, Julie had to start her life over in Witness Protection—fortunately, right there in D.C., where she had come to work for the F.B.I. And there, Sam Morgan and she had become reacquainted, fell in love, and eventually married.

Looking back on it, Bill guessed it could be argued that God had allowed much to be taken from her, but had truly given her a great deal in return for what she'd lost. She now had a loving marriage, two fantastic children, and an excellent support system in their friends and family at the ranch. So, maybe Julie was right for being thankful. But it sure had been a lot to go through to get to where she was now.

Julie turned and pointed toward a couple of comfortable-looking chairs situated in front of the fireplace. "Let's sit and chat a bit. I've been so busy, I haven't had time to catch up on what's going on in your life."

Bill plopped down in the nearest chair and struggled to hold back a bitter laugh. Like there was anything good going on for her to want to know. Besides, Bill was sure Sam had already filled her in on his pathetic life.

After she settled in her chair next to his, Julie turned her blue eyes on him.

"So, Sam said you and Zoey broke up. I'm sorry to hear that."

The familiar shot of pain went through Bill's heart at hearing Zoey's name, but he quickly pushed the pain aside as he sat up a little straighter in his chair. He was pleased that the pain he felt this time wasn't as sharp, but it was still there.

"Thanks. I'm fine." He tried to give Julie a smile to prove how fine he was but wasn't sure he convinced her.

"So, what happened, if I may ask? You two had been dating a long time."

Then Julie waved her right hand in the air and gave her head a little shake. "No, never mind, Bill. I had no right asking that. It's your life, and I don't have any business prying into your private life. Sam scolds me all the time for being too nosy about other people's lives."

He shook his head and released a sigh.

"It's okay, Julie. And if anyone has a right to know, you and Sam do. You're the only family I have."

That statement was true. Bill had no one other than the Morgans as his own family—like Julie's—was long gone.

"Truth is, I don't know what happened that caused the breakup. I mean, you're right. Zoey and I dated for several years. And even though I'd asked her to marry me, and she'd said yes, I could never get her to settle on a wedding date." He sighed again. "I guess I should have seen that as a red flag right away, huh?"

Julie gave him a little smile that looked as sad as he felt.

"Not necessarily, Bill. You and Zoey have hectic lives. I know how much time working for the Bureau takes in your life. It's difficult to form a relationship when you work so many hours and are in so many different places in a year."

Bill nodded as he raised his eyes from the floor to glance over at her.

"But you and Sam made it work."

She slowly nodded. "Yes. But you have to remember, I was just a clerk—not actually working out in the field. I was always there for him to come home to."

It was quiet between them for a few seconds before Bill voiced his other thoughts. Thoughts he hadn't discussed with anyone before. But he'd been thinking a lot the past few days about Zoey's and his relationship, and there had been red flags for months. But he'd just ignored them.

"I think it was more than our respective work hours."

He could feel Julie's eyes on him—even though he wasn't looking directly at her. Sam and Julie had both known Bill longer than most of his friends, so he knew he wasn't going to be able to withhold information from her. The way she was able to get people to open up about themselves, you could almost say she'd picked up some of Sam's interrogation skills over the years.

"The past few months, it was as if Zoey was pulling farther and farther away from me. I can see it now in hindsight, of course. But back then, I didn't recognize the signs."

Bill clenched his jaw as he tried to get control of his emotions. His grief over losing Zoey had now turned more to anger than anything else. Anger than he'd wasted so much of his life chasing after a woman who didn't want him.

"I don't know what she wants out of life anymore, Julie. I just know it's not me."

It was silent again a moment before Julie's soft voice caught his attention.

"Well, as hard as it is for you to go through this, I have to say, I think it's for the best. Better to find out now than after the wedding vows have been spoken."

Then a second later, she added, "What about you, Bill? What do you want to do with the rest of your life?"

He brought his head up, and his eyes locked on Julie's blue ones. It might have been worded differently, but it was the exact same question Jess had asked him a few days earlier.

"I don't know."

He heard her soft chuckle and couldn't help but smile himself a little at the sound. He sounded like a three-year-old that didn't know what he wanted for lunch.

"Okay. Let me rephrase my question then. What did you want to be when you were younger? Maybe when you were in college? What were your plans after you graduated?"

Bill dropped his eyes to the floor and thought about her question. Again, it was almost a duplicate of Jess's question. Was God trying to get his attention? Well, He had it.

"Back then, I had dreams of wanting to teach Physical Education. Or History. Or both." He grinned, feeling a little surge of happiness at the pleasant memory of a simpler time in his life.

"I loved working with the kids at the Youth Center near the college. Three different summers before I graduated, I volunteered at the center, and it was a blast."

Then he frowned. "But that was when I was a lot younger, Julie. It was a different time and a much different life."

Julie shook her head. "Bill. You talk like you're seventy-years-old and your life is over. I mean, really? That dream can still be feasible for you. There is always a need for good teachers. What would you have to accomplish to get your teaching credentials? You finished your Bachelor's degree, right?"

He chuckled. "You sound just like Jess when we talked about this." He gave her a wink. "Have you been talking about me behind my back?"

The woman sitting next to him grinned. "Scouts honor, Bill. Jess and I have *not* talked about you at all." She gave him a gentle smile. "But you know, God does use other people to get us to listen to His still small voice sometimes. Now, back to my question. Your degree, did you finish it?

"Yeah. I graduated just before I decided to join the Marines. But I never completed the necessary testing for certification. I *did* complete my student teaching, but that was about it. And anyway, I don't even know if my degree would be valid now after all these years or if I'd have to take additional classes to qualify for getting my certification."

"Well, you could always check."

Bill rubbed his hand across his freshly-shaved chin and thought about Julie's idea as he stared into the depths of the unlit fireplace in front of them. Could that be what God was calling him to? It did seem rather provident that both Jess and Julie had brought up the same subject to him in just a matter of days.

All Bill knew was that the work he did at the Bureau had recently lost its appeal—even before Zoey had dropped her bombshell on him. And, if Zoey was still going to be there, Bill wasn't thrilled with the prospect of working in a building where he could run into her at any time. Yet he didn't want to think he was just running away from a bad situation by quitting.

But was going after his teaching certification and starting a new career at this point in his life the right thing to do?

"I think you should pray about it, Bill. And Sam and I will be praying for God's guidance for you too."

He nodded as he allowed his mind to drift to old dreams—dreams about working with youth, coaching, and teaching. Perhaps, God had him come to Montana for this very purpose. Maybe God hadn't deserted him after all but was simply leading him to something better for his life.

Something Bill had never imagined.

♫ ♫ ♫

Bill and Joy went on one more horseback ride the day before he was scheduled to leave Montana. This time, Bill felt more comfortable on the back of old Bess, and Joy appeared to be more relaxed around him.

She even shared with him about her own dreams while they rested the horses for a while at the river.

"I don't know if Sam told you or not, but I'm trying to complete my Bachelor's degree. It's long been a dream of mine—so I can get a good job someplace and better my life.

Bill nodded—not surprised to hear Joy's aspirations. It hadn't taken him spending much time around her to discover the young woman was not only courageous but also smart.

He picked a blade of grass off the leg of his jeans and wondered how much of his own dreams he should share with her.

"Sam hadn't mentioned it, but I think that's great, Joy." He gave her a smile and a wink—hoping to make her understand he was really proud of her dreams. "Actually, I've decided to chase after my dream too."

Will that statement, Bill found himself telling Joy all about his long-time dream to be a coach and a school teacher.

"That's wonderful, Bill!"

Joy's dark eyes sparkled, and for a second, Bill forgot what she was congratulating him about as he found himself enthralled by her beauty. And unlike so many women he'd known, she didn't even realize how gorgeous she was.

"I think it's awesome that God brought you here to Montana to find your dreams."

Bill nodded, wondering suddenly where or if the young woman sitting next to him fit into those dreams.

Because if she did, he wouldn't mind that at all.

CHAPTER 12

The following morning, Sam drove Bill to the airport. This time, it had been bittersweet for him to say goodbye to everyone at the ranch. For some reason, Bill had started to think of the place as more of a home than just somewhere to visit. Perhaps it was because he'd stayed longer than he ever had in the past. And saying goodbye to Samantha and C.J. had been especially hard as he'd gotten close to them during his short time there.

"You keep working on your layup, Samantha," he'd encouraged the willowy girl. He'd been giving her hints on her basketball moves every night after supper for the past week, and she wasn't too bad. If she kept growing like she was, Samantha Morgan was going to be tall enough to have a real presence on the basketball court when she hit high school.

He'd leaned over to give the eleven-year-old girl a high-five before feeling his legs tackled in a hug.

"And you keep practicing your dribbling, C.J., my man."

"I'll miss you, Uncle Bill." C.J.'s high-pitched voice had touched his heart.

Yeah, he was gonna miss the kids the most. Especially those two rug rats of Jess's and Zeke's. Charlie and Ben were such a joy to be around. How could you have a bad day with them in your lives?

"You know you can always come back, Bill. Anytime."

Almost as if he'd known what Bill was thinking about, Sam's voice cut into his thoughts and turned his attention back to the road ahead of them. They were getting close to the city limits, so it wouldn't be long now, and they'd reach the airport.

"I know." He sighed. "Did Julie tell you what we talked about? About me, maybe checking into teaching?"

He glanced over long enough to see Sam's nod.

"Yup. And we've been praying about it—and we'll keep praying for you until God gives you a firm answer one way or the other." His former boss looked over at him briefly before turning his eyes back to the road. "You know that, right?"

Bill nodded. "I know. And I thank you both for those prayers."

He sighed. "I feel a little lost right now. I'd kinda turned away from God after Zoey broke up with me, so it's taking some time to get back to where I feel worthy to ask Him for anything. I'm not sure what God has planned., but I guess I'm willing to wait for Him to let me know."

He gave Sam a grin. "In the meantime, I'll just keep going after the bad guys."

Sam's deep chuckle filled the cab of the truck. "Yeah, well, somebody's gotta do it. And my family and I thank you for being there to do it. I *do* know it's not the easiest or safest job in the world."

Well, Sam was right about that. How many times had Bill been shot on the job so far? There was the most recent bullet to his arm that had barely been a scratch. And, of course, there had been the time he'd almost died. He and Jess and Sam had been involved in a shootout at a drug house. Jess had been shot in the leg in two places but had recovered without any trouble. Bill, on the other hand, had been shot in the leg and neck and had almost bled to death before they got him to the hospital. He'd gone through extensive rehabilitation and fortunately, had eventually recovered completely.

It was all part of the job, Bill knew. As previous agents had before him, he took his mission very seriously to find and bring to justice those people who were involved in drug trafficking, money laundering, cybercrime, and other crimes.

But did he want to do it for the rest of his life? That was the question.

Even the great Special Agent Sam Morgan had known when it was time to turn in his gun and his badge. And he appeared to be completely content with his present life. Bill couldn't remember a time when he'd ever seen his former boss so seemingly happy.

"You doing okay running the ranch now, Sam?"

The other man swiveled his head briefly at Bill's question, then faced the road again.

"Yeah. Why do you ask?"

"I was just wondering if you ever regretted leaving the Bureau. I know you were the sheriff in Denning for a short time, too, and I wondered if you sometimes miss having an active role in law enforcement."

Sam shook his head, a crooked grin on his face.

"Absolutely not, Billy-Boy. Especially now that I have a family to take care of. There is no way I would want to be involved in that type of job anymore."

He smiled, and Bill noticed that ever-present dimple that Jess always talked about appearing on the other man's face.

"If you'd told me years ago that someday I'd be living in Montana and running the family ranch, I would have told you there was no way that was going to happen. But you know, God orchestrated each and every moment that got me to where I am today. They weren't always easy moments, as I'm sure you'll recall. I went through some pretty tough times back after we all got shot."

Bill heard Sam's sigh from across the cab and knew he was remembering, as Bill was, the PTSD Sam had suffered after that awful shoot-out. Thankfully, Sam had gotten through the ordeal and fully recovered through a lot of counseling and prayers, and was now back to the Sam Bill knew and loved.

"But now, I know I'm right where I'm supposed to be…doing exactly what I'm supposed to be doing. And I have to tell you, there isn't any better feeling than that."

As Sam pulled onto the road that led to the airport, Bill sighed and wondered if he'd ever know that feeling. He prayed he would.

♫ ♫ ♫

The flight to D.C. was quiet and uneventful for Bill. The airline must not have been able to sell the seat next to him as no one had ever shown up to take it—which was okay with him. That meant he had more space and didn't have to deal with someone trying to make conversation with him the whole trip.

And it gave him more time to think and pray.

One of the first things he wanted to do when he got home was to find out what he needed to do to be certified to teach. He'd completed most of the requirements for teaching certification back when he was in college—but he'd never taken the necessary final exams and tests to gain his certification.

Instead, he'd joined the Marines and gone to war.

Of course, he would also need to decide if he wanted teach in the D.C. area or move someplace else and start over. Maybe a smaller town where his teaching could make a difference would be a better choice.

Perhaps it *was* time for him to leave D.C.—especially if he wasn't going to work at the Bureau. After all, that was the only thing keeping him in the city. Now that his relationship with Zoey was history, there wasn't much of anything for him there anymore. Oh sure, he had friends and people he knew from the workplace. But no family. No real ties to the place.

Not anymore.

Just thinking about running into Zoey once he was back at work caused Bill to squirm in his plane seat. He had to somehow get over these feelings he had for her. He also knew that sometime down the road, he was going to have to find the strength and the courage to forgive her. But he wasn't quite that brave yet. It was going to take him a while before he got to that point. And his heart needed to heal a little more first.

Thinking about healing brought to mind someone else who was doing some of her own healing. Joy Whitefox. Yeah, if Joy could heal and deal with what had happened to her, then the tough FBI Agent Bill Parker ought to be able to deal with a little bit of rejection and go on with his life.

Just the thought of Joy's cute face framed by that wavy black hair took away some of the sorrow at losing Zoey. Joy had been through a whole lot more than Bill Parker ever had. Yet, she didn't seem to harbor any hate for the maniac that had hurt her. She was still afraid of her attacker, though. That was easy to tell just by the way she'd acted when she'd told Bill the story of her attack. And that fact made Bill feel awful for her. It would be great if he could somehow give her the freedom of knowing peace again, but he knew that kind of peace had to come from God—not him.

So, he'd do all he could do for Joy, and that was to pray.

♫ ♫ ♫

Bill's first day back at work at the Bureau was crazy. He spent most of it getting briefed on the open cases his team was working on. Nate Jorgenson, the member of his team who had run the show in Bill's absence, was very detail-oriented, and by the time Bill had been brought up to speed on everything that had happened while he was on vacation, Bill's mind was spinning, and his brain felt half-dead.

That afternoon, Bill met with Director Roberts, who, in addition to filling him in on what had happened in his absence, also wanted a complete update on how Sam and Julie and their family were doing. Meeting with the Director took a considerable chunk out of Bill's day, and by the time the clock on the wall in the squad room said it was time to go home, he was more than ready.

He was walking across the parking area toward his car, wondering what he would fix himself for supper when he got back to his apartment, when he saw a familiar female figure cross the lot.

Zoey

Bill waited for the sharp pain to appear in the region of his heart and was surprised when he only experienced a dull ache. He paused to stand next to his own car, gazing across the top of the vehicle and watched as she unlocked her car and got in. She never even looked his way, which was a good thing. He wasn't ready to talk to her. Yet. Maybe in time, he would get over her. But at least seeing her this time hadn't hurt as much as it had in the past. Perhaps there was hope for him after all.

When he arrived home, Bill changed into a comfortable pair of jeans and a T-shirt. He was more than ready to shed the suit and tie required for his job. After eating the sub sandwich he'd bought at a local deli on his way home, Bill sat at his desk and opened his laptop.

It was time to pursue his dream.

It had been over a dozen years since Bill had received his college diploma. After so much time had passed, he worried that he'd waited too long to do something with his education. Looking back, perhaps he'd been foolish to join the Marines right out of college instead of taking the necessary exams to complete certification for teaching.

At the time, though, the country had been reeling from the after-effects of the attack on the World Trade Center and the Pentagon on 9/11. And Bill had felt the need to do something to join in the fight to protect the country he loved. So, he'd gone to the nearest recruiting office and joined the Marines—and had never looked back.

When the Allied forces joint invasion of Iraq had happened on March 29, 2003, Bill had been right there in the midst of the action. He'd served a second tour and spent time in both Iraq and Afghanistan before being discharged and returning to the states. The one good thing that had come from his time in the military was the chaplain who had led him to the Lord after the loss of one of Bill's buddies in battle.

Upon his return home, Bill had felt the call to try out for the FBI. It wasn't the military, it wasn't regular law enforcement—yet serving in the FBI had allowed Bill to still stay involved in protecting the country he loved.

After months of training, Bill had been assigned to the FBI field team supervised by one Samuel Clemens Morgan, and from the first day, he had known that Sam was something special. Under Sam's tutelage, Bill had learned how to find the clues, follow the leads, track down the suspects, and then interrogate them until he uncovered the truth. And because Sam was also a born-again Christian and lived his faith daily, Bill learned how to go about doing his job with honesty, integrity, and an unfailing determination to see it through to the end.

When Sam had decided to leave the Bureau and move to Montana to help run his family's ranch, he'd recommended to Director Roberts that Bill take over the field team. Bill had jumped at the opportunity to show the guys in charge what he was capable of doing and had loved the challenge of hunting down the criminals and bringing them to justice.

But lately, the job was no longer as appealing. Bill had hoped that a couple of weeks off would give him needed rest and bring him back to the squad room, raring to go again. But that hadn't happened.

Instead, the seed of making a change in his life had been planted.

Online, Bill searched for information on how to go about completing the requirements to get his certification to teach in the District of Columbia—even though he wasn't sure he wanted to stay there. But he had to start someplace. As he went through the requirements, he quickly ticked off the items. He already had a Bachelor's degree and had completed the state-approved educator program. It appeared the only thing he had left to do was take the required Praxis Exams. There were several he'd have to take, including the Core test and one for History, and an additional one for Physical Education—if that was the direction he decided to go.

He printed off several pages of information about where the tests were given, along with a couple of the offered study guides. There were also practice tests he would be able to go back and take. Once he was ready.

Bill released a sigh as he thought about what he was going to attempt. It had been a lot of years since he'd gone to college. Perhaps he was a fool to believe he could become a teacher now. Then he felt the quiet assurance that what he was thinking about doing was what he'd dreamed about doing all those years ago—a dream he'd never really given up.

He'd done a lot of praying about this. And the spark of interest in pursuing it had never wavered.

But he also knew he wasn't going to be able to do it without the Lord's help. He sent up a short prayer while he turned off his laptop and readied for bed. It had been a long time since he'd hit the books.

He sure hoped everyone back in Montana was still praying for him because he was going to need all the prayers he could get if he were going to accomplish this.

CHAPTER 13

It had seemed an unsurmountable task when Joy had first decided to go back to school and complete her Bachelor's Degree. Now, she could almost see the faint light at the end of the tunnel.

With God's help, she might actually be able to finish.

Joy hit the send button on the email containing her most recently completed coursework to her professor and closed the laptop. Releasing a sigh, she leaned back in her chair.

She was in the upstairs loft bedroom of her Uncle Jack's house. When Joy had moved there, they'd created a small bedroom for her that included a bed, bedside stand, and a small desk and chair. It wasn't big, but it was cozy and clean. And safe.

And it was all hers.

She spent most of the hours she didn't work at the diner, up in her room studying for her college courses. Taking twelve to fourteen hours a semester while working full-time at the diner wasn't easy, but Joy was determined to finish her schooling and receive her Bachelor's degree in Accounting and Business as soon as she could. Once she had that education, nobody could ever take it away from her, and she should be able to go anywhere in the country and get a good-paying job.

When she'd first come to Bluecreek Ranch, Joy had tossed around the idea of going back to college to complete her degree. She already had an associate's degree and had always wanted to get her B.A. But even with all the hours she'd been working at the diner job, she didn't see how she would ever be able to save enough money to travel someplace to attend college.

Then she'd done some research and discovered she could take the courses she needed online. But even with the Tuition Waiver for Native Americans, she didn't know if she'd be able to manage it.

Then one day, Sam Morgan had overheard her talking to her Aunt Mary in the main house kitchen about wanting to finish her degree, and that had been all it took. Mr. Morgan had stepped in and offered to not only pay for any fees, books, or other expenses she might have for taking the required college classes, but also had arranged to have wireless internet installed at Aunt Mary's cabin so Joy could take her classes online.

Joy had been entirely overwhelmed by Mr. Morgan's generous offer, and had promised herself right then and there that someday after she got a good-paying job, she was going to pay back every cent to the Morgans. She knew them well enough to know they didn't expect her to repay them, but she wanted to. It was important to her that she did this on her own.

She was currently taking the necessary classes to complete her last semester. If all went well, she should be finished in January and would then receive that long-awaited diploma. Then Joy would have to decide what she was going to do with the education. She certainly didn't intend to wait tables at *Peggy's Place* for the rest of her life.

After changing into her pajamas, Joy pulled her Bible off her bedside stand and plopped down on her bed. It was a nighttime ritual for her to read a little scripture before turning off the light and going to sleep. Hearing the words of her heavenly Father just before bed always gave Joy a measure of comfort and peace to get her through the nights—although, after more than a year and a half, the evenings weren't nearly as terrifying for her as they had been right after the attack.

Tonight, she was reading in the Book of Joshua, the first chapter, telling how Joshua had been commissioned by God to lead his people to the Promised Land. Several verses popped out at Joy as she read the part where God told Joshua to be strong, three different times. But it was the ninth verse of the chapter that touched Joy's heart the most:

Have not I commanded thee? Be strong and of a good courage; be not afraid, neither be thou dismayed: for the Lord thy God is with thee withersoever thou goest.

Reading through the words a second time, Joy couldn't help but think how the words made it sound as if Joshua were a warrior, heading out to face his enemy. And she supposed he was.

Thinking of warriors immediately brought to Joy's mind a certain non-cowboy she had recently met. Bill Parker reminded her of what a warrior should be like—tall and strong and brave and ready to fight for what he believed in. That was the way she saw Bill.

Why she was thinking about Bill Parker at that point in her devotions, she had no idea. It seemed to Joy that she thought about the man way too often. He'd been gone from the ranch for over a month—back to his exciting life in the city—and Joy was sure he never thought about her, so why couldn't she forget about him?

She sincerely hoped he was happy doing what he was doing with his life, though. One thing she'd learned in her short life was that the days passed quickly, and if you didn't watch it, you'd be waiting tables the rest of your life—and feeling miserable about it.

With that thought, Joy reached over and turned off the small light on her bedside table, pulled up the covers, and rolled over on her side. It had been a long day, and tomorrow was going to be equally as long.

It was time for some shuteye.

♫ ♫ ♫

A week later, Bill contacted the college where he'd graduated and was actually able to speak to a couple of his former professors. They both stated they'd be able to provide him with letters of recommendation, and one of his history professors actually remembered him, which made him feel a little better about how long it had been since he'd been in contact with anyone at the college.

After many phone calls and some serious investigating, Bill was also able to find the teacher at the middle school where he'd completed his student teaching. Margaret Williams had retired two years earlier, but fortunately, Bill was able to find her phone number. Sometimes working for a government agency came in handy.

After several minutes of explaining who he was and why he was calling, Mrs. Williams had finally understood who she was talking with.

"Oh, yes—Bill Parker. I remember you." He heard the older woman's chuckle on the other end of the phone. "The girls in my class probably remember you too. If I recall, they all thought you were quite a hunk."

Bill shook his head and closed his eyes as he felt the heat crawl up his neck at the memories. It seemed like every girl in that class had professed to have a crush on the young student teacher that semester. If he'd ever needed a boost for his morale, those girls had given it to him.

"Yeah. Unfortunately, I remember that too, Mrs. Williams. Thanks for reminding me." Bill chuckled, then went on to explain to her why he was calling.

"Why, I'd be happy to provide you with a letter of recommendation, Bill. I always thought you'd make an excellent teacher. Why didn't you ever complete the rest of your requirements, if I may ask?"

He grinned as the tone of the older woman's voice fell into what he remembered as her 'teaching voice.'

"I joined the Marines, Mrs. Williams. Served two tours over in Iraq and Afghanistan before coming home. Then I went to work for the FBI."

"Really? My, how exciting. Well, thank you for your service, young man."

She paused a second before she added. "But now you want to become a teacher?"

Bill chuckled. "Guess I haven't had enough excitement in my life."

She joined him in his laughter. "Well, teaching is never boring, Bill. I'll agree with you there. It can be frustrating, tiring, exasperating, and depressing. But in most cases, it's also the most rewarding thing a person can do, because we train the future adults of this world. I never took my job lightly, and you shouldn't either if you actually do become a teacher. It's truly a calling."

After chatting with Mrs. Williams a few more minutes, the two of them said their goodbyes, and Bill ended the call. He'd enjoyed talking with his former mentor, and hearing her love for a job she'd done for almost forty years led him to believe he wasn't making a mistake by going after what had always been his dream.

He'd made enough mistakes in his life, and he prayed this one wouldn't be another one.

♫ ♫ ♫

Weeks passed, and Bill's days settled into a routine. He worked the required long hours at the Bureau, then went home and spent his evenings studying the manuals he'd sent for to prepare for taking the necessary teacher certification exams.

Since his breakup with Zoey Beckett, Bill hadn't gone on even one date, and now that he was focused on his certification, he also declined any offers from his coworkers to go out for a late dinner after work. His focus was on one thing and one thing alone—getting the necessary credentials so he could teach.

Then one Monday morning, his team, along with another field team, was called into the conference room for a briefing from Director Roberts himself. Bill took a seat around the highly polished wooden table and wondered what was going on. The last time they'd had such a meeting had been right before the takedown of a big drug ring outside Chicago.

His eyes studied each person as they wandered through the doorway and into the room. There were his two team members—Nate Jorgensen and Tyler Caldwell—both good men and men he could trust with his life—had in the past, and probably would in the future.

Then there was the other team, consisting of Milt Bauers, Vic Page, and Cliff Brown. All were long-time employees of the Bureau. Vic had actually been working at the Bureau when Bill had first hired on, so Bill knew the man had to be close to retirement age.

When Director Roberts entered the room, the others grew quiet, and Bill turned his attention to whatever the man was about to tell them. Bill knew the Director was an Army veteran and had been the head man at the Bureau for many years. His paneled office was decorated with photos of him standing next to famous and important people—such as the President of the United States and the Secretary of Defense. He was a man of influence in the city, and even though he'd always been firm and sometimes harsh with Bill, Director Roberts was a man Bill had always respected.

But Bill knew the man well enough to know he hadn't called them there for a friendly chat. Something was up.

"Thank you for coming on such short notice. I know you're all busy working on your own cases, so I'll try and keep this brief."

The Director's eyes were dark as they turned on each person seated around the table. Bill sat up a little straighter as the tone of the man's voice hit him. Whatever it was, the boss was not a happy man, so that meant it was serious.

"We've been contacted by the Montana State Police and informed that they've found contraband in a prison that leads them to believe a man is running a drug operation from there. The prison is near Bozeman."

He turned toward a large screen on the wall and nodded at his assistant, who was sitting at the far end of the conference table in front of a laptop. The other man clicked a couple of keys on the computer and brought up a map of Montana on the screen in front of them.

Director Roberts pointed to the map to show the location of the city he'd mentioned, then hesitated as if he'd just thought of something, and turned and looked directly at Bill.

"Agent Parker, former Agent Morgan lives in Montana now, correct?"

Bill glanced around as all eyes were instantly directed at him. Being explicitly addressed in a briefing by the Director was something new for Bill, and he felt sweat running down his back as his nerves took over. Then he took a deep breath to steady himself. The man had simply asked him a question.

"Yes, sir. Sam Morgan's ranch is east of Billings. Quite a distance from Bozeman, Director."

The older man turned back to gaze at the map, then turned back and spoke to Bill again, his finger on the map projected on the screen.

"His ranch isn't far from the Native American Indian reservation near Billings, though, right?"

Bill gave a slow nod, not seeing the connection, but was sure the Director would soon fill in the blanks. He was well aware the man had a reputation for getting to his point in a roundabout way, but he always arrived there—and just assumed everyone else would be able to keep up with him when he did.

"Yes, sir. I believe so."

Director Roberts stared at the map a few moments, then turned back to the table as a whole.

"Here's the deal, gentlemen. The state boys in Montana have found a contraband phone and what looks like a drug ledger in a prisoner's cell. The prison authorities returned everything to where it was hidden and contacted the police, and they, in turn, contacted us, asking how we wished for them to proceed. We don't want to spook the guy in the hopes that he can lead them higher up the food chain."

The older man stepped closer to the table, where he glanced down at what appeared to be notes.

"The suspect is scheduled to get out of jail at the end of this year, and the authorities in Montana don't want to blow the chance to bring down this ring, so he is of great interest to them—and to us."

He paused and looked up, his eyes locking on Bill, who immediately wondered what was coming next. When he saw the firm set to the Director's jaw, he knew it wasn't going to be anything good.

The Director gave a nod to his assistant, who hit a key on the laptop to put a photo on the screen. A mug shot of a man—dark complexion, a high broad forehead, long black hair, and dark eyes gazed out from the photo. Some could say he was a good-looking man, except for the obvious hate radiating out of the man's eyes.

"He's a Native American—a member of the Crow tribe. Upon release, it's assumed he'll be returning to the reservation near the city of Billings. The very same reservation which Agent Parker has just reminded me is not far from former Agent Morgan's ranch."

Bill blew out a breath as a sick feeling built in the pit of his stomach. The guy they were discussing was being released at the end of the year.

It couldn't be. It just couldn't.

"Do we have a name, Director?" Bill struggled to even ask the question.

Director Roberts glanced down at the paper again.

"His name is Ernie Wolffe. The Montana boys tell me he's a real piece of work. Guess they interviewed the guards at the prison a few months ago and they told them the guy treats the other prisoners, the guards—everyone the same— like they're all nothing but dirt to him. Guess he's got a mouth on him too, and the guards try their best to avoid getting him riled."

Bill felt as if he'd been punched in the stomach. *Ernie Wolffe.* The same man who had attacked Joy.

"Where does the Bureau come in, Director?" Cliff Brown, one of the members of the other team, spoke up, voicing the question Bill had been hesitant to ask.

"Montana State Police just wanted to brief us on the situation and have us be aware what was going on. If we hear any chatter of something doing down in that part of the country, we're to contact them first. They, in turn, will keep us appraised of any information they uncover. They're going to be watching Wolffe closely when he's released to see who he has contact with and where. They want to catch the ringleader of this operation and they aren't sure if he's the guy at the top or not. But for sure, they don't want to spook him or anyone else involved."

"If I may ask, sir, what made them do the search in the first place? Or was it just a random one?" Bill finally found his voice.

The Director glanced down at his notes again. "According to the prison authorities, they got a tip from...his cellmate, it looks like. Evidently, the snitch isn't a fan of Mr. Wolffe and decided he would be willing to use his knowledge of Wolffe's operation in return for being moved to another facility closer to his family."

Director Roberts frowned. "By the sounds of things, the informant was terrified of Wolffe and wanted to get as far away from him as possible."

Bill almost groaned out loud. And *he* was the man who would be freed in a few months to return to the reservation where he'd be closer to Joy. Where he could hurt her. Again.

Someone else spoke up. "Bozeman, Montana? Really? What makes the cops think there's that sort of operation running there?"

Director Roberts ran his hand through his thinning hair. "It all stems back to this Wolffe character and his drug ledger they found hidden in his cell. They believe he's been using a contraband phone from inside the prison to contact his outside partner, and orchestrating when and how to have the drugs shipped in from Mexico and China for distribution."

The big man paused for a moment before continuing. "We think we've found the cartel he's been involved with in Mexico, and we've been watching them closely. They're well known for transferring their drug money from bank to bank to bank through a series of innocent-looking accounts before it finally leaves the country. We know there's been a large influx of money transferred to a small bank in Bozeman, which is what set off alarms in the first place and made us start investigating. So far, we've been able to trace it from there when it was transferred to Canada, then overseas to Hong Kong. After that, we lost the trail, but our computer teams are still working on it."

Nate Jorgensen, a member of Bill's team, chose that time to speak up from where he sat next to Bill. Bill knew the young man was a computer genius, and was always surprised he hadn't chosen to work in the Cybercrime unit, but was thankful he was on his team instead. He was a brilliant investigator and never gave up a search.

"The cartels can get incredibly complex with how they structure these things to hide the money, sir. One LLC in Connecticut might own another LLC in the Cayman Islands, which owns a shell company with an account in a bank in Hong Kong," Nate paused as if to make sure everyone was listening before adding. "That same bank in Hong Kong can then transfer the fund into another LLC, which in turn transfers it back here to an account in the U.S. owned by another anonymous shell company. Tracing it all can take weeks…months. And finding the true owner of the company can take even longer."

Bill shook his head. "I still don't see where this Wolffe character fits the profile of someone involved in running a big drug operation or being involved in money laundering. And I'm certainly not sold that he's smart enough to run the whole operation. There's gotta be somebody else on the outside that's helping him."

The Director turned his dark brown eyes back on Bill. "You know something about this gentleman we don't, Agent Parker?"

Bill once again felt the pressure as all eyes turned on him.

"Yes, sir. I mean, no, sir. I just know what he was originally incarcerated for—and it had nothing to do with drugs, or phony bank accounts, or money laundering. He attacked and raped a young woman living on the reservation. This guy is a goon—evil and malicious as they come. But intelligent enough to pull off something like this?" Bill shook his head. "I'm not sure he's that smart."

Director Roberts took a deep breath and released it, then turned back to look at the map.

"That would lead me to believe someone else is running the show, but regardless, we need to keep our eyes and ears open, people. If you hear anything that even vaguely sounds like it might have something to do with the Montana case, we need to let the state boys know about it."

135

He looked pointedly at Bill. "As for Mr. Wolffe, we'll let the cops in Montana keep eyes on him when he's released. If he's involved in any way, it won't take long for him to show his true colors."

Bill gave his boss a nod of understanding, all the time feeling sick in his gut at the thought that the danger for Joy just kept getting worse. If Ernie Wolffe was really involved with money laundering and drug cartels, Joy was never going to be safe again.

CHAPTER 14

It didn't matter how much time had passed, Joy never felt safe when she returned to the reservation to visit her father.

Joy drove her car up the short dirt drive of the house she grew up in and put it in Park. Her dad's rusty pickup truck was sitting next to the house, so she knew he was home.

She'd put off coming to visit him for as long as she could, but Christmas was only two weeks away, and Joy had promised herself she wouldn't let the holiday pass without making an effort to see her father. Not that he cared if he saw her or not, but it would make Joy feel better as she knew it was the right thing to do.

Turning off the ignition, Joy stuffed her car keys in the pocket of her coat and stared through the windshield at the only home she'd ever known until the Byrds had taken her into their hearts and home. The small square one-story house had once had been painted a bright white, but years of weather and neglect had taken most of the color off the wood siding. The boards now looked more dirty gray than white.

She knew inside the little house were two small bedrooms, a tiny bathroom, and an open area that acted as both a living room and kitchen. Joy also knew, that even though the yard was covered with the most recent snowfall, the grass underneath had probably only been mowed twice the previous summer, if that often.

Her dad was not exactly what you'd call an ambitious individual. About the only thing he cared about was his involvement in the Crow Reunion that he participated in yearly on the reservation. Oh, and of course, there was the book he was supposedly writing about the history of their tribe—and how badly they were misused by the white man when he came to their land.

She sighed. There was no doubt the white man had changed life for the Native American Indians—not just their tribe. But why did her dad think it would make everything better if they could go back to the old way of life? Did he really want to live in a teepee in the middle of winter? And she knew he enjoyed watching all the shows on his television too much to want to give that up.

No, Joy was sure his bravado and outspokenness were more for show than anything else.

But it *had* been enough to finally drive away Joy's mother. The year Joy had turned eleven—the same age Samantha Morgan was now—while Joy had been at school, Judy Whitefox had packed her few belongings and caught a ride to Billings. Later they'd learned she'd taken a plane east.

Joy had never heard from her again. Other than the short scribbled letter her mother had left for her—explaining why she had to get away from her husband and the reservation—Joy had received no phone calls, no letters, and no cards from her mother. Nothing.

What little she could remember about her mother, Joy was positive Judy Whitefox had never been a happy woman. She often wondered why her mom had married Clark Whitefox in the first place. But to hear her dad tell the story, the two of them had met at a restaurant in town and had instantly fallen in love.

Well, that feeling obviously hadn't lasted.

What hurt Joy the most, though, had been that her mother had simply left—leaving not only her husband but also her daughter. Would Joy had gone with her mother if the opportunity had been given her? She had never been able to answer that question. She still couldn't. At the time her mother had left, Joy had been old enough to recognize that things hadn't been right between her parents for years. But to simply leave behind everything she knew to go live with her mother in the big city someplace? Joy wasn't sure what she would have done. But it was a moot point as her mother had never asked her to go with her.

Joy and her dad had never heard from her again. But they had been contacted by the authorities five years ago who informed them that Judy Whitefox had died from cancer. Other than that, Joy had no idea what type of life her mother had lived after she left them. Had she ever found true love? Had she been happy?

What about her relationship with God? Joy could remember her mom used to take her to church when she'd been little, and Judy had seemed to enjoy the services. When she left, had she turned her back on her faith too? Joy would never know.

Heaving a tired sigh, Joy exited the car, taking the time to grab her purse and the sack out of the back seat she'd brought with her. She came bearing gifts for her dad. Not that he'd appreciate it, but it was Christmastime after all, and she wanted to give him some things she knew he'd enjoy having. One wrapped parcel held a warm plaid flannel shirt for him. The other package, a box of home-made chocolate chip cookies—his favorite. Joy didn't have a lot of money to buy gifts but was determined she was going to make sure her dad had at least a little festivity for Christmas—even though she knew he wouldn't return the gesture.

Stomping her feet on the front steps to try and remove most of the snow before entering, Joy gave a cursory knock on the door and entered.

"Dad, are you home?"

Of course, she knew he was probably home as his vehicle was out front, but by calling out to him, she would make *him* aware she was home. Even if she hadn't lived in this house for almost two years, he'd told her to still consider it her home—which was getting more and more challenging to do.

She heard muffled footsteps coming from one of the bedrooms in the back of the house, and shortly, her dad walked through the doorway into the living room. He was wearing a yellowed undershirt and a worn pair of jeans and was in his stocking feet. His black hair was pulled back into a tail at the nape of his neck and didn't look like it had been washed in weeks—which it probably hadn't.

"*Daásitche Úuxdaake*, it's so good to see you."

As she placed her purse and sack of parcels on the floor next to the worn sofa, Joy shrugged out of her coat. Her father was the only person in the world who called her by her official Crow name—*Happy Fawn*.

When she turned around, her dad unexpectedly pulled her into a quick hug, then just as quickly released her. But it had been a long enough hug that it had taken Joy back to the days of her childhood. The smells of cigarette smoke, clothes that needed to be washed, and a faint whiff of her father's aftershave—although by the look of the whiskers on his face, he hadn't used it in a while.

She pointed to the sack at her feet.

"I brought you a couple of things." Joy gave him a smile, hoping he wasn't going to get on her case about spending money on him. "I know it's not Christmas yet, but I probably won't get back to see you before the actual holiday since I'm scheduled to work a lot of hours at the diner."

Her dad reached out and took the offered bag from her, then pointed toward the sofa, while he sat in his well-worn, overstuffed chair. Joy reluctantly sat on the couch, pushing aside a stack of old magazines and newspapers to make room, and hoping there weren't any bugs crawling around under the cushions. Giving the house a cursory glance, it looked like the place hadn't been cleaned since the day she'd walked out the front door and moved to the ranch. Books and papers and dirty dishes sat on the small wooden dining table near the kitchen. What looked like dirty clothes were piled in the farthest corner of the living room. No wonder it smelled so bad in the house.

Joy turned her eyes back on her father as he almost shyly took the two wrapped parcels out of the bag.

"I don't have anything to give you, girl. Why'd you go spend your hard-earned money on buying stuff for me?"

She gave him what she hoped was a loving smile. Her father was nothing, if not predictable. He'd complain if she'd buy him something, but if she hadn't, he would have whined about her not caring about him.

"I didn't spend much, Dad. Just a couple things I knew you could use and wouldn't buy yourself."

He held the two parcels in his lap as if he were afraid to open them.

"You don't have to wait until Christmas Day to open them, Dad. I probably won't be able to get back to see you again, so why don't you open them while I'm here?"

Her father raised his dark eyes to her, a small smile appearing on his face. The smile almost made him look like the younger father she remembered from her childhood. Almost.

"If you're sure it's okay."

She nodded, hoping to encourage him to hurry and open them. Joy didn't want to stay on the reservation long. There were good things here—and good people, but it always made her uneasy being there—even after all the time that had passed. She still felt as if everyone's eyes were judging her for what had happened to her on that terrible night when her life had changed forever. As if somehow it had all been her fault. The only mistake she had made had been getting involved with Ernie Wolffe in the first place.

But Ernie had been a smooth-talker, and Joy had been a sucker for a man that appeared to care about her.

Joy turned her attention back to her father as she watched his large hands rip open the cheap, gaudy wrapping paper she'd purchased to wrap the gifts. He opened the flannel shirt first, and when he saw what it was, immediately stood and unfolded it.

"Nice shirt!"

He shot her a quick grin, and Joy felt her nerves unwind. At least today, her father was in a cordial mood and appeared to not be on one of his belligerent rants about how life had cheated him of everything he deserved.

Her dad sat back down, then reached for the next package. While she watched him tear off the wrapping paper, Joy found herself smiling. At least he hadn't shaken this package. If he had, he would have been disappointed when he discovered what was inside.

"Cookies!"

Clark Whitefox gave his daughter a huge smile—one Joy hadn't seen in recent history. She allowed herself to relax and actually giggled like a little girl. At least for a few moments, she'd brought her father some happiness.

"I know they're your favorite, Dad. I thought you might enjoy them."

Her father was already eating one of the treats, smiling all the time.

"Oh, these are good. Did you make 'em yourself?"

Joy nodded. "Aunt Mary let me use her kitchen so I could bake them."

At the mention of his sister, her dad's smile evaporated, but he continued to chomp away at the cookies. She could tell he was thinking when he dropped his head and appeared to gaze at the worn wooden floor in front of him. Not waiting for him to start ranting about how his sister had stolen away his only daughter, Joy decided to go on the offensive and speak first.

"Things are going okay for me, Dad. I still have the job at the diner in Denning. It doesn't pay a lot, but I'm still taking college classes, and hope to eventually graduate and get a better job."

Her father's head went up and down slowly as he sat quietly in his chair. Then he raised his eyes to her.

"I'm glad for you, girl." He paused a second or two before adding. "I know I don't tell you very often, but I'm proud of you. After everything you've gone through..."

It was silent in the room as the words unsaid bounced from wall to wall.

Joy wiggled a little on her spot on the worn sofa, then stood. It was time for her to go before things got more uncomfortable between the two of them.

"I probably won't get back to see you again before the New Year, Dad. I hope you have a great holiday."

Putting the tin she'd packed the cookies in on the small stand next to his chair, her dad stood.

"Thanks again for the gifts, my daughter. I hope you have a good Christmas too."

Joy nodded and turned to exit the house of her childhood. Somehow, leaving today didn't seem as difficult as it had in the past. Every time she came to see her father, it was just another reminder of why she had left in the first place.

And another reason for her to never return.

♬ ♬ ♬

An hour later, Joy drove her older model sedan into the parking area near her Aunt Mary's cabin and parked. Visiting her dad hadn't been nearly as bad as she'd worried it might be. Not that she was in any hurry to return to living on the reservation. After the incident that had destroyed her life, Joy had made the decision that it was best for everyone concerned if she left the place of her birth and never returned. There was no question, that it was the best thing for her.

When she entered the cabin, it was to the aroma of fresh-baked bread and what smelled like chili simmering on the stove. As Joy came through the back door, her Aunt Mary was just coming out through the back bedroom door and into the central part of the cabin.

"You're home." Aunt Mary gave her a big smile and walked over and engulfed Joy in a warm embrace. "I've been praying for you ever since you told me you were visiting your father today."

She pointed toward the small table and chairs in the kitchen. "Go ahead and sit down, and you can tell me how it went while I finish up supper."

Knowing there was no use trying to stall the discussion with her aunt, Joy pulled out one of the worn wooden chairs and sat at the table. It was Aunt Mary's way, Joy knew, to try and keep abreast of what was going on in Joy's life. Aunt Mary was the closest thing Joy had ever had to a mother since her own mother's departure from her life.

"It went better than I thought it would."

Her Aunt Mary turned a little from where she stood in front of the stove, the wooden spoon she'd been using to stir the chili held above the pot. Her right eyebrow raised a little as if in question.

"Really?"

Joy smiled. "Really. I mean, the house is a disaster." Joy wrinkled her nose as she quickly recalled the smells. "I don't think he ever cleans anything."

She released a sigh, feeling a moment of sadness at what her father's life had become. She shouldn't be surprised that he lived the way he did. After all, Joy had always been the one to do the cooking and cleaning when she was still living at home.

"But he seems content with it, so I guess as long as I don't have to live there, I won't worry about it."

Aunt Mary gave her a gentle smile and a small nod before turning back to the stove.

"So, Clark is well?"

She gave her aunt a nod. "Dad looks good." Joy chuckled. "By the looks of his belly, he's getting plenty to eat—someplace. Maybe he's eating all his meals at the local restaurant or something. He never was much of a cook. I had to do all the cooking when I was still living there."

Joy allowed her memories to take her back to those days when her life had been very different from what it was now. She'd gone to school, then come home every night to cook and clean. Even though it was not the usual way for a child to be raised, Joy had never known any different, so she had been relatively content with her life.

"Did he mention if he'd heard anything about Ernie's upcoming release date?"

Even though she tried not to, Joy felt herself shudder at the mere mention of the man's name. She hoped and prayed she'd never have to see or speak to the monster ever again, and just knowing his time for release from prison was fast approaching, caused fear to rush through her.

"No." She swallowed hard. "We didn't talk about that. I just gave him a couple of things I'd gotten him for Christmas."

Aunt Mary placed the wooden spoon down on the counter next to the stove and sat across from Joy, then reached across the tabletop and took hold of Joy's hand.

"That was nice of you to do that for your father, Joy."

Her aunt's eyebrows went up again as her eyes gazed across the table at Joy. "I'm sure he didn't return the gesture, though."

Joy dropped her eyes to their joined hands.

"No. But I know Dad doesn't have much money."

Her father worked at a job on the reservation and had for many years, but Joy also knew he had never been good about handling what money he had.

Aunt Mary's humph was quiet but loud enough, Joy heard it. She knew her Aunt Mary thought Clark Whitefox wasn't much of a father to Joy. Well, maybe he wasn't. But he was the only father she'd ever had, and she'd learned years ago that she wasn't going to change the man.

Then her aunt released her hand, patting it once before she stood back up.

"Well, I'm proud of you, sweetheart." The smile she turned on Joy looked almost wistful as she stood and stared down at her. "I couldn't be any more proud of the young woman you've become if you were my own daughter. I hope you know that, Joy."

Feeling tears building up behind her eyes, Joy blinked a couple of times and tried to smile. Where would she be without Aunt Mary and Uncle Jack? They had been so good to her.

"I *do* know that, Aunt Mary. And I'm so thankful I have you and Uncle Jack." She stood and gave her aunt a gentle hug. "I hope you know how much I appreciate you and all you've done for me. The Morgans too. Everyone here on the ranch has done so much for me."

Her Aunt Mary sniffed back obvious tears. "I love you, girl. Don't you ever forget that."

Joy smiled and nodded. "I won't. I love you too."

God had blessed her immensely when he'd sent Jack Byrd to the reservation the day after the attack. He'd scooped Joy up and brought her home to Bluecreek Ranch and told her she was going to stay with them for a while. Joy had never left.

Someday she might leave the ranch, but at least in the meantime, here on Morgan land, she felt safe.

CHAPTER 15

He'd avoided talking to Zoey Beckett for months, but the day finally came when Bill could no longer evade her.

It was just a typical day with Bill and the rest of his team sitting in the squad room at their desks. He was working at his computer with his head bent down when he caught the movement in the corner of his eye of someone walking toward his desk. Bill didn't look up right away, concentrating on finishing the email he was typing before dealing with the next problem walking in the door.

Then he heard Nate Jorgensen clear his throat.

"Uh, boss?"

Finishing the last few letters of the email, Bill hit the send button and raised his eyes to find his former fiancée standing patiently in front of his desk, a small smile on her face as she watched him.

"Sorry to bother you, Agent Parker."

He kept his eyes steady on her face, refusing to let any facial expression show what a turmoil his emotions were in at having her show up at his office.

"No problem, Agent Beckett. What can we do for you?"

Bill allowed his eyes to lock on her green ones, noting in the few seconds he allowed his eyes to really look at her, that she was doing something different with her brown hair. Instead of allowing it to hang around her shoulders, today, it was pulled back at her neck with some sort of decorative clip. He also noticed that it looked as if she'd lost a little weight—not that she needed to. She'd always been slim and trim.

At his question, he saw her lips turn up in a little smile that looked more forced than usual, and she dropped her voice to barely a whisper.

"If it's possible, I'd really like to have coffee with you after work tonight, so we can talk. I know you more than likely aren't interested in doing so, but I thought it would give us a chance to air a few things."

Air a few things.

Did Zoey have any idea what he'd like to say to her?

Bill released a puff of air and glanced over long enough to see both Nate's and Tyler's eyes watching them, and proceeded to give them each a glare. Thankfully, they both dropped their eyes and turned their attention back to their own computer screens. He certainly didn't need anybody sticking their noses in his personal life—what little of it there was any more.

Zoey still stood in front of his desk, and he forced himself to look her in the eyes, trying to remain neutral in his emotions.

A cup of coffee and a talk. I don't know why she wants to talk to me, Lord, but I'm an adult. I guess I should be able to handle that.

"I think I can manage to fit that into my schedule, Agent Beckett."

She gave him a nervous little nod, and they quickly made plans to meet at a little coffee shop two blocks from their building at a particular time, which Bill hoped would work. If not, he'd have to call and reschedule their meeting for another time. As Zoey was well aware, the job had to come first.

Fortunately—depending on how you looked at it—his workday ended on time, and Bill immediately made his way

148

to the coffee shop, all the time wondering what he was doing, agreeing to meet with her in the first place. What could Zoey want? Did she want to get back together with him? Somehow he didn't see that happening, and frankly, if that was what this was all about, he wasn't interested. Not after all she'd put him through.

Focused on finding her in the busy coffee shop, Bill tried to steady his nerves, sending up prayers as he elbowed his way through the crowd around the counter. He needed to feel God's presence right then if he was going to be able to calmly sit down and talk to the woman who had shattered his dreams for a marriage and a future family.

Zoey saw him first and waved him over to a small table where she was seated. A paper cup of coffee sat in front of her, and another one already sat on the table in front of him when he took his seat.

"I too the liberty of ordering yours. I hope that's okay."

Giving her a little nod, Bill lifted the cup to his lips and took a sip. Black, just the way he liked it. At least she remembered that much about him.

"Thanks, Zoey."

She gave him a little smile, her glance drifting over to the line of people in front of the counter.

"Well, I figured if I didn't order it when I got here, you would be in line forever."

Bill took another sip, taking the time to study his former girlfriend. She looked beautiful, as always, although there was something different about her. She was still the slim, petite, brown-haired dynamo he remembered—almost exuding nervous energy that spoke of how vibrant a personality she had. But today there was a humbleness about her Bill couldn't recall seeing there before. Perhaps it was because she was feeling guilty about the way they had parted after their last conversation.

"So, what did you want to talk about?"

He decided they might as well get to it. If Zoey wanted to talk, there was no sense filling in ten minutes with idle chit-chat.

His question garnered a little grin.

"In a hurry, Parker?"

"Maybe." He sighed. "I *do* have a life, Zoey. Regardless of what you might think about me."

She dropped her eyes from his, and he immediately felt like a jerk. There was no sense stirring up trouble. Zoey had been brave enough to confront him; he needed to be man enough to sit here and listen to her.

"Sorry." He sighed. "Let's start over. How are you doing?"

Her eyes brightened as she raised them to look across the table at him again.

"I'm doing well." She sighed. "I'm leaving the Bureau."

"What?"

How did the Bureau's grapevine manage to fail him so badly?

She giggled, a sound that caused Bill to loosen up a bit, and he released a smile at hearing it. It had been a long time since he'd heard Zoey giggle.

"Can't believe you hadn't already heard that news."

"Nope, not a word."

"Hmm. Well anyway. I'm leaving the end of the month. I've accepted an assignment as a short-term missionary to Ukraine. If this first trip goes well, I'll raise funds to do it on a full-time basis."

Bill stared across the table and wondered if he had heard correctly. A missionary? To Ukraine? That was about the last thing he would have thought the Zoey Beckett he had known would be interested in doing.

"Well, aren't you going to say anything?"

He gave his head a little shake. "I'm not sure what to say. I'm in shock."

There was that giggle again.

"Yeah, I know. It's happened so fast, it still feels a little surreal for me too."

"Are you positive you know what you're getting into, Zoey? I mean, this isn't going to be a vacation. You'll be living in a foreign country with strangers, doing work no one else wants to do."

Her green eyes turned serious.

"I *do* know that Bill, and I'm positive. I've been restless for quite a while—feeling there was something…more important out there for me to do than work at the Bureau. But it wasn't until I went to a meeting with one of my friends from church that the pieces all fell into place."

She sighed, her face getting a wistful look on it. "When I was a kid, I used to love it when missionaries came to the church to speak. I remember listening to them tell about going into other cultures and learning to live there—learning how best to help the people—and having the opportunity to not only share the Gospel but to live it out each and every day."

She gave him a nod. "I'm sure about this, Bill.

"At first, I'll be working in administrative work at the headquarters. Then I hope to be sent out into the field to work—either at a school, where I'll help youngsters learn English—or I'll work at an orphanage. It sounds like there's plenty of work to do over there—even by someone as new as I'll be." She paused for a second before adding, "I just know this is what God wants me to do, and I won't have any peace until I do it."

Bill released a breath. It sounded as if she'd put a great deal of thought and prayer into her decision. It sure wasn't what he'd been expecting from her, though. But was it any different than him going after his dream of teaching?

"Well then, if you feel that is where God is leading you, who am I to argue the point?"

She raised her eyes to his, and he couldn't help but notice there was a little extra moisture in the corners.

"Thanks, Bill."

It was quiet between the two of them for a few moments while Bill moved his empty coffee container around on the table in front of him.

"You know, I really do care about you, Bill. I never meant to hurt you, but I'm smart enough to know I don't love you the way you deserve to be loved. Can you forgive me for taking so long to decide what I wanted to do with my life? You know as well as I do, that if we'd gone ahead with the marriage, we both would have been miserable."

Her voice was so quiet, he almost hadn't caught all the words, but he had, and they brought his head up to stare over at her. She was looking back at him with a soft glow in her eyes, an expression that told him she was sincere. He knew he probably needed to say something, but he didn't know what to say. This woman had held his heart in her hands for three years and then had shattered it. How could she sit there and say she cared about him?

And then he realized somewhere along the way, he had already forgiven her. Because, when it came right down to it, Zoey had done the right thing.

He dropped his eyes back to his coffee cup and gave a reluctant nod. It was still going to take some time to forget how it had felt to be rejected, but he could forgive her. And maybe, hopefully, someday he'd be open to a new relationship with a woman.

Almost as if she'd read his mind, she continued.

"Somewhere out there is a gal that will appreciate you and love you for who you are. She'll need you in her life. She'll need the man you are to step up for her and be her hero."

She released a little sigh, which made him look back up at her. "I just know I'm not that person, Bill. I'm sorry." Then she gave him a little smile. "But whoever she is, I hope she realizes what a great guy you are."

A multitude of feelings went through Bill while he gazed into Zoey's eyes. Pain, a sense of loss, and the simple realization that Zoey wasn't the person God had picked out for him. Even as attracted to each other as they'd been, even as much they'd enjoyed spending time together, they were two very different people with two very different views of where their lives were going.

Bill wanted to marry and settle down and have a couple of kids with the woman he loved, and a perhaps have a dog, and maybe even become a school teacher. Zoey…Zoey wanted to travel and see the world and do some good out there to make the world a better place. She didn't appear to want to settle down and have a family—at least right now. And who knew, maybe she never would.

"Thanks, Zoey." He cleared the hoarseness out of his voice before he continued. "I wish only the best for your life too. I hope you find everything you're looking for. And I hope you're happy when you find it. And know I'll be praying for you."

Zoey reached her hand across the table and lightly touched the back of his hand.

"Thanks, Bill."

Giving him a small smile, Zoey stood and gazed at him a few seconds. Then she leaned over and gave him a quick peck on the cheek before she grabbed her purse off the floor next to where she'd been sitting and turned and walked out the door.

Bill sat for a moment and pondered everything she'd told him, sending up a silent prayer of thanks that God had stopped them from going ahead with the marriage. It wouldn't have been a good one; their goals and dreams were too different, and there was no doubt in his mind now that they wouldn't have been happy together.

Zoey had been right to break things off. And he was glad he'd come today to talk with her. Somehow, it had set him free, and the old feelings of rejection and inadequacy were gone.

He wasn't sure when it would happen, but when it did, Bill was ready for the woman God had picked out for him.

And this time, he would listen to God more than his own heart.

♫ ♫ ♫

When Bill returned to the office, it was to find a voice mail message on his desk phone. It was the Director's secretary, asking him to report to the Director's office as soon as possible.

Holding back a groan as he wondered what had happened now, Bill told his team where he'd be and headed for the elevator that would take him up to the proper floor. Once there, Bill exited the elevator and entered the receptionist area outside the Director's office. Director Robert's secretary, Teresa, gave Bill a smile and motioned toward the open door.

"He's waiting for you, Agent Parker."

He gave the woman a quick nod and took a deep breath. It wasn't often an agent was ordered to the Director's office, and when it did happen, usually something was wrong, or there was something big going on. With the Christmas holiday coming upon them soon, Bill hoped it wasn't anything too terrible.

But he'd learned years ago that evil took no holidays or vacations.

Giving a knuckle-knock on the door jamb, Bill waited in the open doorway for the Director to look up from where he sat behind his desk.

"Agent Parker, come on it. I've been expecting you."

Bill almost smirked at the statement. Of course, the man was expecting him. After all, he'd been the one to request Bill's presence.

When offered by the Director, Bill took a seat in one of the leather chairs at the conference table in the office and worried again why he'd been called there. Was he about to get called on the carpet for something he or one of his team had done wrong on one of their recent cases? His mind ran through the cases they'd just closed and he couldn't think of anything that would warrant a scolding by the Director or anyone else. And it bode well that there was no one else from the Bureau waiting in the office for this impromptu meeting. It couldn't be too bad if just the Director wanted to talk to him. Hopefully.

"Is there a problem, Director?"

Whatever the issue, Bill decided to attack the problem head-on. If he hadn't learned anything else from Special Agent Sam Morgan in the years he'd worked under him, it was that trying to avoid a problem never worked.

"Right to the point, Agent Parker. I've always like that about you."

The other man pushed a case file across the polished table toward him.

"Take a few moments to review that, please."

Bill felt a moment of shock at the 'please' added on at the end of the Director's request, then picked up the case file folder and opened it. The photo on the top of the stack of papers in the folder immediately caught his attention.

Ernie Wolffe

After staring at the mug shot of the man he'd enjoy spending just five minutes with, Bill took a few more moments to scan through the reports included in the file, all the time feeling dread. *This* was the man who had destroyed Joy Whitefox's life. And *this* was the man who was due to be released from prison—all too soon.

After a few moments had passed, Bill raised his eyes to find those of the older man watching him.

"You're aware Wolffe is due to be released the end of the year."

Bill nodded. "Yes, sir."

"And you'll also recall our earlier meeting about his possible ties to drug trafficking and money laundering?

"Yes, sir."

"Well, Mr. Parker, I believe it's time for you to fill me in on everything you know about him, and how you know it. Something tells me you weren't totally open with us when the subject of Wolffe first came up. You stated you knew why he was incarcerated in the first place—something about him attacking a young woman."

Releasing a sigh of frustration, Bill tossed the folder of papers back on the conference table. He really didn't want to talk about it, but knew the Director wouldn't let up on him until he did.

"I became acquainted with the man's reputation when I last visited Sam out in Montana."

Director Roberts gave him a nod.

"The ranch's wrangler, Jackson Byrd, and his wife Mary, have a niece who came to live with them on the ranch." Bill hesitated as he wondered how much to tell and still protect Joy's privacy. Then he made the decision it might be best to just tell the other man everything he knew.

"This niece had previously lived on the reservation, but they felt it was no longer safe for her to live there."

He sighed, remembering the terror he could recall seeing in Joy's eyes the first time he'd met her.

"She had been assaulted and raped by a man she'd been dating a short time. He was found guilty by the Tribal Council and given two years of prison time for his crimes. That man was Ernie Wolffe."

He saw the Director's eyes narrow. "So that's the connection."

It was quiet between the two of them a few seconds, but Bill could almost hear the gears turning in the Director's brain.

"You know this girl he attacked? You've met her?"

Bill nodded, wondering what the other man was thinking.

"Yes, sir."

Director Roberts gave him a little nod, and it was quiet between the two of them for a few moments. Bill wondered what was going through the Director's mind. He knew the man well enough to know he was processing everything Bill had just told him and would soon be making a decision of some sort.

"I think it might be in everyone's best interest if you were to take some time off and pay a visit to the Morgan ranch again—perhaps stick around for a month or so after Wolffe is released—paid time off, of course, as you will actually be there in an official FBI capacity."

Feeling confused, Bill sat up a little straighter in his chair. "I'm sorry, Director. I don't understand what you're asking me to do."

The other man picked up the closed case file and waved it in front of him.

"Once this Wolffe character is released, he's likely to go after this young lady, don't you think?" The older man's right eyebrow raised in question. "After all, she's the one who has cost him the last two years of his life, and I'm guessing he's the type of man to hold a grudge. All we need to do is catch him doing something illegal, and we can take him back into custody and bring him here. Once we get our hands on him—off the reservation—perhaps we can get him to spill the beans on the operation in order to save his own skin."

"Director Roberts! That almost makes it sounds as if you want me to use Joy Whitefox as bait to catch this guy!"

The Director shook his head. "That is *not* what I'm asking you to do, Agent Parker. But we *do* know he'll go after her, so why not be there to catch him when he does."

Bill nodded, although he still didn't feel right about it. It still felt as if they'd be using Joy to get Wolffe to come out into the open where they could catch him—hopefully, doing something illegal that would warrant arresting him again.

The older man sighed. "Since you're going to be there anyway, I also want you to contact the sheriff in that town near Sam's ranch." He opened the folder and his eyes squinted as he tried to scan the contents. "What was the name of the place?"

"Denning."

"Yeah, that's it. Let the sheriff there know what we suspect so he and his deputies can keep an eye out for the guy too. They, in turn, can also let the law enforcement on the reservation know what's going on. It's going to take a joint venture if we're gonna take this guy down. And hopefully, in the process, we can also take down the cartel he's working with."

Bill gave a little nod. He wasn't sure how him going to Montana was going to make any difference in the situation, but if that's what his boss wanted him to do, then that's what he'd do.

"How much do I tell Sam?" He gave the older man a little grin. "You know his radar's going to be going full blast as soon as I arrive. I was just there a few months ago. He's gonna know something's going on."

Director Roberts nodded. "He's no longer an agent, but go ahead and fill Sam in on all of it. Everyone else on the ranch will need to be kept in the dark as we don't know if Wolffe has any accomplices somewhere. I know we don't need to worry about Sam. He's one of us—even if he is retired."

Bill nodded. He hated to think anyone on Bluecreek Ranch might be even remotely involved in the mess with Wolffe, but he understood the Director's need for secrecy. You couldn't be too careful.

"When do you want me to leave?"

His boss stood, signaling the meeting was over, and Bill did likewise.

"Go home and pack your bags, Agent Parker. The sooner you get there, the sooner we have eyes on the ground."

"Yes, sir."

The other man put his hand on Bill's shoulder as Bill walked beside him toward the office door. "Look at it this way, Bill. At least you will be able to spend the holidays with Sam and his family."

Bill allowed himself to smile as that thought sunk in. The Director was right, of course. For the first time in a very long time, Bill would have a family to spend Christmas with. Almost made the upcoming trip worth it.

"What do I tell my team, sir?"

"You let me worry about that. You have your mission. I'll take care of everything here."

Shaking the older man's hand, Bill gave him a nod and left the office.

He needed to go home and get online to purchase a plane ticket. Then he had to pack his bags and arrange to be gone from his apartment for at least six weeks—possibly longer. Then he needed to call Sam and Julie and let them know they were going to have a visitor over the Christmas holiday.

Chuckling to himself, Bill shook his head. Nothing like inviting yourself to someone's house. Hopefully, Julie wouldn't scold him too much for showing up at the last minute.

Bill's thoughts then turned to the petite niece of Jack Byrd and wondered what she'd think of him reappearing at the ranch. Suddenly, with the thought of seeing Joy Whitefox again, the idea of spending a few weeks in Montana—even in the winter—didn't sound so bad to Bill.

Not bad at all.

CHAPTER 16

Sam Morgan stood in the airport terminal and waited for the flight from Washington, D.C. to unload and the passengers to come through the gate. After Bill's unexpected phone call, Sam had thought at first about sending Zeke or Jack to pick up Bill at the airport. Then he'd made the decision to come himself. It hadn't been that long since Bill's previous visit, so Sam was sure something was going on. Whether it had to do with Bill personally or was Bureau business, Sam didn't know.

But he was going to find out. And soon.

The sight of the large former Marine striding through the door into the terminal made Sam smile. Bill Parker was hardly a kid anymore, but he still had that cocky, confident walk about him that he'd had the first time Sam had ever seen him. Sam was glad to know the Bureau hadn't changed that about his old team-mate.

He knew precisely when Bill spotted him in the crowd as a huge smile crossed the other man's face. Seconds later, Sam was engulfed in a brief hug after a quick pound on the back.

"Sam, my man!"

He chuckled at the younger man's familiar greeting. Bill might be getting older, but the young agent who had been a 'probie' under Sam's tutelage was still there.

"Billy-Boy. Did you have a good flight?"

Sam heard Bill's groan and bit back a smile.

"I hate airplanes. It doesn't matter how many times I fly, I will always hate being encased in an uncomfortable seat in a steel box thirty-thousand feet in the sky."

The two of them laughed as they left the terminal and headed to where Sam had parked the ranch's SUV. Knowing it was much warmer in D.C., Sam was happy to see Bill had at least dressed for the Montana weather. The other man was wearing what looked like a warm winter coat with a hood and had on boots. Even if they weren't insulated, they'd keep the snow off his feet. The temperature had dropped into the low twenties overnight, and even with the sun shining, the high temperature was only supposed to be hovering around freezing. Winter had arrived in Montana.

Once Bill had tossed his luggage into the back seat, and the two of them were strapped into their seatbelts in the front, Sam started the vehicle. A few moments later, they were on the main road heading out of town, and Sam felt comfortable enough about driving in the traffic to talk with the man seated next to him.

"So, I have to say—the phone call from you saying you were coming back to the ranch for another visit was a real surprise."

He glanced over long enough to see the frown on Bill's face, which was quickly replaced by a blank look. So that was how it was going to be, huh? Bill was pulling out his poker face for him.

"Yeah, well. I thought it might be nice to be here over the Christmas holidays since Zoey and I aren't together anymore."

Sam noted Bill's left foot was tapping on the floorboard of the SUV. The man might be trying to appear all calm, cool, and collected, but something was definitely bugging him.

"Well, you know you're welcome at Bluecreek anytime, buddy." Sam paused for a moment to take the upcoming exit that would lead them in the right direction, then added. "But I know just by the way you're acting that there's more to this story than what you told Julie on the phone when you said you were coming."

He actually heard the audible release of air from Bill's lungs as the other man sighed—almost as if in relief.

"I told the Director you'd know right away there was an ulterior motive for my coming. I knew I would never fool you."

"Yeah, well, now that we've gotten that out of the way—how 'bout you tell me what's really going on?"

Sam listened for the next fifteen minutes while Bill briefed him on everything Director Roberts had told him. Listening to what they suspected this Ernie Wolffe of being involved in, caused Sam's heart to drop to his stomach. He'd been through this all before and dreaded the fact that such evil had made its way to this part of Montana and the reservation. He'd always hoped and prayed to keep Bluecreek Ranch a safe haven for his family and friends, but it looked like once again, evil had come to them.

"So, what's the Director expecting you to do while you're here?"

Bill shifted a little in his car seat and turned to look over at Sam.

"He wants me to connect with the sheriff in Denning and update him so he and his deputies will be aware of the situation. And also he wants the sheriff to notify law enforcement on the reservation, so they know what's going on."

Sam nodded. "I can take you into town in the morning and introduce you to Sheriff Wilson. He's a good man. Worked under me when I was sheriff and then took over the job after I retired."

Releasing a sigh, Sam thought again about what Bill's news meant for Denning and the surrounding countryside.

"And, of course, there's Joy."

Bill's statement confused Sam for a second.

"What do you mean?"

"Like the Director told me, you can be fairly sure that Wolffe isn't too happy that Joy pressed charges and testified against him. He will see her as the main cause for him spending the past two years in a prison cell."

Sam glanced over at his friend long enough to see the frown on Bill's face.

"And you and I both know, Sam, that he's the kind of man who doesn't even know what the word forgiveness means."

Sam slowly nodded as Bill's words sunk in.

"You mean, he's going to come after Joy."

"Yup."

He took his left hand off the steering wheel long enough to run it across his face while he thought more about what Bill was telling him. No, it didn't look like even Bluecreek Ranch was going to be safe enough for Joy when Wolffe got out of prison.

"So, you're here to find out more about Wolffe and keep an eye on his movement, and try to catch him in the act of doing…something. And you're here to make sure the local police know about it so they can help. And you're here to keep Joy safe."

Bill shot him a crooked grin.

"That about sums it up, boss."

Sam chuckled, feeling an unexpected joy at hearing the old nickname from his former team member. The ranch hands occasionally called him boss, but hearing it from Bill reminded him of the old days when Sam and his team fought crime together and went after the people who committed them.

"Any ideas on how to accomplish all those goals the Director has set for you?"

There was another smile from the man on the other side of the vehicle.

"Well, that's where you come in, former Special Agent Morgan. I'm kinda hoping we can work as a team on this one. The Director specifically requested we not tell anyone else on the ranch what's going on, though. Even Julie can't know about this. I was carefully instructed to tell only you."

Sam saw Bill hold up a hand as if he knew what Sam was about to say next.

"I'm not saying any of your ranch hands have anything to do with this, Sam. But like the Director said, the fewer people that know about it, the less the chances are that the word will somehow be leaked back to the wrong people. It's gotta be just you and me, Sam. You okay with that?"

Sam slowly nodded, realizing the wisdom in keeping it hush-hush. The Director was correct when he said it would lessen the chances of something slipping to the wrong people. But it was going to be difficult for him to keep it from Julie. He told her everything, and Sam particularly hated hiding something like this from her. She'd faced danger too many times in her life already.

"I mean it, Sam. Not even Julie."

He nodded again. "I know. Although she's already curious as to why you're back for another visit when you were here just a few months ago."

Bill chuckled. "Maybe we'll have to pretend I'm back because I'm so attracted to a young lady here, I just couldn't stay away."

Sam quickly glanced over at Bill, then turned back to the road.

"You mean Joy?"

Bill didn't deny it, and Sam couldn't help but wonder if Bill was just using that as an excuse to give Julie or if Bill really did feel some attraction to the beautiful young woman staying at the ranch.

"Well, we can tell Julie that story, can't we? Do you think she'll buy it, Sam?"

Sam laughed, knowing his friend had no idea what he was setting himself up for.

"Oh, she'll buy it. You realize, though, that once Jess gets wind of that story, she and Julie both are going to do everything they can to make sure you and Joy have a whole lot of time to spend together—just to help the romance along."

He grinned at the look that appeared on Bill's face at that statement and decided to tease the big guy even more.

"I never knew anyone so intent on playing matchmaker than those two."

Sam shook his head, remembering all the times the two women had plotted with each other to try and get some of their friends at the local church to start dating in the hopes that they'd fall in love. And, of course, his dear wife had been instrumental in getting Zeke Mosher and Jessica Thorne together in the first place.

"Guess when you're happily married, you want that for everyone else too, huh?"

Bill's cheery voice brought a smile to Sam's face.

"Yeah, something like that." Sam couldn't deny marriage had been kind to him.

It was through the FBI that Julie and Sam had met more than thirteen years earlier. They didn't share the exact details of their meeting with most people, but Bill had been there when the whole incident had played out, and in the end, had actually been the person who had ended up saving Julie's life. Of course, she hadn't been Julie Henderson back then. She'd been Sarah Masters, and that day, her life had changed forever. Sam's had changed too.

Sarak a/k/a Julie had been taken into the FBI Witness Protection Program and had been trained on how to begin her life under a new identity. She'd taken a job at the FBI in the digital archives section, and there, she had once again met up with Special Agent Sam Morgan. They had begun dating, had fallen in love, and had eventually married.

Now, Sam and Julie weren't just husband and wife. They were best friends. They had taken their time getting to know each other during the year they dated and had shared the past thirteen plus years together. When Sam had gone through a rough patch after a shootout which had injured not only him but also Bill and Jess, Julie had stood by his side until he got better. When Sam had decided to leave the FBI and move the family to Montana and take the sheriff's position there, she'd supported his decision one hundred percent. And after his Uncle Fred's death and his dad had gotten old enough that he needed help, Julie had supported Sam wholeheartedly when he'd resigned his job as sheriff and taken up the running of Bluecreek Ranch full-time.

Yes, marriage had been good for Sam. And he wanted that for his friend, Bill Parker too. Whether with Joy Whitefox or whoever God had picked out for his friend.

As they came to the two tall wooden posts with the familiar faded sign hanging above the road that announced they'd reached the ranch, Sam heaved a contented sigh. It didn't matter how many times he turned onto the dirt lane that led him to Bluecreek Ranch, Sam never got tired of the feeling that rose up in him.

It was the feeling of coming home.

CHAPTER 17

Later that evening, Sam once again wished he could tell his wife Julie the real reason Bill was there. The two of them had just come upstairs to their bedroom, and while Sam was unbuttoning his shirt and tugging it out of his waistband, he was listening to his wife's excited voice talk about Bill's surprise visit.

"So, do you really think there's something between Bill and Joy?"

He watched as Julie sat in a chair at the end of their bed and brushed out her brown hair. She'd stopped dying it years earlier and had finally let it grow a little from the way she used to wear it, and this current style was cute. Although it really didn't matter to Sam. He'd always feel his wife was the most beautiful woman in the world.

"I guess so," he finally muttered as he sat on the edge of the bed and pulled off his socks and tossed them across the room, feeling a sense of accomplishment when they both landed in the laundry basket.

"Well, I remember how surprised I was when he was here the last time—that Joy and he seemed to spend a lot of time together. Joy's so shy around everyone, yet she seemed to like spending time with Bill right away."

She nodded her head as she placed the hairbrush on the small stand next to where she was sitting.

"Has Bill said much about it to you, Sam? I mean, other than he's attracted to her?"

Sam had the overwhelming need to groan. He'd known that his dear wife would jump on the matchmaking bandwagon as soon as she caught any hint of a budding romance between Joy and Bill. The biggest problem, as far as Sam was concerned, was that Joy was entirely in the dark as to what was going on. And he certainly didn't want the young woman to get her feelings hurt when she discovered Bill wasn't really there to romance her into falling in love with him.

"Listen, Julie. I'm sorry I even mentioned it to you. Please don't say anything to Joy, or Mary, or Lottie—or anyone. Okay? Just let Bill and Joy work it out between the two of them. Please promise me you aren't going to start playing matchmaker or something."

His wife turned her big blue eyes on him as if she was appalled at his concern.

"Sam, of course, I'd never say anything to Joy. Don't want to scare the poor girl off, after all."

As Sam crawled into bed a few moments later, shortly joined by his wife, he reached out to turn off the bedside lamp. He settled down under the covers and relaxed his head into the pillow, letting the worries of the day evaporate.

"But that doesn't mean I can't pray about the situation, does it?"

Sam felt his lips turn up into a small smile. He might as well surrender. His wife was on a mission, and once Julie Henderson Morgan was on a mission, there was no stopping her.

"Praying is good, Julie. Always."

He pulled her over toward him for a quick kiss before closing his eyes again.

"I love you, sweetheart. Now it's time for sleep."

"Love you too, Sam."

♫ ♫ ♫

It was still dark when Joy walked across the back porch toward the door of the Morgan house, pausing long enough to stomp the snow off her boots. She had today off from her diner job and had promised her Aunt Mary she would come over to the main house early enough to help serve the ranch hands their breakfast. It had been months since Joy had been free to do so, and she was actually looking forward to it. It was always entertaining to hear the menfolk sitting around the long trestle table, drinking their coffee, and chatting about their plans for the upcoming workday. And, of course, razzing each other about this and that. She'd never had brothers, but if she had, she liked to think they'd be like the Morgan men and the men who worked for them.

As she entered the warm house and shucked off her winter coat and boots and hung her coat on one of the many hooks near the back door, Joy could already smell coffee brewing and bacon frying. She lifted her nose and felt her lips turn up in a smile before she headed in the direction of the ranch kitchen.

Her Aunt Mary was already there, apron strapped around her waist, and hands flying as she rolled out biscuits on the countertop. She looked up as Joy walked through the open doorway between the kitchen and the great room, a smile creasing her face.

"Good morning, sweetie."

Joy walked over and gave her aunt a quick kiss on the cheek before pulling a matching apron off the hook along a back wall. She swathed it around her waist and reached back to tie the ties, all the time taking in what needed to be done.

"Good morning, Aunt Mary. Where do you need me?"

Giving Joy a smile, her aunt pointed a floury finger toward a pot on the stove. "Can you stir the sausage gravy for me? And then we need to get the table set."

Joy gave her aunt a nod and grabbed the wooden spoon resting on the counter next to the stove.

"Consider it done."

After giving the gravy a good stir, Joy started taking plates, silverware, coffee mugs, and glasses to the other room to prepare the long trestle table for breakfast. She had just started placing the plates around the table when Julie came through the doorway from the other part of the house that led to the upstairs.

"Joy!"

The other woman quickly came over and gave Joy a hug, smelling faintly of the floral shampoo Joy knew Julie always used.

"Good morning, Mrs. Morgan."

As Joy knew she would, Julie gave her a scolding look. "Good morning to you also, Joy. But how many times do I have to tell you it's not necessary to call me Mrs. Morgan. Please call me Julie, dear. You can call my mother-in-law Mrs. Morgan if you wish, but I'm simply Julie."

"Yes, ma'am."

When Julie headed to the kitchen to help Aunt Mary, Joy turned back to her work. Once the table was set to her satisfaction, she returned to the kitchen and started to get the large pitchers of milk and juice ready. It had been a while since Joy had helped her aunt in the kitchen of the big house, but she remembered the drill. Feeding the men before they went out to work for the day was a big job, but she knew how much these guys could eat, so there had to be a lot of food cooked for them. Her Aunt Mary had been doing it for so many years, though, she took it all in stride. To Joy—even after working in a diner—it always seemed like a miracle that her Aunt Mary could somehow manage to have everything ready when the crew arrived.

About that time, Clay Morgan's wife, Lottie, arrived in the kitchen from their downstairs bedroom, just off the kitchen. She was followed by her husband. Joy had always thought Clay Morgan looked like an older version of his son,

Sam, and even though she knew the man had to be in his early seventies, he still appeared to be healthy and vibrant.

He stopped long enough to give his daughter-in-law Julie a quick hug and kiss on the cheek, greeted Mary and Joy, then pecked his wife Lottie on the lips before giving Joy a wink that made her face warm. Joy watched Lottie watch her man walk from the kitchen and sighed, wondering if she'd ever find a love like that. The Morgans and her Aunt Mary and Uncle Jack had found it, but it sure didn't seem to Joy like she'd find it anytime soon. She'd thought once upon a time that she'd found it. But, boy, had she been wrong.

A part of her wondered what it would be like to have a man cherish her and protect her the way these Morgan men did their women. Not that Joy couldn't take care of herself. But just the idea that a man could ever love her that much sent her heart into overdrive.

Oh well, maybe someday.

Joy had just walked through the doorway toward the table with a pitcher of orange juice in one hand and a pitcher of milk in the other when Sam Morgan himself entered the room. His wife, Julie, had followed Joy from the kitchen with a bowl of fruit which she placed on the table before turning to meet her husband. When the two of them embraced and shared a quick kiss, Joy felt her face once again grow warm, and she quickly turned her eyes away from them, feeling a little embarrassed as they expressed their evident love for each other. Still, a part of her wondered again what would it be like to have a man look at her the way Sam Morgan looked at his wife. And it was easy to tell, Julie felt the same way about her husband as she gazed up at him in adoration.

Heading back to the kitchen, Joy prepared to help her aunt carry more platters of food to the table. The second trip from the kitchen, the sound of the ranch hands coming into the house greeted her ears as the men removed their coats and pounded snow from their hats before hanging them on the waiting hooks.

Feeling shy in the presence of all the men, Joy stepped back in the entry to the kitchen, watching as they took their seats around the table. She had known all the men for over a year and a half, so they didn't seem so scary to her anymore, but their rowdiness still left her unsettled.

There was Buck Buchanan—a man about Sam Morgan's age—short and stocky, but Joy knew his strength as she'd seen him wrestle calves and toss bales of hay as if they were feathers. Like most cowboys, he wore his graying hair a little long and always looked like he needed a shave—other than when Joy saw him at church on Sunday.

Then there was Wade Williams, tall, lean, and dark-haired. Joy guessed him to be older than her by about ten years and knew he was married and rented a small house about two miles from the central part of the ranch. Both Buck and Wade were both longtime employees of Bluecreek, and Joy felt safe around them.

There was also the younger blond-haired man named Jimmy Martin, who hadn't worked at the ranch for many years but appeared to practically worship her uncle and Sam Morgan. Her Uncle Jack had told Joy that he'd taught Jimmy a lot about the care of the horses, and he had appeared to pick up on it quickly.

And, of course, there was Zeke Mosher, who had been with the ranch for almost as many years as her Uncle Jack. Joy adored Zeke and his wife, Jessica, and their two little boys.

Then Joy's eyes were pulled toward the sound of heavy footfalls coming from the direction of the doorway leading into the other part of the house. She couldn't stop her mouth from falling open at the sight of Bill Parker, dressed in jeans and a flannel shirt, walking across the room to join the other menfolk seated around at the table.

"Hey, Bill!"

Joy's Uncle Jack immediately stood to shake the other man's hand, also taking hold of his forearm as if to make sure it was a firm handshake. Joy recognized that as what it was. Her uncle liked this man and wasn't just going through the motions of a polite handshake. Somehow that warmed her heart. The others already seated around the table also greeted Bill, who found a seat on the other side of the table where Joy could clearly see his face.

What a surprise to find Bill at the ranch again. Neither Joy's Aunt Mary nor Julie had mentioned anything about him coming back for another visit.

The men at the table all got settled and then quieted as Clay Morgan, Sam's father, stood from his usual spot at the end of the table to lead them all in a blessing for the food. Joy also closed her eyes and dropped her head as the deep voice of the elder Morgan echoed through the room. His words were those of thanksgiving and praise to the heavenly Father, and Joy felt a real peace sweep over her as he finished. Everyone around the table echoed his 'amen,' and then the chatter started back up as the platters and bowls of food were quickly passed around the table.

Joy felt her Aunt Mary come to stand beside her and turned her head enough to see the gentle-looking smile cross the older woman's face. It was easy to tell her aunt loved each and every one of the men seated at the table. All the work she did preparing the food for each of their meals wasn't work for her—it was an act of love.

Joy felt her aunt's hand on her arm and turned to look at her.

"I noticed we have another guest at the table this morning."

Feeling the warmth spreading across her cheeks again, Joy glanced quickly at the table full of men, then back at her aunt.

"I saw that. Do you know if he's here for very long?"

"Nope. Seeing him at the table this morning was the first I even knew he was here. Just like you. Perhaps he's here for the Christmas holiday?"

"Hmm." Joy nodded. "That makes sense, I guess—especially if he doesn't have any family of his own. Does he?"

She turned and looked at her aunt as she asked that question, wondering if that might be true. Maybe Bill was here because he didn't have any place else to go for the holiday season. Somehow that saddened her.

"Don't know."

Aunt Mary pushed away from the door. "How about you top off their coffee while I take some of the empty platters off the table to give them more room."

Joy went back to the kitchen and grabbed the coffee pot and followed her aunt across the room toward the table. She hadn't gotten very far before Bill's head turned her way, and his blue eyes locked on her face. Joy gave him a smile, then turned her attention to the mugs on the table, carefully filling each one with the hot brew. All the time, she could feel Bill's eyes following her movements as she slowly made her way around the table. When she came to Bill's side, she reached around him and carefully poured his mug full. Once she finished, she stepped back, but not before Bill had turned to look up at her.

"Thanks for the coffee, Joy."

Her face involuntarily broke into a broad smile as she looked directly at him. What was there about this man that made her want to let down her guard? Ever since the attack, she had been so careful to not get near any man—or let any man get near her. Yet, Bill Parker seemed to have broken down the wall she'd so carefully built around herself.

"You're welcome. Surprised to see you back."

He grinned.

"Is it a good surprise?"

Joy laughed at the little-boy look that appeared on his face. The man was actually flirting with her.

"Jury's still out on that, Cowboy," she quipped as she moved on down the table to pour the next man's coffee.

She could feel Bill's eyes on her, though, as she made her way slowly around the table. Bill didn't need to know how much of a pleasant surprise it had been for Joy to see him again. What he didn't know couldn't hurt her. At least that's what she kept telling herself.

CHAPTER 18

Bill finished the last bit of food on his plate and reached for his almost empty mug of coffee. His eyes raised to glance across the room toward the entryway to the kitchen, wondering if Joy would be back out with the pot of fresh coffee to refill his mug again.

Seeing Joy this morning had been a great start to the day. As she always did, she looked so cute. Today she was dressed in a dark blue sweater over a pair of worn blue jeans, and her glossy black hair was pulled back into a single braid down her back. He wondered if she had to go to work later, although he thought she looked more as if she was ready to go for a ride on her horse, instead of going to the diner.

"Hey, Pops," Sam's deep voice pulled Bill's eyes back to what was going on around the table. "I'm gonna run Bill into town after a bit. Is there anything you need me to pick up while I'm there?"

Bill watched as Clay Morgan sat down his own mug of coffee and gave his son his full attention.

"Yeah, will you check at the vet's office and see if that order of Aminoral came in?"

"Will do." Sam swiveled his head back toward Bill. "You good to leave right after we finish eating?"

Bill nodded. "That'll work."

A short time later, the sound of the other men pushing back their chairs and readying to leave signaled that the meal was done. Bill noticed Mary Byrd and Joy coming from the kitchen and also stood. He was finished eating anyway and didn't want to hold them up from cleaning up after the huge meal.

"Thank you, ma'am, for another good breakfast," he addressed Mary, all the time his eyes wanting to drift over to watch the younger woman as she stacked up dirty plates.

Mary gave him a smile as she also picked up several empty platters and bowls.

"You are most welcome, Bill. I do love to see my boys eat heartily."

Bill chuckled, feeling a warm spot in his heart at being included as one of 'Mary's boys.'

"Well, you sure know how to feed 'em, ma'am."

Mary laughed and headed toward the kitchen with Joy trailing after her. Bill's eyes followed the two women as they left, then turned to find Sam's eyes resting on him, a big grin on the other man's face.

"Won't have to put on much of an act, will you, Parker?"

Bill scowled and shook his head, refusing to take the bait. It was bad enough that he felt such an attraction to the young woman. But now, he'd have Sam ribbing him all the time about it.

"You 'bout ready to leave, Sam?"

The sound of Sam's quiet chuckle caused Bill to think about his mission. He really needed to be careful and remember the real reason he was there. What was supposed to be an act could quickly get out of control, and he certainly didn't want anyone's feeling hurt over this whole thing. He was here for one reason alone—because his boss in Washington, D. C. wanted him to oversee this Wolffe character, and to guarantee that when he was released from prison that he never got anywhere near Joy Whitefox. That was it.

Bill just needed to keep his head on straight and focus on his job. Then he could go back to D.C. and his real life.

"Ready when you are, Billy-Boy."

♫ ♫ ♫

The drive into Denning was quiet. Sam seemed content to concentrate on navigating the snow-covered roads, and that was fine with Bill. His mind was racing with what he should tell the sheriff about the Ernie Wolffe mess, and concerned about what Joy was thinking with him showing up so unexpectedly on the ranch for another visit.

He had seen the look of surprise on her face that morning when she'd first spotted him sitting at the breakfast table. And he was reasonably sure his face had reflected that same feeling of shock when he'd seen her standing there, looking as cute as he remembered. Then to have her stand so close to him as she'd refilled his mug of coffee had made him surprisingly nervous. Thus he had taken to teasing her, which had only made her act even more flustered. She was probably furious with him, which bothered him. And the fact that it bothered him worried him even more.

It wasn't long before they reached Denning, and Sam was parking his SUV in front of a brick storefront on the main street of town. Bill looked through the windshield toward the front of the structure as he unbuckled his seatbelt. The building kind of reminded him of the sheriff's offices they always had in the old black and white westerns his Dad used to watch when Bill was really little. Although, this was a much larger building and looked like it was in excellent condition.

As the two of them went through the front door, two uniformed deputies looked up from their desks, and another tall man was just walking out of a back office. He was wearing the same dark brown pants and light brown shirt uniform as the deputies, with a sheriff's badge pinned to his chest. At the sight of the two of them coming into the office, the tall man's strides lengthened as he walked toward them, his hand outstretched.

"Sam Morgan, as I live and breathe! How ya' doin', old man?"

Bill glanced over at the man beside him long enough to see his lips turn up in a dimply grin at the greeting. Obviously, these two were old friends.

Sam shook the offered hand, then turned toward Bill.

"Sheriff Wilson, this is Special Agent Bill Parker from Washington, D.C. Bill, meet Sheriff Chad Wilson—the man who took over keeping this town safe after I decided to hang up my badge."

Bill shook the offered hand, then noticed Sam's face sober.

"You got a minute for a little chat, Chad?"

The smile also left Sheriff Wilson's face, as if realizing their visit wasn't purely social.

"Sure, Sam. Come on back to the office."

Bill followed the other two men to an office at the rear of the building—a small room that thankfully had a window, or it could have felt somewhat claustrophobic to Bill. So, this was the office Sam had used when he served as Sheriff of Denning for a few years. It wasn't much after the modern conveniences they enjoyed in the squad room back at the Bureau.

The Sheriff pointed to a couple of old plastic-covered chairs in front of his desk, then took his own seat in the worn desk chair behind his desk.

"What's up?"

Sam glanced over at Bill, then turned his attention back to the sheriff.

"I think I'll let Agent Parker fill you in, Sheriff. It's really his story."

Bill shifted in his chair while his mind raced with all the information he had to share with the man. The Director had told him to make sure the local law knew how dangerous the situation was with Ernie Wolffe, but Bill wasn't sure how to make his case in such a way that the Sheriff would understand the full extent of the man's reach.

"You are aware that Ernie Wolffe is due to be released from prison at the end of this year?"

At Bill's question, the Sheriff's eyebrows raised, and he glanced quickly from Sam back to Bill as if trying to figure out why they were there and what it had to do with someone currently in prison. Well, the man just needed to hang on, and Bill was going to tell him.

"Sure. As you can imagine, we're not too happy about that, but the man's served his time. What's the FBI's interest in him?"

Bill sighed. The man hadn't served nearly enough time for what he'd done to Joy as far as he was concerned, but that was another story.

"Wolffe's name has been linked with possible counterfeiting, money laundering, and several other crimes involving a drug cartel working out of Mexico. It's a drug ring we've been trying to take down for years, and we're hoping that by watching every move Wolffe makes when he gets released, we'll be able to flush out his bosses."

The Sheriff nodded his head. "Doesn't surprise me to find out he's involved in something like that. He'd bad news all the way around."

Bill swallowed hard as he thought about just how rotten the guy actually was. "We're also concerned about the safety of the young woman he attacked and raped—the entire reason he was finally put behind bars. We're afraid he's going to try and make her pay for testifying against him and sending him to jail."

Sam spoke up. "Joy Whitefox is currently living on our ranch, and we feel she's safer there than when she lived on the reservation. But we can't be with her twenty-four hours a day, Sheriff. We're hoping you can help keep an eye on her when she's here in town working. And, of course, if Wolffe is looking to harm her, you'll also be able to keep track of him at the same time. We'd also like you to let the law enforcement force on the reservation know about what we suspect of Wolffe's involvement with the drug cartels."

The Sheriff nodded. "Well, you have my complete cooperation and access to anything you need from us."

He shook his head and looked over at Sam. "Of course, you know we don't have a huge force—there's just a couple of deputies and me—so what we can do to help you is rather limited. Sometimes I wish you were still the man sitting at this desk, Sam. The job hasn't gotten any easier over the years since you retired."

Bill saw Sam frown, then give a little nod before he addressed the Sheriff again.

"I'm afraid it's that way everywhere. Evil seems to be becoming more widespread. Even small towns are fighting crimes like this now."

"We just want the local law enforcement to be aware of the situation, Sheriff," Bill added. "I'm going to be at Sam's ranch for the near future—until we can find out what Wolffe's next move will be once he's released. Trust me, we're going to be keeping an eye on him too."

Sam stood, and Bill joined him as the two men took turns shaking the Sheriff's hand.

"I appreciate you gentlemen stopping by and letting me know what's going on. Please keep me updated on anything new you find out, and I'll do the same."

"Thanks again, Sheriff," Sam replied.

Bill and Sam exited the Sheriff's office and walked back down the sidewalk toward where they'd parked, neither of them saying anything while Bill replayed the conversation they'd had with the Sheriff. He couldn't think of anything he'd left out when he'd updated the lawman on the situation. Hopefully, with the Sheriff's Department, the reservation's law enforcement forces, and Bill and Sam aware of what was going on, they would be able to stop Wolffe before something more happened.

"I'm going to run across the street to the vet's office and pick up that medicine for Pops, then I've got a couple more errands to run for Julie. If there's something else you want to do while we're in town, go ahead and do it, and I'll meet you back at the vehicle—say in about forty-five minutes or so."

Bill gave him a nod and watched as Sam strode confidently across the quiet street, his Stetson firmly on his head. It had taken a while for Bill to adjust to seeing former Special Agent Samuel Morgan decked out like a cowboy, but he'd finally gotten used to it. Now, seeing Sam dressed any other way just didn't seem right.

He stood there on the sidewalk a few more moments and wondered what to do to pass the time until Sam finished his errands. If Joy were working, he would have stopped into the diner to grab a cup of coffee and tease her a little bit, but he knew from seeing her at the ranch earlier that morning that she must not be working. He was glad she finally had some time off. From what Jack had told him, Bill knew she put in long hours at the diner.

Finally, he turned in the direction of a clothing store down the street he'd noticed when they'd come into town. If Bill was going to be in Montana for a while, he needed to start fitting in more. Which meant he needed to buy some more jeans and blue denim shirts. And maybe even a cowboy hat.

And he also needed to do a little Christmas shopping since Christmas was less than two weeks away. He already had one item in his luggage—a little something he'd brought with him from D.C., but he still needed to get a few things to give to the Morgan family. Since the Director had dumped this trip on him at the last minute, he hadn't had much time to prepare.

As he stopped in front of the clothing store, Bill gazed at the window display, which consisted mostly of cowboy hats. Spotting one he kind of like, Bill grinned, wondering what Joy would think of him the first time he wore it.

Yeah, he really needed to buy himself a new hat.

CHAPTER 19

After a quiet lunch with her Aunt Mary and Uncle Jack at their cabin, Joy wandered across the ranch yard to the barn, intending to spend a little time with her horse, Spirit. With her working so many hours recently, she'd neglected the poor animal, and he was probably feeling abandoned.

The inside of the barn was cool but not as cold as it was out in the wind as the animals helped to warm the interior. Joy was sure it was going to snow again, though. She could almost smell it in the air.

Joy entered Spirit's stall and greeted him, rubbing his nose and talking to him in a quiet voice. The horse nudged her hand as if appreciating the attention. Spirit could be temperamental with others, but Joy had always treated the horse with care and love, and the animal seemed to understand that and responded well to her. She led him out into the aisle between the stalls on either side of the barn and attached lead ropes—one from each side of the aisle to make sure the horse stayed put while she groomed him. Spirit was a calm horse most of the time, but there was a reason why her Uncle Jack had given him that name when he was born. He could be somewhat obstinate at times, so Joy had learned to be careful when handling him, even though he was usually good for her. Her uncle had taught her years ago you could never be too cautious around livestock.

Once the horse was secure, Joy ran her hand down his front leg and lifted his foot. Using a hoof pick, she checked the hoof carefully to make sure any rocks or debris were removed. Then she did the same thing with the other feet, all the time singing quietly to help calm the horse. Joy had always loved music and loved to sing. It was such a part of her, she couldn't help herself—especially when she was at peace with her life.

Today, she was humming and singing a song of praise, based on the fourteenth verse of Psalm 27:

Wait on the Lord: be of good courage, and he shall strengthen thine heart: wait, I say, on the Lord.

There was no real tune to her song as it was more of a chant in the way of her people, sung quietly and reverently, her voice going up and down as her emotions warranted.

Joy frequently sang when she felt the presence of the Lord around her. Often after her morning prayers, she wished she had time to ride through the pastures to loudly sing out her praises. But today, she didn't want to spook Spirit, so she kept her praising more subdued.

When she finished cleaning the horse's hooves, she grabbed a curry comb from a shelf on the wall behind her and began currying the horse, starting at his neck. At the sound of someone coming through the barn door, however, Joy stopped what she was doing and turned her head to see Bill Parker entering the barn.

♫ ♫ ♫

Bill stood outside the barn door for several minutes before entering, enjoying the unexpected sound of Joy's beautiful voice singing a rather strange tune. Bill had heard her singing once before when she hadn't known he was listening, and he loved the sound of the pure musical notes. Her voice was beautiful, even though this melody sounded almost ethereal. Perhaps it was a Native American Indian tune she was singing. But he'd quickly recognized the words for what they were—straight from the book of Psalms.

When the singing stopped, he pushed the door open enough to enter. Joy stood in the aisle between the stalls, grooming her horse. Her head came up at his entrance, and he shot her a quick smile, hoping he hadn't frightened her. He hadn't seen her since that morning at breakfast, and when he'd decided to visit the barn, he hadn't known she'd be there. Not that he was upset to find her there. Quite the contrary.

"Sorry, I didn't know you were out here."

He stopped where he stood, just inside the doorway, and waited for her to give him some signal so he'd know whether he should go or stay.

She turned and started running the curry comb across the horse's back, using circular motions like Jack had shown him to use. Joy didn't say anything for a few seconds, and Bill took a step backward toward the door. Maybe he'd best come back another time.

"You can stay."

She turned long enough to shoot him a small smile before returning to her work. "Although I have to say, I wouldn't have thought you'd want to spend time in the barn when you didn't have to."

Bill chuckled and strolled across the barn floor to where he was standing closer to her, taking care not to stand behind the horse.

"Yeah, well, I've spent enough time out here working with your uncle that I'm starting to feel like it's my second home."

He was happy to hear her answering chuckle.

"Never thought I see the day when I'd hear you say those words, Cowboy."

189

When nothing more was said between them, Bill turned and walked over to Bess's stall, greeting her in a quiet voice, and leading her out into the aisle. He noticed Joy had stopped what she was doing and was standing beside her horse, watching him while he went through the motions of snapping lead ropes on Bess's bridle and then over to the hooks on the walls to keep her in place for grooming. Then he grabbed a curry comb from the shelf behind him and went to work.

The two of them worked quietly on their own horses for a few moments before Joy's soft voice broke the silence in the barn.

"I have to say, I was surprised to see you back here at the ranch. I figured you'd want to spend the holidays with your family."

Bill frowned at her question, then realized that, of course, Joy would think that. She didn't know his history.

"No family to spend it with, I'm afraid."

She straightened and looked down the aisle at him. "I'm sorry."

He shook his head, not wanting her sympathy nor wanting to make her feel bad for him.

"It's not a big deal. I lost both my parents when I was very young—young enough, I barely remember them. I spent most of my childhood being raised by foster parents."

He smiled at the memory of his last foster family. It had truly been a family as his foster parents had taken in more youngsters than just Bill. There had been six children of various races and ages raised in that household, and for the most part, it had been a happy home.

"I can't imagine what that would be like." She gazed at him, her dark eyes looking large in her face. "My dad may not be much, but he was still my dad, and was there when I needed him. Most of the time."

Bill digested that information, wondering what Clark Whitefox was really like. Jack Byrd didn't seem very impressed with the man. And from what he'd heard from

Sam, her dad hadn't been much help after she'd been attacked by Wolffe.

"I had good foster parents. Well, the last ones were always good to me." He paused for a moment before adding. "They've both passed away now."

Joy looked over at him a few more moments before turning back to her horse.

"So, that's why you're here then."

Bill paused, wondering how he should respond. Joy hadn't asked a question. It was more of a statement as if she now understood the reasoning for his sudden appearance on the ranch again. Which meant she'd been thinking about it— wondering why he was there. He didn't know whether that was a good sign or not. Perhaps she was just curious about him.

Bess shifted a little on her feet, and Bill took a step back from the horse he was grooming until she settled, then went back to work, rubbing the comb in a circular motion in the direction opposite the hair growth, like Jack had shown him to do. Surprisingly, Bill found grooming a horse to be almost as relaxing for him as it appeared to be for the animal.

"Decided it's better to spend my holiday with people I care about then to spend it alone, don't you think?"

Joy turned her eyes on him, her face getting that distressed look on it again as if she were feeling sorry for him. He really wished she'd quit that. He was perfectly happy with having grown up the way he had. He'd never known anything different. Perhaps it was time to switch the topic of conversation to Joy.

"How about you? Will you be spending the day with your dad?"

Even though she'd turned back around, he heard the unexpected snort and tried not to smile. It sounded so unladylike coming from such a little thing like her.

"I already went and visited my dad and took him his gifts. Besides, I have to work on Christmas Eve. Thank goodness, the diner is closed Christmas Day, so I'll be able to spend that day with Aunt Mary and Uncle Jack."

He nodded. "Good."

Part of him wanted to ask more about her visit to her father but knew it was really none of his business. He was glad to know she'd be on the ranch Christmas Day, though. He had something to give her but needed to somehow work it out so it wouldn't appear to mean more than it did.

Yeah, good luck with that, Parker.

Because he certainly didn't want Joy to get hurt by anything he said or did. Somehow along the line, the young woman had become extremely important to him. As a good friend, if nothing more. And he didn't want to lose that feeling.

"Is your dad the only family you have then—other than your Aunt Mary and Uncle Jack?"

He watched as Joy finished grooming her horse, then led Spirit back into his stall. As he waited for her answer, he unhooked Bess's lead rope and led her back to her own stall. He made sure she had feed and water, and then closed the stall door and went back out to the center part of the barn.

There, he found Joy waiting for him, seated on a bale of straw. He walked over and sat on another bale near her, hoping to have more time to talk with her, but not wanting to scare her away.

"In answer to your earlier question—Yes. I have an uncle. Uncle Tate. He used to live in Denning when I was younger but has since moved to Wyoming. He's married and has two kids, so I have cousins. I never see them anymore, though."

She paused for a moment. "Uncle Tate and my dad don't talk. Dad was always mad because Uncle Tate went to college and then moved off the reservation. He said Uncle Tate turned his back on his people. I never saw it that way, though. Uncle Tate just wanted a better life than what he would have had if he'd stayed."

He could hear her sigh from where he sat.

"Dad's probably going to feel the same way toward me when I finish my degree and leave."

Bill shifted where he sat on his bale of straw, so he was a little closer to her. It sounded as if Joy didn't have any intention of staying in this area.

"How's that going, by the way? Isn't this your last semester?"

Joy's face brightened at that question, and Bill felt a catch in his chest at the sight of her smile. She didn't smile nearly often enough, and when she did, she was so beautiful, she took his breath away.

"Yes. I've actually finished my exams, and I'm waiting for my final test scores. I know I'll graduate. I just don't know what my grade-point-average will be."

Her face grew wider. "I can't *wait* to get that diploma in the mail. Then I can get out of here and find a real job someplace."

Bill heard the yearning in Joy's heart. But did she really want to leave Montana and the only world she'd ever known, or was she just running from what had happened to her here? Somehow he couldn't imagine her living in a city. She belonged here, riding Spirit across the open landscape.

"Where will you go?"

She raised her eyes to lock on his. A look of surprise passed over her face, which was quickly replaced with a blank stare. She didn't answer and immediately dropped her eyes from him, and for a while, Bill wondered if she would respond to his question.

"I don't know. Just someplace far away."

He nodded, wondering how much to say to her about what he thought of the idea. Running away from your past never worked. He'd learned long ago that his past had made him the man he was today—even the bad things that had happened to him.

"And here, I was just thinking about moving to Montana and starting over here."

Joy's head came back up, a surprised look on her face.

"You're joking, right?"

Bill grinned. He sure did enjoy pulling her chain. Then he changed his silly grin to a smaller smile. She had no way of knowing his plans.

"Not really. I haven't said a word to Sam or Julie or anyone else yet, though, so this is just between us. Okay?"

Her head bobbed in a little nod, her eyes still large in her face.

Feeling more nervous talking about what he'd done than he thought he would, Bill took a deep breath and released it. So far, he hadn't mentioned his plans to anyone else. It was all too new—too exciting.

"Just before I came back to Montana, I took my Praxis exams—the tests I had to take to become certified to teach." He lifted his lips into a broader grin. "I passed."

Much to his surprise, Joy launched herself at him in a quick hug as she screeched in happiness.

"Congratulations, Bill! I know how much that must mean to you!"

Then, as if realizing what she'd done, Joy quickly moved back to her bale of straw and sat down, her hands clasped tightly together between her knees. She stared at the floor as if afraid to look at him again after her unexpected show of emotion.

"Thanks." Bill felt a little unsteady himself after having her wrap her arms around his neck—albeit very briefly. But she *had* hugged him. And he had to admit, he'd liked it. A lot.

"And you're thinking about moving here?" Joy's raised her eyes back to his face, her eyebrows rising in unbelief. "Why?"

Bill chuckled. That was a question he'd been asking himself ever since the notion had first come to him. He had to believe it was God leading him, but for the life of him, Bill couldn't figure out why God would want him to come to Montana to teach. There were thousands of other places Bill would have thought of moving first.

"Good question. And I don't really have an answer yet."

He released a sigh. "I just feel as if God is telling me here is where He wants me to teach. We'll see.

"I'm still an FBI agent, so I haven't put anything into motion that will bring me here. If I'm supposed to be here, I'll have to start applying for some jobs and see what happens."

Joy nodded. "Denning has an excellent school. I know Jess Mosher taught there for several years before she and Zeke got married."

Bill could remember Jess had done that, although he'd forgotten about it. Making a mental note to check out the school before he left town, Bill thought of something else.

"What about the schools on the reservation? Are they good schools?"

She paused for a second before answering him. "I had good teachers, but I'm sure they're always looking for more." Her lips lifted in a small smile. "Not everyone wants to teach on a reservation."

Yeah. Bill wasn't sure he'd be up for that either—especially as a new teacher.

It was quiet between the two of them for a few moments, and Bill wondered if right then might be the best time to give her his gift. It wasn't really a gift, of course. It was meant to help keep her alive if—God forbid—Ernie Wolffe ever came after her. He reached into his pants pocket and pulled it out, holding his hand fisted as he moved over closer to her. He reached out his closed hand toward her, his eyes searching her face as she turned a questioning look on him.

"What's this?"

He smiled, feeling surprisingly nervous. He didn't want Joy to get the wrong idea, yet it was imperative that she wear it all the time.

"I have something for you."

When her eyebrows went up, he quickly sobered and shook his head.

"It's not a big deal. It's just something I found when I was in D.C., and it made me think of you and everything you've been through."

He reached over with his left hand and took hold of her right one, then placed the item in it. Her eyes dropped to the palm of her hand, where the item rested.

"I just wanted to give you something—as a friend only. No strings attached."

Bill watched as Joy lifted the necklace from her hand and let it hang in front of her. It was a heart with a tiny cross in the center. On the back was inscribed the words Hebrews 13:8, reference to a verse which Bill hoped would give Joy comfort.

Jesus Christ, the same yesterday, and today, and for ever.

"Oh, Bill." Her eyes raised to his. "This is beautiful."

Then she shook her head. "But I can't accept this. I mean…"

He raised his right hand and shook his head.

"I mean it, Joy. It's just something I want you to have. I don't want you to feel it means anything other than what it is. A gift—from a friend to a friend."

He sighed. "There's a good reason I want you to have it." He pointed to the necklace. "Inserted inside it is a tiny GPS chip. If you were ever to disappear, we could track the necklace and find you."

Her eyes grew big as she stared at him.

"The only reason I'd ever turn on the app on my phone to track you is if I really needed to, Joy. I promise it's not to invade your privacy. And if you'd rather I never did, just tell me now, and I'll give you my word I won't ever turn it on."

She didn't say anything for a few seconds as she dropped her head and gazed at the necklace in her hand. When she turned it over and saw the scripture reference inscribed there, he saw her lips raise in a small smile.

"That's one of my most favorite verses about the constancy of Jesus and His love. How did you know?"

He chuckled. "Guess God told me it was the one I should have put on there. I've always liked it too."

She finally released a sigh and gave him a small smile.

"Thank you, Bill. It's beautiful."

He nodded, satisfied. Thankfully, it appeared she was going to accept it.

"There is one request I have, though."

Again her eyes raised to his, and a fleeting look of suspicion crossed her face.

"Just promise me you'll wear it. Always. And whenever you begin to feel fearful, you look at it and remember God is with you, and you're never alone. And remember, I'm praying for you."

Her eyes brightened, and she quickly nodded her head.

"I can do that."

Bill watched as she unzipped her jacket and reached around both her hands to fasten the clasp of the necklace. It made him feel good to see it hanging around her neck. Now, if something were to happen to Joy, and no one could find her, Bill would be able to track her down and save her from harm.

To protect her from Ernie Wolffe.

Because there was no way, Bill wanted anything to ever happen to her again.

♫ ♫ ♫

That evening, Joy sat in her loft bedroom and looked down at the necklace hanging around her neck. She was still in shock that Bill Parker had given her such a gift. And she'd felt terrible that she had nothing to give him in return, even though he'd assured her that he didn't want her to give him anything. And there had been a good reason for the gift. The gift didn't mean anything. It was just so they could find her if she were to disappear for some reason.

At that thought, Joy shivered.

But it had been kind of Bill to think of doing something like that for her. Even though he'd assured her, it was just an expression of friendship.

So, why did she feel the stirrings of something more for him?

Joy had never known a man like Bill Parker before. The only man she could think of that even came close was Sam Morgan. And she had never felt as comfortable around Sam as she did Bill. In just a few months, Joy's initial fear of him had disappeared. In fact, she found herself enjoying his company.

A lot.

Which led to why she was staring down at the necklace. Joy had felt something much more than friendship when Bill had taken hold of her hand and placed the piece of jewelry in it. He had stirred something in her heart and soul—a need to get close to another person again. Since being attacked, Joy had pulled back from other people. Even physical contact with her Aunt Mary and her Dad had become an effort.

But then Bill Parker had come into her life.

She allowed the necklace to drop back to its resting place and closed her eyes, a quick prayer on her lips.

Lord, please don't let me fall in love with a man You don't want in my life. I believe Bill is a good man, a Christian man. But I don't want to do anything to interfere with Your plans for his life. Or for mine either, for that matter. But I do thank You for his friendship.

Because that was *all* there was between the two of them, and Joy was sure that was all there would ever be. After all, what man would want anything to do with a woman who had been sullied the way she had?

No. Friendship would have to be enough.

CHAPTER 20

The next evening, Bill helped Clay, Sam, and Jack haul a huge spruce tree into the great room of the main house. They'd already delivered a smaller version of the tree to Jack's cabin, and another one to the bunkhouse. Zeke and Jess had assured the three men they had plans to get their own tree, so Bill was relieved that at least they wouldn't have to haul one to their house too.

Once the tree was set up in the corner of the room and met Lottie, Julie's, and Samantha's expectations, the men sat in chairs in front of the fireplace and relaxed with cups of coffee and watched as Julie, Lottie, and Mary, with Samantha and C.J.'s assistance, decorated the tree. The women had just finished putting on strings of lights when the backdoor opened, and Joy Whitefox walked in.

"Oh, good." Mary went over and gave her niece a quick hug. "You're home from work in time to help decorate the tree."

Julie joined Mary in encouraging Joy to stay and help. Bill could tell Joy was unsure if she wanted to or not, and waited anxiously for her decision, hoping beyond hope, that she'd stay. She'd been working so many hours recently, he hadn't had the opportunity to see her for days.

When he heard her quiet voice finally agree, Bill released a sigh of relief. Not wanting to be too obvious, though, he turned his attention back to the other men who were discussing horses...or cattle...or something like that, Bill was sure. It seemed that was all they ever talked about. But then, he *was* on a cattle ranch, so he guessed that wasn't surprising. Even while half-listening to the other men's discussion, though, Bill kept his eyes trained on the activity around the Christmas tree.

Julie and Mary were carefully removing decorative balls and baubles from a wooden box where it was apparent they were stored from year to year. He listened as Julie explained to C.J. that he had to be very careful with the glass ball she'd just handed him.

"That one is extremely old, C.J. Your great-great-great-grandparents brought that with them when they moved here from Illinois in 1915."

Bill felt his lips raise in a smile when he saw the young man's eyes grow large.

"Wow! That's like a hundred years ago, Mom!"

Upon hearing C.J.'s exclamation of wonder, the women's laughter echoed through the room as they all returned to their work. Bill had to agree with C.J. It was amazing that something that fragile had survived all these years—especially during the initial journey to Montana. Back in those days, that trip must have been a grueling one.

His eyes drifted from the tree to the young woman helping Samantha reach a higher branch to hang a decoration of some sort. His lips lifted a little in amusement as he watched them. Neither of them was tall enough to reach very high, so it wasn't going to be long, and they were going to be finished decorating the lower branches. Then someone much taller was going to have to step in and help.

Pushing himself out of his comfortable chair, Bill headed in that direction. It had been a long time since he'd help decorate a Christmas tree. Too long.

♫ ♫ ♫

Even though he and Jack and his dad were deep in a discussion about a horse that had developed a sore on its foreleg, Sam caught movement in his peripheral vision. Bill was strolling across the room in the direction of the womenfolk decorating the tree.

Like a moth to a flame.

He'd wondered how long it would take before Bill would cave and go help them, especially after Joy had shown up to help. Usually, Julie hounded Sam to help decorate the upper part of the tree, but maybe this year, he'd lucked out.

Good for Bill. Sam didn't think his old partner had many occasions to get involved in family activities like this. It would do the lonely man good. And, of course, Sam had been sure once Joy started helping, it would just be a matter of time before Billy-Boy would step in to add his assistance.

Sam had been carefully watching his friend as he'd settled into living on the ranch, and Bill had definitely changed from the man who had come for an unexpected visit several months earlier. There was something more...settled about him. Sam didn't know if Bill had finally come to grips with his break-up with Zoey, or if it were something else. From a couple of things Bill had said to him, Sam couldn't help but think most of the change in him had to do with his restored relationship with the Lord.

But whatever it was, Bill appeared to be happier than he had been in years and that did Sam's heart good.

He heard Bill's laughter ring out as he reached above Joy's head to hang a couple of ornaments, and Sam felt his own lips raise in response as he heard Joy's answering giggle. Sam wasn't attuned to matters of the heart the same way his sweet wife was, but it would take a blind and deaf man to not realize there was more than a growing friendship between those two. He couldn't decide if that would be a good thing or not. Joy was a country girl—born and raised on the Crow Reservation not far from the ranch. Bill was a city boy—and an FBI agent to boot—with his life firmly entrenched in D.C.

Sam sighed and turned his attention back to his dad, who had asked him another question about some of the livestock. It was a good thing Bill and Joy were friends, but there was no way anything else between them would ever work.

♫ ♫ ♫

The days passed quickly for Bill as activity around the ranch ramped up. Christmas was in less than a week, and everyone seemed to be in a frenzy, getting ready for it. He spent some of his time in the house, helping the women as they moved furniture around and finished their decorating. Some of his time was spent out in the barn—usually with Jack Byrd.

Disappointingly, because she was putting in such long hours at the diner, Joy was rarely around. And Bill couldn't believe how much he missed her company.

He also felt a sense of frustration as the days flew by, bringing the time of Wolffe's release ever closer. So far, Sheriff Wilson and his deputies hadn't come up with any new information for Bill. He'd checked in with Director Roberts a couple of times too, and he didn't have any new information for him either. It was as if everything in the investigation had come to a standstill as they all waited for Wolffe's release.

Bill knew the upcoming freedom of the man who had violated and beat her had to be weighing heavily on Joy's mind, but whenever he did see her, she never showed it. He'd seen her just that morning at breakfast as she quickly ate her food and then stood to leave for work.

Before she'd left, though, it had touched Bill deep in his heart to see her throw him a quick smile while reaching down with her right hand to take hold of the piece of jewelry hanging around her neck. He was glad to see she wore it all the time. That was what he'd prayed she would do. If she'd left it at home on the top of her dresser and something happened where she came up missing, it wasn't going to do him any good.

Sam, with his eagle-eyes, had already asked him about the necklace. Bill had awkwardly explained his reasons for giving Joy the piece of jewelry, all the time feeling Sam's steely gray eyes studying his face. Yeah, there wasn't any sense in trying to get anything by Sam Morgan. Hopefully, though, Sam thought the necklace was just a way to protect Joy and didn't realize how much the young woman was beginning to mean to Bill.

♫ ♫ ♫

Three days before Christmas, right after breakfast and just before he headed out the door to join Jack in the barn Mary Byrd stopped Bill.

"Mr. Parker, may I have a word with you, please?"

Bill raised his eyebrows in confusion as he glanced over at Sam, who was already at the back door, his hand on the handle. Sam just gave him a shrug and a grin, then grabbed his hat off the hook and left.

"Yes, ma'am."

Mary walked in the direction of the kitchen, and Bill dutifully followed her, wondering what he had done to cause the small woman to address him so formally. Had she gotten wind of the necklace he'd given Joy? If so, what did she think it meant?

Bill swallowed a couple of times and tried to breathe. The last thing he wanted to do was cause trouble for Joy and her family. Or him and Joy's family.

And he certainly didn't want to get on the wrong side of Jackson Byrd.

Once in the kitchen, Mary pointed in the direction of one of the stools at the counter.

"Go ahead and have a seat, Bill. And wipe that look. You aren't in trouble with me. I just need to ask a favor of you."

Bill took a seat and released a sigh of relief. A favor. He could handle doing her a favor. He hoped.

"Yes, ma'am. What can I do for you?"

Mary took a seat on the stool next to him. "As you probably know, our Joy has finished her college education and has been awaiting the arrival of her diploma." The woman gave him a crooked grin. "What my girl doesn't know is that it arrived in yesterday's mail. I hid it from her because Julie and I have decided to throw a graduation party for her. We hope to keep it a surprise, as something to show her how proud we are of her."

A warm feeling rushed through Bill at the thought of them doing something special for Joy. She'd worked hard to get her degree and deserved a little celebrating.

"I think that's a wonderful idea. What can I do to help?"

The woman's eyes narrowed as she continued to look over at him, and Bill instantly worried about what he was getting himself into. Visions of putting up crepe streamers and blowing up balloons suddenly rattled around in his head. Not at all his idea of fun.

"I need you to take Joy someplace off the ranch for a few hours so we can decorate the house and get ready for the party."

Bill nodded. That didn't sound so bad.

"I guess I could do that. Do you have any ideas of where I could take her to spend a few hours? You have to remember, I'm not a local."

Mary's eyes lit up. She apparently hadn't thought he'd be so quick to agree. She pulled her stool over a little closer as if to keep their conversation private—even though everyone else had left the house right after breakfast. Julie had run into town with Lottie, Samantha, and C.J., and the men had all headed to the barn to do chores.

"I have a plan, Bill. I want you to ask her out and take her into Billings and treat her to dinner."

Dinner. She wants me to take Joy out to dinner. Like a date.

"Dinner?" Bill gulped and swallowed hard as he struggled to wrap his mind around what Joy's aunt was suggesting.

"Yes. That will give us plenty of time to get things ready here. Take Joy someplace nice for an early dinner, and by the time you get home, we'll be ready to surprise her. What do you say?"

What *could* he say? Bill's mind raced with the implications of what others would think of him taking Joy out on a date. He and Joy had become good friends over the past couple of weeks. But a date? That would change everything. But he couldn't very well refuse to do what her aunt was asking of him as that would send out all kinds of signals: that he didn't like Joy; that they weren't as good of friends as he'd told Joy they were; that he didn't want to help with the surprise…

No, he had to accept the mission.

"I think I can arrange that, Mary."

The older woman practically jumped off the stool she'd been sitting on and reached out to give him a quick hug.

"Fantastic. I told Julie you were just the man for the job. I'll leave all the details to you, but just remember, you can't be back here at the ranch until after six-thirty."

Bill nodded. No problem. Dangerous and impossible missions were his specialty.

205

CHAPTER 21

Joy glanced up at the sound of the bells jingling over the diner entrance and almost dropped the coffee pot when she saw who was coming through the door.

Bill Parker.

She watched as he pulled off the Stetson hat he'd taken to wearing and held it in his hands while he looked around the diner. Then the man at the table she was standing in front of brought her attention back to her job.

"Uh, Miss. My coffee?"

Feeling flustered, Joy apologized to the man and quickly re-filled his coffee cup, then turned and watched as Bill made his way through the restaurant to take a seat at a small table near the back. Taking a deep breath, she headed in that direction.

"Bill, I didn't know you were coming into town this morning."

Blue eyes locked on hers, and Joy caught her breath. This morning, Bill's eyes were a deep blue like the waters of Bluecreek River—the way the water looked on days when the sun shone brightly and make it look as if God had sprinkled diamonds across the top of the river.

"Well, it was kind of a last-minute decision." He gave her a crooked smile, and she couldn't think of what she was supposed to do next.

Finally, she was able to pull her mind back into action.

"Coffee?" She up-righted the overturned mug on his table, and at his nod, poured him a mug-full. "Can I get you anything else?"

His chuckle warmed her to her toes. "You *do* know I just ate one of your Aunt Mary's breakfasts, right?"

She couldn't help but grin back at him. There was no way he'd be hungry for at least a couple of hours.

"Right. Sorry."

His eyes were still locked on hers. "That's okay. Hey, do you have a minute to talk?"

Joy glanced around the diner, noting everyone already had their meals, and there hadn't been any new patrons come through the door since Bill's arrival.

"Sure, I guess I can. What's up?"

Bill motioned to the chair across the table from him. "Will you get in trouble if you sit with me?"

She shook her head, knowing Peggy wouldn't give her a rough time as long as Joy didn't let it interfere with her getting the work done. Joy slid into the chair, placing the now half-full pot of coffee on the table in front of her.

The good-looking man seated across the table continued to gaze at her, almost as if he were trying to figure something out. Well, Joy was trying to figure something out too. She was confused. Why was Bill in Denning anyway? He never came to town unless he tagged along with Sam or Zeke when they came for supplies. And she was reasonably sure they hadn't mentioned anything at breakfast about needing to go into town for anything.

"I want to ask you something, and I hope you say yes." He paused a moment and chewed on his lower lip as if he were searching for words. "I'm asking you as a friend, and I hope you accept as a friend."

Joy nodded, not knowing what else to do. This was reminiscent of the day Bill had given her the necklace. It was almost as if he were repeating the words to himself as much as to her.

"O-kay," she finally said, wondering where this was leading.

She saw Bill's Adam apple jump as he swallowed and had to hold back a smile. Whatever it was, the big, tough FBI Agent across the table from her was actually nervous. It was a side of him she hadn't seen before, and she kind of liked it.

"Will you go out to dinner with me tomorrow night?"

Joy felt a sense shock go through her as his words finally registered. Bill was asking her on a date?

"What?"

"Dinner. Tomorrow night." Bill acted a little less nervous now that he'd gotten out the first words. "I thought we might drive into Billings and find a nice restaurant there. I know you've finally finished your studies and will soon be getting your diploma, and I'd like to buy you a nice dinner in celebration."

Celebration. Well, taking her out to a nice restaurant was a kind thing to do, but then Bill was a nice guy. Joy only had to think about it for a couple of seconds.

"Sure. I think that would be great!"

She gave him a smile, feeling relieved that what he'd come to tell her hadn't been something terrible—like he was leaving and going back to D.C. For some reason, Joy wasn't looking forward to that day.

"Thank you for asking, Bill. That's nice of you."

His signature grin appeared on his face as he quipped, "I keep tellin' you. I'm a nice guy, Joy Whitefox. When are you gonna believe me?"

♫ ♫ ♫

Bill stood in front of the mirror on the back of the guest bedroom door and tried to decide if he should lose the tie. He'd decided not to wear a suit but had added a tie to his plain white shirt and dark blue dress pants at the last minute to dress things up a little bit. The restaurant where they were going didn't require a suit and tie, but he wanted to look nice for the evening. The truth was, he wanted to look extra-good for Joy.

He finally heaved a sigh and shook his head. He was overthinking everything about tonight. It was time to go and quit worrying about how he was dressed. Reaching out as he passed his dresser, Bill grabbed his wallet and stuck it in his back pocket. At the last minute, he decided to go ahead and wear a sport coat, as it would hide his holstered gun. When he was on the ranch, he never bothered to carry his weapon. But tonight they were going to be out in public, and he'd feel much safer knowing if something were to happen, he'd have his trusty Sig Sauer with him and be able to protect Joy.

When he reached the great room, all eyes turned at his entrance. Sam released a low whistle, and even Jack gave him a nod of approval, although his eyes were stern as they gave Bill the once-over.

"You clean up good."

Bill released a nervous laugh. "Thanks, Jack."

Picking up his booted foot, he added. "I kept the cowboy boots. After all, I'm still in Montana."

That brought laughter from everyone in the room. The place was hopping as Jack, Clay, Sam, Mary, Lottie, and Julie were all busy decorating the room for Joy's upcoming party. Mary had been baking all day, and a beautifully iced cake rested in the center of the long trestle table. Julie stood on a small ladder, tying crepe streamers around in various places.

Bill couldn't help but smile at the sight of her. At least he'd gotten out of streamer and balloon duty.

Sam turned toward him, hand outstretched.

"Take the SUV. It's four-wheel-drive in case you need it. They're not calling for more snow tonight, but at least you'll have traction on the snow-covered roads."

Julie piped up. "And make sure you dress warm and have plenty of warm hats and gloves in the car—along with extra blankets in case you break down."

She smiled, then gave him a wink. "Although you do have cell phones so you could always call for help."

That resulted in a chuckle from Clay, who was immediately elbowed in the side by his wife, Lottie.

"What? I didn't say anything."

Lottie just looked at him and shook her head, then turned back to Julie. "They're all like little boys, aren't they?"

That resulted in more laughter, and Bill decided it was an excellent time for him to make his escape before things got any more embarrassing than they already were.

Before he reached the door, though, Mary came to his side.

"Now, you two have a good time and be careful on the roads. And remember. Don't bring Joy back home too early, Bill."

He nodded. "Got it."

Heaving a sigh, Bill took the opportunity to exit the house before anyone else had some smart to add to Mary's comment.

As much as he was looking forward to the evening, Bill also couldn't believe how nervous he was. He hadn't dated anyone in months—ever since his breakup with Zoey. And it had been years since he'd taken anyone out on a first date. He just hoped he could make it an enjoyable evening for Joy, and not spoil the surprise that everyone was trying so hard to pull off.

The air outside was cold—so cold it almost hurt to take a deep breath. According to the thermometer in the vehicle, it was ten degrees below zero. Bill wondered if it could even snow when it was that cold. But this was Montana, so who knew.

He let the vehicle warm up good, so there was actual heat coming out of the vents before he drove the short distance to Jack's and Mary's cabin to get Joy. It was still early enough in the evening, there was a little daylight left, and he was thankful they wouldn't have to make the drive in the dark. Coming home would be another story.

Once he reached the cabin, Bill put the car in park while he hopped out and went up the steps to the small front porch and knocked on the door. Seconds later, the door opened, and there stood Joy. She wore dressy black slacks covered with a beautiful toga-length royal blue sweater. Her black hair hung loosely around her shoulders. And she was gorgeous.

"Right on time, Mr. Parker."

He gave a nervous laugh. Joy didn't look a bit nervous, which wasn't fair at all as far as Bill was concerned. But then again, maybe she was just good at hiding it.

Taking a moment to help Joy put on her coat, Bill was standing close enough to her to catch a whiff of a flowery scent. He didn't know if it was a perfume or a floral shampoo she'd used, but being that close to her was sending his senses into overdrive.

She buttoned up her coat and turned from him and grabbed a purse from a nearby stand.

"Ready when you are, Cowboy."

Bill swallowed hard and offered his arm. He wasn't sure if he was ready or not, but regardless, they were on their way.

CHAPTER 22

It was quiet in the vehicle as Bill drove the backroads toward Bridgeman. He'd decided after talking with Julie that it would be wiser to take Joy someplace closer than Billings. With the winter weather being unpredictable, he didn't want to get too far away from the ranch. He'd just have to make sure not to bring her back until the time stated by her aunt. Even though they weren't driving all the way to Billings, it was still going to be a long drive, so he didn't foresee any problem with getting done with dinner early.

As he carefully drove the snow-covered roads, Bill's mind drifted to a phone call he'd received earlier in the day from the Bureau. Director Roberts had called for an update from Bill and to let him know the latest they'd learned about Ernie Wolffe. Wolffe was still scheduled to be released on January 2nd. Unfortunately, there didn't seem to be any way to stop his release as the man had appeared to not give anyone much of a problem in prison the past two years. Bill had a difficult time believing that, but evidently, Wolffe was a good actor.

Director Roberts had also stated they'd been pulling Wolffe's attorney's financial records in the hopes they'd find something that might explain how Wolffe was still running the show from prison. Since the hot-shot attorney from

Bozeman was Ernie's only visitor during the two years he was incarcerated, he was the obvious choice as a partner-in-crime. So far, they hadn't found anything suspicious, but they were still digging.

Realizing he wasn't acting very cordial to his passenger, Bill pulled his mind away from the Wolffe case and back to the present—and the beautiful young woman riding along in the vehicle with him. He still wasn't sure how he'd let Mary and Julie rope him into the date, but since he'd asked Joy out, he was going to enjoy each and every moment. Joy deserved to have a special night just for her, and Bill wasn't going to do anything to spoil it.

"Any big plans for the holiday?"

He watched as Joy swiveled her head toward him.

"Nope. Just working Christmas Eve, and then I suppose I'll spend the big day with Aunt Mary and Uncle Jack." She shot him a grin. "Of course, I can sleep in if I want. That will be a treat."

He chuckled, remembering when he thought getting to sleep a little later in the morning was a big deal.

"Good. It sounds like you should have a nice day."

It was quiet between them again for a few miles, the glow from the sun going down in the western sky casting a rosy glow over the snow-scaped countryside around them. Bill had finally gotten to the place where he enjoyed the sight of the Montana wide open spaces. He remembered during his first visit to Bluecreek Ranch, how huge and strange it had all seemed. Now he longed for the openness. The land was starting to grow on him, although he didn't think he'd ever like winters here.

"How about you? I'm assuming you'll spend the day with the Morgans."

Bill nodded, glancing over long enough to see Joy's face turned his way. The sight of her dark brown eyes almost made him forget what they were talking about.

"Hmm, yes. And Zeke and Jess and the boys are coming to the house later in the day too, I guess—after they have their family time at home."

"That's good."

Again, the conversation between them stalled, and Bill was thankful when they reached the outskirts of town. The way things were going, he didn't feel as if he was doing a very good job of entertaining Joy. Unless he upped his game, it was gonna be a long few hours.

Somehow, he had to get over this nervousness he felt each time he was near her. It surprised him, unsettled him, and confused him. She was such a little thing. So, why did she tie him up in knots every time they were together?

♫ ♫ ♫

Joy exhaled a nervous sigh as they pulled into the parking lot of the restaurant. She'd heard about this place but had never been there.

She was still in shock Bill had invited her out for dinner—let alone brought her to someplace this nice. But then again, maybe he hadn't wanted to be seen with her anywhere near Denning. She couldn't blame him, she guessed. Who would want to be seen dating a young woman who had been accosted and defiled the way she had?

Just thinking of the way the people on the reservation had treated her after the attack made Joy feel a little sick. If it hadn't been for her Aunt Mary and Uncle Jack—well, she hated to think what her life would be like if she were still living with her father.

Which was why she was already making her plans to leave the area. She'd applied for several jobs—all of them not in Montana. It was time for her to find a life someplace else where she could start over. Someplace where no one knew who Joy Whitefox was and what had happened to her.

In the meantime, though, Joy intended to enjoy this evening and the time spent with the handsome man seated in the driver's seat. After two years of wanting to hide away in a hole someplace where no one could find her, Bill Parker had pulled her out of her shell and made her want to live again. He'd been a good friend, and she was thankful God had brought him into her life when He had.

But, she had to keep reminding herself that was all Bill was ever going to be to her. Just a friend. She couldn't afford to let anyone derail her from her plans for her future. Even a good-looking FBI Agent with a ready smile and the bluest eyes she'd ever seen.

♫ ♫ ♫

Their meal was delicious, and Joy couldn't believe how much she enjoyed sitting and talking with Bill. They talked about everything—Montana weather, her growing up on the reservation, his growing up in a foster home, his dreams for finding a job teaching and coaching, and her happiness at finally being finished with her college classes.

When the waiter brought the check, Joy glanced at her watch long enough to note the time. She couldn't believe two hours had passed.

"I've really had a good time, Bill. Thank you for this. It's been great."

He flashed her a brilliant smile as he placed his credit card with the bill and handed it back to the waiter, who indicated he'd be right back with Bill's receipt.

"I've really enjoyed it, too, Joy."

Once the bill was paid, the two of them made their way out to their vehicle in the parking lot. The night was cold, and Joy raised her eyes to look up at the sky, which was one of the clearest she'd seen all winter. Even with the lights from the parking lot, she could still see the multitude of stars streaking across the sky.

"What a beautiful night sky God created for us."

After pushing the vehicle's key fob to unlock the car doors, Bill paused next to where she stood on the passenger side of the vehicle. Noting the direction she was looking, he too raised his eyes to the heavens.

"Wow. You don't see a sky like that in the city."

She sighed at that and gave him a smile as he opened the car door so she could get in. His statement was true, of course. Life would be different for her in the city. When she left here, she'd be leaving behind not just the people, but also the way of life.

But that was okay. Joy gave a little nod. She was more than ready for a change.

The drive back to the ranch was silent as if they were both so caught up in their own thoughts they didn't need to talk. When they crossed the cattle guard signaling they'd reached Morgan land, Joy sat up a little straighter, wondering what the end of their evening together would look like. Would Bill kiss her good-night? Just the thought of that made her nervous, although the nervousness was not because of fear but due to excitement. She hadn't had a man touch her since the attack. How would she react? Whatever happened, she just prayed she wouldn't embarrass herself or Bill.

Then Joy realized that instead of taking her directly to her Aunt Mary's cabin, Bill had driven to the main house and pulled over and parked. She turned to look across the darkened vehicle toward him.

"Why are we here?"

His deep voice was teasing. "Just wanted to stop here for a minute before I take you home. Come inside with me, please?"

Wishing she could see his face clearly to know what was going on, Joy finally agreed.

"Okay. But I don't want to be too long and worry Aunt Mary."

Bill helped her out of the SUV, gently holding her arm as he led her up the sidewalk to the front door of the old farmhouse.

"I promise we won't do anything to worry your Aunt Mary."

The front part of the house was dark, but the door was unlocked, and Bill led her through the large wooden front door into the entry hall where she could see the light pouring down the hallway from the back of the house where the main living area of the house was located. Muted voices drifted down the hallway as they made their way through the house.

When they reached the arched entry that led to the great room, Bill stopped her, his hand still holding to her arm.

"We're here, folks," he called out, and before he could say anything else, and before Joy had a chance to register the fact that there were a lot of people in the room, everyone was calling out "Congratulations, Joy!"

She turned and looked at Bill, sure that her face reflected her confusion.

"What's going on?"

Bill simply grinned, his blue eyes twinkling as they looked down at her.

"It looks like a party to me." He added in a husky voice. "Totally in honor of you, Joy, and your recently completed college education."

There wasn't time for Joy to ask anything further as she was quickly pulled into the room by her Aunt Mary, who helped her remove her coat. Then she was receiving hugs from her Uncle Jack, and Sam and Julie Morgan. Clay and Lottie Morgan congratulated her, Lottie giving her a gentle squeeze and telling her how proud they were of her. And Zeke and Jess with their two little guys were also there to give her hugs and congratulate her. Samantha and C.J. were practically jumping up and down in their excitement for her.

Finally, Joy's Aunt Mary pulled her over to a table that had been set up in front of the fireplace.

"I hope you aren't going to be angry with me for not letting you know it arrived."

That was when Joy noticed the framed diploma sitting on the table, surrounded by photos of Joy as a little girl all the way up to current.

"My diploma! It finally came!"

She gave her Aunt Mary a hug, then turned her head, her eyes immediately finding Bill standing there watching her from across the room. She gave him a smile, then turned back to her aunt.

"So, that was why Bill asked me out to dinner. It was a ploy to get me off the ranch so you all could plan this."

Bill had joined her and her aunt by that time, his blue eyes staring at her intensely, and a gentle smile on his face.

"Well, that was *one* of the reasons. I mean, you *did* enjoy our dinner together, didn't you, Joy? I know I did."

Feeling warmth rush into her face, Joy swallowed hard, then tried to smile, his eyes drawing her into their depths.

"Well, of course, I did, Cowboy."

Then she gave a nervous laugh. "But you all were kinda sneaky, planning this behind my back."

Her Aunt Mary, who had been standing next to Joy and watching Bill and her interact, quickly spoke up.

"You can blame me, dear. Don't get mad at Bill. I roped him into spiriting you off the ranch long enough we could pull this all together. It wasn't his fault, so please don't be angry with him."

Joy swallowed back the disappointment she felt at her aunt's words. It was apparent that Bill hadn't volunteered for the job, and that their 'date' hadn't been a real one after all.

"Well, thank you all," Joy said as she pasted a smile on her face and turned to take in the rest of the people in the room. "I can't tell you how much this means to me."

Julie pulled her over to another table where there was a beautifully decorated cake in her honor, and everyone got a piece, with Joy having the honor of being given the first one. While she sat at the long trestle table where she'd eaten so many meals, she looked around at all the familiar happy faces and felt a sense of belonging.

Then she quickly reminded herself that this was not her home. Her real home was back on the reservation where she didn't want to be.

This was all very nice, but Joy had other dreams—other aspirations for her life. And no matter how happy she was at this moment, none of those plans included staying in Montana.

CHAPTER 23

Bill helped Joy put on her coat and walked her to the door, wishing he could finish the evening the way he would have if it had been a regular date. But Joy was walking back to the cabin with her aunt and uncle. It would have seemed too forward for him to insist that he walk her home—although that was really what he wanted to do.

"Sorry about being sneaky about it all. Your Aunt Mary had it all planned, though, and I sure didn't want to cross her."

Joy gave what sounded like a nervous little laugh. "No, you don't want to get Aunt Mary's ire up."

Then she turned her dark eyes on Bill, and he felt his heart race. "Thank you for the nice dinner, Bill—even though you did ask me under duress."

He reached out and pulled her hair loose from the collar of her coat, relishing the silky feeling of the black tresses running through his fingers. He'd wanted to do that for ever so long.

"Trust me, Joy, it wasn't under duress."

He would have liked to say more, but her aunt and uncle were ready to leave, so Joy gave him another smile and a little wave, and he watched as the three of them went out the back door to walk home to their cabin. It wasn't far, and with the full moon glowing down to reflect off the white snow, it almost looked like daylight outside, so he knew they shouldn't have any trouble making their way down the familiar trail.

But it still didn't seem right to him to let her leave like that. The thought of giving her a good-night kiss had been with him all evening, and he felt robbed.

Turning back with the intent of helping Julie and Sam clean up the remainder of the party, Bill found several sets of eyes on him. Sam stood tall, his arms crossed on his chest and a look of understanding on his face. Julie stood beside him with a big grin on her face and a sparkle in her eyes. Clay and Lottie Morgan also stood across the room, watching him with smiles on their faces.

"What?"

Sam just shook his head, and Bill readied himself to be ribbed by his friend. Jess had already given him several teasing looks before she and Zeke had scooped up their boys and left the party earlier.

"We're just happy you and Joy had a nice quiet dinner together, that's all." Julie finally said, her eyes still twinkling.

Bill walked over to a table and started picking up a few plates and pieces of silverware to take to the kitchen. They could rib him all they wanted, but Bill wasn't going to let it bother him.

"We *did* have a nice time."

Thankfully, nothing more was said as the rest of them joined in the clean-up, but Bill knew that sooner or later, his relationship with Joy Whitefox was going to be brought up again. In the meantime, Bill needed to decide just what that relationship was, where it was going, and what he was going to do about it.

♫ ♫ ♫

Christmas Eve day, Bill had a chance to think about that question again. Mostly because he had no choice.

They were enjoying an unseasonably warm day, so with the sun shining, Bill knew it would be a good one to get out of the house. Clay, Sam, and Zeke had saddled their horses earlier and had left the ranch yard to go check out the herds and make sure they had food before the next winter storm arrived.

Bill had hung around the house for a while and then wandered out to the barn in the hopes of finding something to do to pass the time. It was there he discovered Jack Byrd, sitting in the tack room on an old wooden chair, cleaning a horse bridle. Jack raised his head as soon as he noticed Bill come through the door and gave a little lift of his chin in acknowledgment.

"Hey, Jack."

The older man returned his eyes to the horse tack in his hands after giving a brief nod in the direction of the wooden stool sitting across from him.

"Pull up a stool, Bill."

Bill did so, wondering at the tone of voice of the other man. Jack almost sounded angry at him.

It was silent between the two of them for a few moments, and Bill watched Jack's large brown hands deftly polish the metal on the bridle with a rag. You could tell this wasn't the first time he'd done the job.

Finally, the other man heaved a sigh and laid the cloth he'd been using on the workbench, then stood and hung the bridle on the empty hook where it apparently went. Then he turned around and came back and sat down across from Bill, who readied himself for whatever was going to happen. Something told him Jack wasn't in a friendly mood this morning. Maybe it had been a bad idea to come out to the barn after all.

"Everything okay, Jack?"

The older man's dark eyes locked on Bill's face, and again, Bill was reminded that this man came from a long line of fierce warriors.

Jack's voice was gruff when he finally spoke.

"What are your intentions when it comes to my niece?"

Bill exhaled the breath he'd been holding and shifted his perch on the stool. So that was what this was all about. Before he could answer, however, Jack continued.

"You gave her that necklace." He held up his right hand. "I know. You and Sam explained to me the reason why, and I can accept that."

Jack gave Bill a steely look. "And then you spend a great deal of time talking with her—even invited her out to dinner at a nice restaurant." He stopped speaking for a second or two as if steadying his temper. "You can see where a young woman might begin to think there is something more happening between the two of you than just being friends."

Swallowing while he tried to find the words to reply to Jack, Bill was reminded of the way Joy had made him feel the night they went to dinner. He hadn't felt that way in a long time. Not even talking with Zoey had ever felt so comfortable—so right.

"I certainly don't want to do anything that might hurt Joy, Jack. You know that." He clenched his jaw before asking, "Has she implied that we're more than friends?"

Jack gave a firm shake of his head. "No."

Then he narrowed his dark eyes again as he glared at Bill. "This is me asking."

The man suddenly stood and sighed, and Bill could read the frustration on his face. For a second, he wondered if Jack was going to take a swing at him. And then Bill wondered what he would do if Jack *did* try to punch his lights out?

"Joy is very important to Mary and me. She has become the daughter we never had, and I just don't want to see her get hurt."

Bill nodded. "I can understand that, Jack. And I don't want her hurt either—in any way."

He swallowed hard. Then he sighed. Maybe it was best if he let Jack know his feelings and see what the reaction might be. That might be the only practical way to find out if he was just dreaming of something that could never happen.

"Jack, I care about Joy. A lot." He ran his hand across the hair at the top of his head, noticing how much his hair had grown since he'd come to Montana.

"The two of us are good friends, yes. But I have to tell you, Jack, that given a chance, I'd like to be more than just a friend to Joy. But I don't know how she feels about me. She's never given me any sign that she wants to be more than friends."

Jack stood in front of him with his hands on his hips, looking down, as if he were thinking about what Bill had just told him.

"You're going back to the city."

Bill sighed. It was more of a statement than a question, and he quickly understood Jack's concern. He didn't want Joy to leave, nor did he want her to be hurt when Bill left.

"I am." Then he held up his right hand as if to stave off any more of Jack's wrath. "But I don't think I'm going to be staying there."

He sighed. Other than Joy, Bill hadn't talked with anyone else about his plans.

"Sam and Julie don't even know this, Jack, but I've applied for a teaching position at the school in Denning. If I get it, I'll be moving to this area and staying here."

The other man looked at him in surprise, then slowly sat back down in the chair he'd previously been sitting on.

"That so?"

Bill nodded, finally feeling as if he could breathe again. He gave Jack a small smile and felt hope when Jack's lips also turned up a little, and some of the darkness left the other man's eyes.

"I've wanted to be a teacher for many years, but life sidetracked me. God has led me back to it, and after much prayer, I've decided to move here—if I get the job, of course."

He knew there was always a chance he might not get the job, but the interview had gone well, and the school board had acted as if they were definitely interested in hiring him. He just wouldn't know for sure until after the Christmas break.

"Hmm. Wouldn't have thought you'd be willing to give up your job at the FBI. Thought that was what you wanted to do."

Nodding, Bill smiled. "It was. I did. And now it's time for me to do something new.

"'Behold, I will do a new thing; now it shall spring forth; shall ye not know it? I will even make a way in the wilderness, and rivers in the desert.'"

Jack smiled as Bill quoted the scripture from the book of Isaiah he was sure the older man was more than familiar with.

"So, where does my niece fit into these plans of yours?"

Shifting a little on the stool, Bill winced. They'd come full circle and had arrived back to the original question.

Joy.

He didn't have a firm answer for Jack. Yet. But that didn't mean he hadn't been thinking about it. A lot.

"I want to spend more time getting to know her better. If God wants us to be together, then I'm certainly not against the idea. But I won't rush her or push her. She's been through enough already."

Nodding his head, Jack reached out his hand, and Bill took it and received a firm handshake. Seeing the look of acceptance on the other man's face, he was left with the feeling that he'd passed some sort of test. And Jack's next words affirmed that.

"I can live with that answer."

Bill heaved a sigh of relief and released a nervous laugh. Looked like today wasn't the day when he'd receive a whipping from Jack Byrd. But he knew the man had his eye on him, and Bill was aware that he'd best watch his step.

Especially when it came to Joy.

♫ ♫ ♫

Christmas morning arrived with a flurry of activity in the Morgan household. After an early hearty breakfast prepared by Lottie and Julie, they all gathered around the tree for their traditional gift exchange.

The last time he'd been in Denning, Bill had purchased items for everyone; warm, lined leather gloves for Clay and Sam, pretty scarves for Lottie and Julie, a new basketball for Samantha, and a couple of books Julie had suggested for C.J. In turn, he also received some lovely items from them— although he certainly hadn't expected gifts. The last time Bill had actually been involved in a family gift exchange had been when he'd been living in his last foster home—many years earlier.

After the gifts had been opened and the subsequent mess from opening them had been cleaned up, they all got ready and headed out the door for the church where there would be a special morning Christmas service. Bill was looking forward to it as Mary had hinted earlier in the week that Joy would be singing. He'd only heard bits and pieces of her songs in the past, but had heard enough to know she had the voice of an angel. Bill couldn't wait to listen to her sing in a church setting.

When they arrived at the church, the pews were already starting to fill up, but they made their way toward the front where there was still plenty of seating. Bill slid into the pew next to Sam and Julie and their kids and looked around for a specific dark head. He finally spotted Joy, seated with Jack and Mary on the opposite side of the church, a few rows up from them.

Pastor Beaumont soon walked behind the pulpit on the stage, and the service began with an opening prayer, thanking God for the gift of his Son so many years earlier. After they all stood and say *Joy to the World*, with Bill's mind drifting to another Joy in his life, the congregation took their seats, and he watched as Joy slipped out from her pew and walked gracefully to the front. She was dressed in a dark green dress, her black hair hanging around her shoulders. He didn't think she'd ever looked more beautiful.

She shyly walked across the stage and took a cordless mic from the pastor, then turned and faced the people. But Bill noticed as the music started playing over the sound system, that she'd already closed her eyes and wasn't looking out at the crowd. He didn't know if it was because she was nervous, or if she was just allowing the Spirit to touch her as she readied to sing.

O come, O come, Immanuel, and ransom captive Israel...

As soon as Joy started singing the words to the old hymn, the congregation became silent as if the Holy Spirit himself had descended on the place.

O come, O Branch of Jesse's stem, unto your own and rescue them!

Bill was mesmerized as he listened to her sweet voice sing the haunting melody, lifting her voice in praise to her God and her Savior. You couldn't doubt her love for her Jesus as she poured all her passion and emotion into the words of the song.

Rejoice! Rejoice! Immanuel shall come to you, O Israel.

When the final note was sung, and the music stopped, it was so quiet in the sanctuary, you never would have known it was filled to capacity. Then the applause began, and Bill watched as Joy gave a humble nod of her head, handed the mic to the pastor, and made her way back to the pew. Bill had never been as proud of her as he was then.

Joy Whitefox was something else. And he was blessed to have her as a friend. The problem was, just as her Uncle Jack had suspected, something more was happening in Bill's heart. And he was beginning to understand that he didn't want to only be her friend anymore.

He just wasn't sure what he was going to do about it.

CHAPTER 24

Two weeks into the New Year, Bill began to get restless. Winter had settled into Montana and it was colder and snowier than he'd ever experience. On top of that, nothing seemed to be happening on the Wolffe case, yet he had a gut feeling all that was about to change.

According to the most recent phone call he'd received from Director Roberts, Ernie Wolffe had been released from prison and had immediately returned to the reservation where he was staying with his mother. The lawmen on the reservation were supposedly keeping a close eye on him, but so far, Wolffe didn't appear to be doing anything illegal that might throw suspicion on him. Ernie was evil, but he wasn't stupid. But Bill was sure sooner or later, Wolffe would get careless. He just wanted to be around when it happened.

In the meantime, he knew Joy had to be feeling some of the same fear she'd felt right after the attack, and Bill felt helpless to take away those fears.

He did finally activate the GPS on her necklace. Bill didn't tell her he had done so, but tried to justify his actions by reminding himself that it was under the direction of his boss that he'd given it to her in the first place. That didn't make him feel any better about it, even though he knew sooner or later, Ernie Wolffe was going to come after Joy.

And when that time came, Bill had to be ready to protect her.

She was counting on him.

♫ ♫ ♫

Bill sat in a dark corner of the parking lot in Sam's cold SUV, watching the lights go out in *Peggy's Place*. When only the bay of lights near the front door was still lit, he straightened in his seat and waited for Joy to come walking out as she did each night about this time. He'd been following her every morning and night since Wolffe's release. She just didn't know it. Whenever Joy was off the Bluecreek ranch property, Special Agent Bill Parker wasn't far away.

After a few more minutes, Bill saw Joy come out the front door, dressed warmly in a heavy winter coat—the hood pulled up against the brutal winter winds that had swept down from the mountains just a few days earlier. She scurried across the snow-covered parking lot to her waiting car and got in and started the car. Moments later, her car drove out of the parking lot onto the road that would take her back to the ranch.

He blew onto his hands before sticking them back in their warm gloves, then started his car and put it in gear. He only drove a few feet, however, when a warning light came up on the dash along with a funny chiming sound.

Releasing a groan, Bill looked down at the dashboard message stating he had a flat tire. Great. Just what he needed.

Throwing the vehicle into Park, he turned off the engine and got out, walking back to where the rear passenger side tire sat, flat as a pancake. Thankfully, he knew Sam always carried a spare, so he just needed to change the tire, and he'd easily be able to catch up with Joy on her way home.

Ten minutes later, Bill was wiping his greasy hands on an old rag in the back of the SUV and was ready to go. That was probably the fastest he'd ever changed a tire, but the clenching feeling in his gut had him worried about Joy. He quickly got back in the vehicle and started it, taking the time to pull up the GPS monitoring app on his cell phone to see how far ahead Joy was on the road.

What he saw made Bill's heart almost stop.

Whereas the little green dot that represented Joy's car should be moving down the road at a steady rate, instead it was stopped along a section of highway Bill knew was rarely traveled. Something was wrong, and instead of following her like he should have been, Bill had been stuck in the diner parking lot with a flat tire.

Gunning the engine, Bill whipped out of the parking lot and raced in that direction—all the time praying as he drove.

Lord, please keep Joy safe. Whatever has made her car has stop, please don't let Wolffe or anyone else harm her.

All the time he drove, the only thing Bill could think of was that he'd promised everyone, including himself, that he would keep Joy safe. And he'd failed.

♬ ♬ ♬

Joy was softly singing to herself as she drove the familiar road leading to the ranch. It had been a quiet day, so she wasn't as weary as she usually would be this late in the evening, and she felt happy tonight. Her life was good, and everything she'd hoped for her future was beginning to fall into place. She had much to be thankful for.

By the time the interior of the car warmed up enough she felt comfortable taking off her heavy gloves, she was just a few miles outside of Denning. The winter weather so far had been brutally cold, but at least they hadn't had as much snow as some winters. Her car didn't do well going through high drifts of snow, so she was thankful for less of the white stuff.

When she was about halfway home, Joy thought she heard a noise behind her and glanced up in her rearview mirror, worried she might be followed. There was often traffic on the roads, but this particular stretch of road she was traveling usually had little traffic, and was her least favorite for that very reason.

Glancing into her rearview mirror was when Joy realized she wasn't alone in the car.

The man she had hoped to never set eyes on again leaned forward from the back seat, his stale breath near her neck. Joy felt for a moment as if she couldn't swallow, her fear was so intense. Then she made herself breathe, and tried not to grip the steering wheel so tightly. The last thing she wanted to do was pass out.

"Slow down the car, sweetheart," the vile voice she remembered from her nightmares ordered.

Joy immediately let up on the gas, wondering all the time how he'd gotten into her car. She was sure she'd locked it when she arrived at the diner that morning. She always locked the car doors now—even when she was at the ranch. Ever since the attack, it had become second nature to her.

Her mind raced with thoughts of what she could do to get away from the man in her back seat. He hadn't shown a weapon yet, but Joy was sure he had one in his possession, and she was also positive that he wouldn't hesitate to use it on her. He'd used his fists during their previous encounter, and just the memories of what those blows had felt like, made her want to throw up.

"Pull over here."

His gruff voice brought her mind back to the present, and she immediately pulled over to the side of the road at a spot where the snow had been pushed back from the roadway to create a pull-off of sorts. Ever since Ernie had made his presence known to her, there hadn't been another car on the road. Although, even if another vehicle *had* come along, Joy wasn't sure how it would help her. No one in the world knew Ernie Wolffe was with her in the car.

She was in this alone—just like the last time.

Once she had the car stopped, Joy tried to think of what to do next. She hadn't put it in Park yet, so if he got out to move to the front seat, she could easily take off and leave him behind. Or, she could throw her own car door open and try to escape, but if he had a gun, she didn't stand a chance of getting away from him that way. For once, she was thankful she had an old car that still allowed you to open the doors, even when the vehicle was still in gear.

"Put the car in Park, turn off the engine, and give me the keys," Ernie's voice was harsh as he spouted off his orders.

Joy swallowed hard, her hands shaking as she followed his instructions. What was he going to do to her? There was no way she was going to go through what had happened before. She'd fight him to the point he had to kill her before she'd let that happen. Emotionally, she couldn't stand to go through that again. She just couldn't.

Lord, help me!

Those three words were all her tortured mind could repeat as she did what Ernie told her to do. All the time, wondering if the time had finally arrived when she was going to die.

♫ ♫ ♫

Even though the roads were snow-covered, Bill drove like a madman with his eyes peeled on the roadway in front of him, searching for taillights of another car in the darkness—either driving ahead of him or parked along the side of the road somewhere. The app on his phone still showed Joy's vehicle hadn't moved from where it had been when it had first stopped. That meant she either was having car trouble, or something else had happened. He prayed it was just car trouble.

As he zeroed in on the spot where the GPS still showed Joy's car parked, Bill's eyes strained through the darkness to try and spot taillights or a vehicle. There was nothing.

That was when he finally spotted her.

Standing along the side of the road, dressed in her coat and boots, stood Joy. Alone. With no sight of her car.

Bill pulled over to the side of the road and stopped. He left the car lights on to help illuminate the area, but got out of the car cautiously, as he didn't want to scare her.

"Joy?"

As soon as she saw him, the look of terror on her face turned to one of relief, then her face crumbled as she ran toward him. Bill immediately took her in his arms and held her as her body shuddered and shook with cold and fear.

"Bill? How did you get here so fast?"

"Shhh, it's okay, darling. I've got you."

He led her over to the passenger side of the SUV and helped her in, noting she had her purse slung over her shoulder. So at least, whoever had taken her car had left her that.

Once she was safely in the vehicle, Bill hurried around and got in the driver's side, turning the heat on full force once he was inside. She had to be almost frozen, although he didn't think she'd been standing out in the elements too long.

"Are you sure you're okay, Joy? What happened? Someone stole your car?"

She was still shaky, but turned and looked over at him with such a look of fear on her face, his stomach clenched.

"It was Ernie." Her voice also shook, whether due to the cold or shock he wasn't sure, but it made it difficult to understand her. "He was in the back seat of my car when I got in it at the diner, and I didn't know it."

Bill almost groaned when he heard that. Wolffe had been right there all the time. He'd probably been the one responsible for Bill's flat tire—intending to delay Bill from being able to follow Joy. That meant Wolffe had been watching Joy—and Bill too, more than likely—probably longer than just tonight.

"He made me pull over and then took the keys and made me get out of the car. And he destroyed my phone, so I couldn't call for help. I thought I was gonna freeze to death out here in the dark."

Joy shook her head, the tears now spilling out of her eyes in torrents. "He told me he needed the car, but that someday soon he'd be back for me. And that when he did, this time I wouldn't live to talk about what he did to me. He told me I was going to pay for putting him in prison."

Bill finally couldn't stand it anymore and reached out to pull her partway into his arms—at least as close as he could with the console between them.

"Oh, Bill, I was so scared." Her tear-filled eyes looked up at him. "I was sure he was going to kill me right then."

"Shhh. You're okay, Joy. I'm here now, and you're okay."

Bill held her tightly for a few minutes while he chastised himself silently. She was okay, no thanks to him. He hadn't been there for her when she'd needed him most.

What would he have done if Wolffe had just kept going with Joy and disappeared into the night? Just the thought of that happening made him want to throw up.

Of course, there was the GPS tracker installed in her necklace. Wolffe couldn't know about its existence, and Bill would have been able to find them eventually. But what would Wolffe have done to Joy before Bill could have rescued her? It turned his heart cold to even think about it.

"Take me home, Bill. Please."

Giving her a gentle kiss on the top of her head, Bill released her, then reached across the seat to help her shaking hands get her seatbelt fastened. After fastening his own, he put the vehicle in drive and headed toward the ranch.

All the time, praising God that he'd reached Joy in time. And that, at least this time, she wasn't hurt.

CHAPTER 25

On the drive to the ranch, Bill put a call through to Sheriff Wilson in Denning to let him know Ernie Wolffe had stolen Joy's car and was on the move. The Sheriff took the information about the vehicle and said he'd get an APB—or All-Points Bulletin—out on it right away.

They didn't know where Wolffe was headed, but at least they knew what he was driving.

Once they reached the ranch, Bill took Joy directly to her Aunt Mary's cabin. It had been difficult for him to turn her over to someone else's care but knew they loved her, too, and would take good care of her. Because if the latest incident with Wolffe had done nothing else, it had shown Bill he loved Joy Whitefox with his whole heart—not just as a friend.

In the meantime, Mary, Jack, Sam, Julie, and Bill had already talked to Joy and told her that for her safety, they felt it was best if she took a some time off from her job at the diner. They all agreed that she needed to stay on the ranch. At least there, they could keep an eye on her, and it wouldn't be as easy for Wolffe to get to her.

The days crept by as they waited for some word of Wolffe's whereabouts. His mother on the reservation had been questioned by the tribal law enforcement officers, and all she could tell them was that Ernie had told her he was leaving town. She said he kept making phone calls to someone in a big city and had talked about needing to go take care of some business there. She was old and rather slow mentally, so the Sheriff told Sam and Bill they were lucky they got that much out of the confused woman.

Bill felt nothing but frustration, and it was only Sam's level head and Jack's endless list of chores for him in the barn that kept him from going crazy. He wanted to find Wolffe, and he wanted to drag his sorry behind back to prison—after he had a few moments alone with the man. While the Christian part of him knew that wasn't a wise idea, Bill couldn't help how he felt.

That monster had terrorized Joy too many times. It had to end.

♫ ♫ ♫

In the days that followed, Joy spent most of the time hiding in her upstairs loft at her aunt and uncle's cabin. When she wasn't there, she was in Spirit's stall, her head resting on the loyal horse's flank while she sobbed.

She had hoped and prayed her nightmare was over.

All the time Ernie had been in prison, she had prayed that he'd change—that he would turn over a new leaf after his release, go on with his life and allow her to go on with hers. But no, the man had come back to do her more harm.

True, stealing her car hadn't hurt her that badly—not physically anyway. It was the mental anguish she was going through since she'd seen him again that was tearing her up inside.

How was she supposed to continue to function in the world knowing he was out there someplace, just waiting for an opportunity to come back and hurt her again? How was she supposed to deal with that? She was so tired of being afraid all the time.

Trust Me.

Those words kept replaying in her head, and she knew God was right. She needed to trust Him to take care of her. God still loved her more than she could ever know. And even though the experience of seeing Ernie again and having him take her car and threatening her had been awful, she was thankful that this time, he hadn't hurt her physically in any way.

God had sent Bill to find her and protect her.

He'd apologized to her over and over again for not getting there sooner. Unbeknownst to her, Bill had been guarding her all that time. And that awful night, the beautiful necklace he'd given her had led him right to her.

So, she had to trust that God would continue to keep her safe. For without that faith, that trust, and that knowledge, Joy would fall apart.

And if she fell apart, then evil would win.

♫ ♫ ♫

Bill was surprised to find Joy in the barn one Sunday afternoon when he went searching for a quiet spot. She was sitting on a bale of straw, bundled up in her winter coat, and when he entered the barn, it was to the sound of her weeping.

His heart almost broke at the sight. What he would give for this sweet gal to have never gone through all she'd suffered.

As soon as Joy saw him, she immediately turned away from him, wiping the moisture from her face with the palms of her hands.

"Bill."

He stopped just inside the door.

"Would you rather be alone?"

The quick shake of her head was all he needed before he strode across the barn floor to her. She stood, and without even thinking about his actions, Bill pulled her into the circle of his arms like he had the night Ernie had taken her car.

"I'm so tired of being scared all the time, Bill."

He slowly rubbed his hand across her back, wishing he could do or say something to take away her pain and fear.

"I'm so sorry, Joy. I failed you. He never should have been able to get that close to you."

Bill felt the movement of Joy shaking her head moments before she pulled away from him.

"It wasn't your fault."

"Yes, it was."

Frustration built up over the past week or so erupted. "It was my *job* to protect you, Joy. And I didn't."

He released her and ran his hand through his hair. Surely she could see that he'd failed her. He'd wanted to be her hero, and he hadn't come through for her when he'd needed to.

Her wide eyes stared up at his face, her head still shaking in denial.

"Bill, you're not God."

Feeling as if she'd punched him in the stomach, Bill stared at Joy as her words sunk in. She was right, of course. He'd tried to protect her, but her safety and life were really in the hands of God—not FBI Agent Bill Parker.

Joy moved to stand closer to him, her dark eyes large as they looked up into his face.

"I'm so thankful you were there that night, Bill. You *did* find me and keep me safe and sane. And for that, I'm ever so grateful. But ultimately, God is in control of what happens to me, so I have to quit hiding away from life. I can't live like this anymore..."

With those last words, Joy's voice cracked, and Bill pulled her back against his chest.

"Have I told you lately what a wonderful woman you are, Joy Whitfox, and how proud I am of you?"

Again he felt the shake of her head.

"Not lately, you haven't, Cowboy. And a girl can always stand to hear it again."

♪ ♪ ♪

Two evenings later, Bill was sitting on the sofa in the great room of the Morgan house when he felt his cell phone vibrating in the pocket of his jeans. When he saw the caller ID, his heart kicked up a notch. He usually ignored a phone call that came when he was with the Morgan family, but this one couldn't be ignored.

He immediately glanced across the room to where Sam was sitting, catching the other man's eye as he answered the call.

"Special Agent Nate Jorgensen, you keeping D.C. in line, buddy?"

There was a chuckle on the other end of the phone. "Hey, boss."

Bill grinned at the nickname. It hadn't been that long ago that he'd called another man 'boss.' And now that same man he'd called boss for so many years was standing next to Bill, having caught on to the fact that someone from the Bureau was calling.

"So, what's up, Nate? I'm pretty sure this isn't a social call."

Nate had taken over the field team as a temporary leader while Bill was in Montana. From all reports he was getting back from the Director, Bill had been right about the young man's readiness to lead a team—even temporarily. Nate was sure to be leading his own team one day soon.

"Director Roberts asked me to give you a call and update you on the Wolffe case."

Bill frowned and braced himself for what this call could mean. Was he being called back to the Bureau? He wasn't ready to go yet. Ernie Wolffe was still on the loose, and Bill felt he needed to stay in Montana where he could protect Joy. The poor girl still jumped whenever there was a loud noise anywhere near her. How could he leave her now?

"I'm listening."

"Boss, they found the car Ernie Wolffe stole from that woman. It was located in a back alley in Bozeman—stripped of anything of value, but his prints were all over it. They talked to a witness that saw him dump it, and through that witness, the local police were able to trace him to an apartment building where Wolffe had been living with a woman.

"Wolffe wasn't there, but the Bozeman police took the woman into custody, and I guess she told them everything she knew about the guy. Long story short—with the information she provided, Wolffe and his attorney were caught in an FBI sting operation in Bozeman earlier this week. In the process, Wolffe was killed, and his hot-shot attorney was taken into custody. Sounds like the sleazy weasel of a lawyer was the master-mind of the whole operation—not Wolffe like we thought. Anyway, the attorney fell apart under interrogation and gave up the whole ball of wax. He provided law enforcement with enough information that the Wyoming Department of the Bureau was able to take down another cell of drug-runners and counterfeiters there yesterday."

Bill released a sigh and stared heavenward.

Thank you, Lord.

"That's great news, Nate. Good to hear. Be sure and thank the Director for keeping me updated. I know it'll be a real relief to everyone here. I'll also let Sheriff Wilson and the law enforcement on the reservation know the good news."

Bill ended the call and turned toward his former mentor with a smile on his face and a sense of relief in his heart he hadn't felt for a long, long time.

"They got him, Sam. Ernie Wolffe is dead, and praise the Lord, he will never hurt Joy or anyone else again."

Before doing anything else, Bill pulled on his coat and tromped through the freshly-fallen snow to the Byrd cabin. This was one piece of news that needed to be delivered in person.

Mary answered his knock and immediately invited him into the warm house and took his coat.

"What brings you out on this cold evening?" Jack asked.

"I'm here to see Joy."

At the sight of Jack's eyebrows raising, Bill quickly added. "I have news for her—good news."

Mary immediately went to the bottom of the ladder Bill knew led to the upstairs loft and called for Joy, who came right down. When she reached the bottom of the ladder and saw Bill, Joy's face broke into a smile.

"Bill. What a surprise."

He couldn't hold back his own smile at the sight of her.

"A good one, I hope."

Feeling the presence of Jack and Mary, Bill quickly added, "Come sit down, Joy; I have news to share with all of you."

It didn't take Bill long to fill the other three in on what Nate's phone call had been about. While he told the story of the FBI sting, Bill watched the different emotions sweep across Joy's face—fear, worry, then relief.

"Ernie Wolffe is gone, Joy. And they caught the rest of the gang too. You have nothing to fear anymore."

As Joy and Mary hugged and cried tears of relief, Jack stood and shook Bill's hand.

"Thank you, my friend. It is good to know this nightmare is finally over."

Bill took firm hold of the older man's hand, feeling better about life than he had in a long time.

Now that the Wolffe case was wrapped up, it was time for Bill to decide what came next in his life. And if Joy Whitefox was going to be a part of it.

CHAPTER 26

Now that the threat to Joy was finally gone, Bill decided it was time for him to make his move. He'd prayed about it, suffered through sleepless nights about it, and finally came to the conclusion that it was time to do something about it.

Joy had returned to her job at the diner and appeared to be more like the happy person she'd been before Wolffe had stolen her car. Hopefully, she'd be able to put the whole experience behind her and could go on with her life.

At least, that was what Bill prayed.

Late one afternoon, Bill hitched a ride into Denning with Wade Williams, one of the long-time hands at the ranch. If all went well, he planned to be riding back to Bluecreek with Joy. If things didn't go as planned...well, he supposed he could always call the ranch, and Sam would come and get him.

He hoped it wouldn't come to that, though.

Once they reached town, Bill asked to be dropped off near *Peggy's Place*. Wade gave him a thumb's up and a wave and drove off to his dentist's appointment, and Bill turned toward the door of the diner.

No time like the present to take action.

He took a deep breath for courage and released it, then tugged open the diner door and entered. It was too early for dinner and too late for the lunch crew, so other than for a few older folks who had a tendency to hang out there all afternoon and drink coffee, the place looked empty.

Bill hadn't taken more than a step or two into the room when he knew Joy had seen him. She finished pouring coffee into the elderly man's mug in front of him, gave the man a smile, and then turned to greet Bill.

"You lost, Cowboy?"

Bill grinned, loving the sound of her teasing voice. She sure had come out of her shell since he'd first met her six months earlier.

"Nope. I know exactly where I am."

"Hmm." She lifted her chin toward the table where he usually sat when he came for coffee. "You want any pie with that coffee?"

"What kind you got?"

She grinned. "Cherry, Peach, Apple, and Blueberry."

He grinned right back. "I'll have a slice of apple then. Ala-mode, of course."

Her quiet chuckle warmed him. "Of course. Can't imagine you eating it any other way. Go ahead and have a seat, and I'll be right there."

Bill slid into the chair, placing his Stetson hat on the empty chair next to him, and nervously moved the silverware around on the tabletop until Joy finally returned with a tray containing a glass of water and a plate with a slice of pie covered with ice cream and whipped cream. After depositing the items on the table, she grabbed the upside-down mug on the table and deftly flipped it over, then filled it with the hot brew.

"So, what brings you into town?"

Bill took a sip of the coffee and then looked up into those beautiful dark brown eyes. He could so easily get lost in the depth of those eyes.

"You."

He saw those same eyes widen and felt like kicking himself. He was coming on too strong, and he certainly didn't want to frighten Joy. She was still like a skittish colt, even though the threat of Ernie Wolffe was gone.

"I mean, I came into town to talk to you. To find out how you were doing."

He dropped his eyes and stared at the pie in front of him, suddenly feeling like an idiot. Because that's sure what he sounded like—even to his own ears.

Surprisingly, Joy slid into the chair across from him.

"I'm doing fine, Bill."

She sighed and smiled at him again, the smile reached into the depths of those brown eyes of hers. She really did look happy.

"I mean it, Bill. I went through what I went through, and I truly believe I'm a stronger person because of it. I'm not going to hide away from people for the rest of my life. It's time to move on."

Her face was solemn as her eyes continued to gaze at him, then she added in an upbeat voice.

"Hey, I get off work in about half an hour. How about I give you a ride back to the ranch. I think we need to talk."

Bill felt a sense of shock go through him. He hadn't even had to ask her for a ride—and it sounded as if she wanted to talk with him too. This might be easier than he'd thought it would be.

"Sure. That would be good."

Giving him a smile and a little nod, she stood and collected the tray and coffee pot and walked back through the diner toward the kitchen, all the time Bill watching her go.

Yeah. Maybe this wasn't going to be as challenging as he'd thought.

♫ ♫ ♫

Half an hour later, Bill found himself sitting on the passenger side of Jackson Byrd's rusty pickup—the vehicle Joy was evidently driving until she could replace her car. She started the vehicle and turned on the heater, fastened her seat belt, and then turned toward him.

"I've actually been wanting to talk with you, Bill, so it's good that you came into town alone."

Well, Bill had some things he wanted to talk about with Miss Whitefox too, although she couldn't know that. While he waited to see if Joy had more to say to him, Bill wondered if now was the right time for him to bring up what he wanted to tell her. He finally decided that since they were together, and no one else was around to interrupt them, he might as well get it over with.

"I've wanted to talk to you too, Joy, but haven't had a chance." He frowned. "You've been working a lot of extra hours."

Joy gave him a small smile. "I know. I wanted to earn as much as I could while I had the chance. Figured I would need the cash one of these days."

He didn't know what that meant but wasn't surprised by her statement. He knew the waitressing job didn't pay the best.

"Anyway, I wanted you to be the first to know."

Joy's head swiveled at his words, and her dark eyes locked on his.

"As you probably remember me telling you, I applied for a teaching job here in Denning at the school. I just found out, I got the job."

She just stared at him as if she hadn't heard him, then her eyes lit up, and she grinned at him.

"Oh, Bill. That's wonderful news! I'm so happy for you."

Bill sighed. That was only part of what he had to tell her, but at least he'd managed to get that part out.

"Yeah, you know I owe it all to you, Joy. You told me to go after my dreams, so I did."

He took a deep breath and released it before continuing. Stepping out in faith had been difficult, but he'd had so much peace after he'd found out he'd gotten the job, Bill was sure he was doing what he was supposed to. And he couldn't wait to get into the classroom and teach and then begin working with the boys on the baseball team. And the following October, he'd be working with the basketball team.

"I start in March, which won't give me a full term to get my feet wet, but it will give me time to go back to D.C. and give notice there, get rid of my apartment, and all that's involved with ending my life there. It won't happen quickly, but I *will* be coming back to Montana. This time for good."

"Oh, Bill. I'm so happy for you."

She gave him a small smile before adding, "That's kind of why I wanted to talk to you, Bill."

He watched as Joy reached up with her right hand and pushed her hair behind her ear, making it so he could see her face more clearly.

"You see, I too applied for a job not long ago. And I got it."

Bill smiled. That *was* great news for Joy as he knew she wanted to get out of the diner in the worst way. That had been the whole purpose for her striving so hard to complete her college degree.

"That's great. So, where will you be working?"

Her eyes were huge as they turned to look at him, and he noticed right away that she wasn't smiling now, almost like she dreaded answering his question.

"It's a position as an office manager in an accounting firm. It's an excellent job. In St. Louis. Missouri."

Bill stared at her, wondering if his hearing was going bad. He *couldn't* have heard what he thought he'd heard.

"What?"

"I haven't even told Aunt Mary and Uncle Jack yet— or my Dad either, for that matter. You're the first to know as I just received the call this afternoon. Isn't it exciting?"

He nodded, feeling numb as he tried to digest what she was telling him. She had a new job. Not here in Denning. Not even in Montana.

In St. Louis, Missouri.

Joy was still chattering about flying to St. Louis in two weeks, that she'd already put a deposit down on an apartment one of her future co-workers had found for her not far from the building where she'd be working.

She sounded so happy.

Bill, on the other hand, was having trouble breathing.

"Please don't tell anyone else, though, Bill. I plan to tell Aunt Mary and Uncle Jack tonight, and then I'm sure it will spread to everyone else on the ranch. I just had to tell someone and when you showed up at the diner…"

He nodded numbly. "Sure. I promise I won't tell anyone."

"Thanks," she gave him a grin, then reached up on the dashboard and grabbed a paper sack and handed it to him.

"I almost forgot. This is for you. I've meant to give it to you for weeks, but with everything that happened…"

Bill looked at the paper sack in his lap and glanced over at her, feeling confused.

"What's this?"

"Open it."

Joy's face was so filled with expectation, Bill automatically unfolded the top of the sack and opened it, peering inside to find something wrapped loosely in white tissue paper.

"Take it out of the sack, silly."

Bill reached in and pulled out the paper, then removed an object. At first, he wasn't sure what it was, then remembered seeing something like it in a gift shop back in D.C.

"It's a dreamcatcher."

Joy gave him a smile as if pleased he'd recognized what it was.

"I wanted to make something to give you so you'd always remember our friendship and how we encouraged each other to go after our dreams."

Bill swallowed hard as he looked from her gift over to her. Like he'd ever be able to forget her. Yeah, right.

"It's beautiful, Joy. Did you make it?"

She nodded. Pointing at it as she talked, Joy added, 'Even though the Crow people weren't the first Native American Indians to make them, I've always thought dreamcatchers were a beautiful symbol of our culture."

Bill nodded, studying the item in his hand. It looked like it had been made from a willow branch or grapevine, twisted into a circle. A web made of string had been created across the ring so as to catch a person's dreams, and a couple of large bird or eagle feathers hung from the bottom of it in decoration.

"You should hang it above your bed, or at least someplace in your bedroom, and it will protect you as you sleep." She grinned. "At least, that is what our culture teaches us. They are meant to filter the good dreams and trap the bad dreams."

He chuckled. It wasn't exactly the type of item he'd typically purchase for himself. But then again, if Joy had made it for him, you'd better believe he'd hang it above his bed. And he'd think of her every time he saw it.

"Thank you, Joy. It's beautiful and even more special because you made it for me."

"Oh!" She reached over and took the sack from him, pulling out a slip of paper and handing it to him. "It's a certificate of authenticity." She grinned. "There are so many of these things that are made in China now, this is proof that this one is a real Native American dreamcatcher. Not some knockoff."

Bill smiled, feeling some of the pain at her news begin to ebb away. She had given him this unique gift—something she'd made with her own hands—just for him.

"I'll treasure it always, Joy. Thank you again."

Before he realized she was going to do it, Joy leaned across the car and kissed him on the cheek, then pulled back and dropped her eyes from him as if embarrassed by her action.

"Well, I suppose I'd best get us back to the ranch, Cowboy."

Still feeling the pleasure of her kiss, Bill gave her a nod and carefully placed the dreamcatcher and certificate back in the paper sack. This little talk certainly hadn't turned out the way he'd hoped, but he had to believe it was the way God intended for it to be.

Bill didn't understand why he always had to fall in love with women who didn't love him in return, but that appeared to be his destiny.

And he'd just have to live with it.

CHAPTER 27

Bill felt the vibration of his cell phone in his pocket and stopped what he was doing to pull it out and look at it. When he saw the caller ID, he grinned and answered it.

Sam.

"Okay, what do you want now, Morgan?"

There was a little chuckle on the other end of the line before Julie Morgan's cheery voice answered.

"I want you to come out to our house for supper Saturday night, Mr. Parker. Do you think you can fit that into your busy schedule?"

He almost fell off the roof when he realized it was Julie on the phone and not Sam.

Her voice continued, almost scolding him. "Bill, we've only seen you twice this summer. I know you're a busy man—especially now that school is back in session—but please, humor me and come for a visit. I promise, Mary and I will cook you a meal you won't soon forget. And Sam's promised to grill steaks."

Bill had to admit, grilled steaks did sound mighty tasty.

"Okay. What time should I be there?"

He heard Julie's giggle on the other end of the phone and smiled. She might be the mother of a twelve-almost-thirteen-year-old, but sometimes she acted and sounded as young as her daughter.

"Come early. We can talk and catch up on what's going on with you."

"Yes, ma'am. I'll be there. And thanks for the invite."

Bill ended the call and stuffed the phone back in his pocket. He just needed to finish this last row of shingles, and he'd be done with the roof.

While he hammered the last few roofing nails in, as they often did, Bill's thoughts turned to the image of Joy Whitefox the last time he'd seen her. She'd been walking out the back door of the Morgan farmhouse, her carry-on bag slung over her shoulder, and a broad smile on her face as she headed to the airport to catch her flight to St. Louis. Bill had to use every bit of his strong Marine and FBI fortitude to keep from running after her and begging her to stay. It had hurt when Zoey had broken up with him, but having Joy walk out of his life had pretty much brought him to his knees.

Which wasn't a bad place to be.

Bill had spent more time during the past six months praying and reading his Bible than ever before. He'd found solace and peace in the Words of the Holy Book, and talking out his pain and frustration with God had given him the wisdom to know that if he loved Joy, he had to let her go.

Bill Parker wasn't what she needed right then. Perhaps he never would be what she needed. But God was still going to be with Joy, no matter where she went, and Bill prayed that God would lead her to His will for her life.

The dreamcatcher Joy had given him had a place of honor hanging over his bed, and was a constant reminder of the woman who had wormed her way into his heart and touched his life in ways he'd never imagined. Joy had given the dreamcatcher to him as a parting gift—as a way to ensure he would always remember her—but Bill knew that memories of her would be with him for the rest of his life.

Even if he never saw her again.

In his own world, Bill had found his place in life in teaching. Bill had thought he'd loved his job as a Special Agent working for the FBI, but he had finally discovered that had just been a job. His teaching job and his coaching job—those were his passions. He loved spending time working with the kids in his classes, opening their eyes to the history that had created the great nation of the United States, and watching as their minds absorbed what their ancestors had gone through to give them the freedoms they enjoyed now.

Bill also loved the time he spent with the boys on the junior-high basketball team as their coach. He had a great group of young men that would go far. Even if they didn't, though, he was determined that they would understand the concept of teamwork being the most essential part of the game. And that even though it was nice to win, it was more important to have fun.

The only thing Bill wished was different was the fact that he was living his life alone. He had once prayed Joy would be a part of his current life, but after she'd left town, he'd finally come to the acceptance that Joy wasn't a part of God's will for his life.

It wasn't was *he* wanted, but who was Bill Parker to argue with God's plans?

After finishing the shingle job, Bill climbed down the ladder and stood once again on solid ground, gazing at the house in front of him. Never would he have believed he'd enjoy being a homeowner, but once he'd settled into his new job, he'd known he was ready to put down roots. He had been renting a room at the local bed and breakfast for several months when he'd driven down a side street in

Denning and noticed the *For Sale* sign in the front yard of a house that had immediately caught his eye. And once he'd seen the inside of it, Bill had known he'd found a forever home.

It was the first real home he'd ever had. And once the mortgage was paid off, it would be entirely his.

The house was a two-story Victorian with a porch that wrapped itself around two-thirds of the house. It sported a fresh coat of white paint, but the decorative pieces of the architecture were painted a dark green, making them stand out. He'd worked all summer to paint the exterior and was more than pleased with the results.

Inside, there were three upstairs bedrooms and a bath, and a smaller room downstairs he used as an office. The kitchen was an eat-in kitchen and reminded him of the last house he'd lived in as a child. He had sweet memories of sitting around the worn wooden table in that kitchen with his foster parents and fellow-foster siblings.

In the front entry of the house was an open stairway leading to the second floor. The entry walls were covered with gorgeous oak paneling and trim. It only needed some touching up in places and a good cleaning, and it would glow.

Other than the kitchen, the inside of the house still needed a lot of work, but his vision for the exterior and the yard had drawn him to it the second he'd seen it. Then there was the two-car garage at its side, which was just icing on the cake. Bill had always wanted a garage to putter around in.

Once school was out for the year and summer had arrived, Bill had poured himself into fixing up the old house. It had helped to keep his mind off of Joy—most of the time.

The weeks and months after Joy had gone to St. Louis had been some of the most difficult of his life. He'd wanted so badly to go after her to make sure she was really going to be safe there. Sure the threat of Ernie Wolffe was gone, but that didn't mean she'd be safe. The world away from Bluecreek Ranch and Montana was a very different one than that she'd grown up with, and Bill couldn't help but worry about her.

He'd reactivated the GPS software on his phone to track her necklace just once. The day her plane was due to land in St. Louis, Bill had turned it on long enough to make sure she'd arrived safely. Then he deleted the app from his phone, not wanting to be tempted to regularly check on her. He'd known right then he needed to let her go, and the temptation would have been too great to stalk her if he'd allow himself. Instead, he'd prayed for Joy and turned her over to God. It had been one of the toughest things he'd ever done.

That, and going on with his life without her.

He couldn't say he was over Joy. The old feelings were still there, and something told him he wouldn't ever be entirely over her. What he felt for Joy wasn't like what he'd felt for Zoey Beckett. This was so much stronger. This was a forever feeling.

But until God brought Joy back into his life—if He ever did—Bill was going to have to live with Joy's decision to leave and search for her life purpose elsewhere.

Even if that life didn't include him.

♫ ♫ ♫

The next Saturday night, Bill drove across the cattle guard and down the familiar lane that led to the center of Bluecreek Ranch. He was looking forward to seeing his friends much more than he'd realized. It would be good to spend time with them again and have some adult conversation.

He'd made a few friends amongst his fellow teachers, and had even thought about asking one of the single female teachers out on a date. But then he'd decided he wasn't quite ready for the dating scene yet, and honestly, Bill wasn't sure when he would be.

Just earlier in the week, his assistant coach Carl Hopkins had commented again on Bill's lack of dating.

"You really need to get out and see people, Bill. There are all kinds of single ladies around who would love to have your attention."

"Hmm. Yeah, right."

Bill had tried to ignore the man and had turned his attention back to the team roster on his desk.

"I mean it." The other man had huffed. "Why the school superintendent just hired a new administrative aide, and I hear she's adorable...and single. Maybe you need to check her out."

Bill had shaken his head and glared at the man on the other side of the desk. He'd never lost his temper with his assistant coach, but that was about to change if the man didn't let up.

"Listen, Carl. I. Do. Not. Need. A. Dating. Service. Okay? If I want to ask a woman out, I'll manage it on my own. Got it?"

He knew Carl had meant well, but everyone trying to control his love life was sure getting tiresome. Not that he had a love life, but it was the principal of the thing.

No, tonight he was looking forward to just spending some quality time with people Bill had come to think of as family over the years. And getting a delicious home-cooked meal out of the deal was just a plus.

And as for Julie, Jess, and Mary—they'd better not start with him or try to fix him up with someone, or he'd be leaving the ranch early. His life was just fine the way it was.

He parked his pickup truck next to Sam's SUV in the yard and hopped out, taking a moment to enjoy the view around him. It was nice living in Denning, and the view of the distant mountains from the upstairs windows of his house was enjoyable. But out here on Bluecreek Ranch, everything was so much more wide open. The sky looked immense above him, and the land around him looked as if it went on forever. It didn't matter how many times he saw it, Bill was always amazed.

After enjoying the view a few more seconds, Bill turned around and reached back into the truck and grabbed the small bouquet of flowers he'd decided to buy at the last minute from the local flower shop. Then he swung his truck door around and shut it. He hadn't felt right coming to Morgan's empty-handed, and hopefully, the flowers would get him out of hot water with Julie for not being around more. He'd planned on spending more time there and hang out with Samantha and C.J., but between his job, attending the local church, and working on his house, it seemed his hours were always filled.

Before he reached the front door, it was swung open by Julie Morgan herself, her face wreathed in a huge smile.

"Bill! You finally made it."

He crossed the porch in a couple of steps and reached out with his free hand and pulled Julie into a quick hug. The woman had always felt like a big sister to Bill, and she and Sam were more like family members to him than mere friends.

After they entered the house and stepped into the front entryway, Julie closed the door behind them, and Bill handed her the bouquet.

"For you."

"Thank you, Bill. They're beautiful."

She lifted the flowers to her nose as they headed down the hallway toward the great room. Bill could already hear the timber of deep voices echoing through the high-ceilinged room as they walked through the arched doorway, and his eyes immediately fell on the men seated in chairs in front of the fireplace. Bill headed in that direction, and Sam rose first and shook his hand, patting him on the back.

"'Bout time you show up, Mr. Parker. You've been MIA long enough."

Clay Morgan also stood and shook Bill's hand, his steely gray eyes gazing at him carefully. "Sam's right, Bill. You've been making yourself rather scarce. I know you're a busy man, but don't forget your friends."

Feeling chagrined at the older man's concern, Bill gave him a sheepish smile and a nod.

"Yes, sir. I *have* been busy, but I sure do appreciate the invite tonight."

He glanced toward the kitchen from where delicious smells drifted.

Sam grinned, then headed toward the back door. "Well, now that you've finally arrived, I best go get that grill fired up. Julie will be nagging me soon, wondering when I'm going to get things ready to do the steaks."

Bill tagged along after Sam and Clay as they went out the back door, all the time listening to the two men take up the subject they must have been discussing before his arrival. While Sam got the charcoal in the grill going, Bill took the time to look around the yard again.

The land of the Morgan ranch spread around them in all four directions. He'd asked Sam once how many acres they owned and was simply given a smile while Sam had explained that out there, it was easier to tell how many miles it was to get someplace. Well, the land of the Bluecreek ranch stretched for miles and miles, so Bill knew there was a lot of acreage involved. He couldn't imagine owning that much land.

He raised his eyes to look through the leaves of the tree they were standing near to gaze up at the crystal clear blue sky. Why did the Montana sky always seem so much bluer than anywhere else? Even after living in the state for a while, Bill was still astounded by the night skies of Montana. How could you not believe in a Creator—a loving God—when faced with such beauty?

A few moments later, Julie came tripping down the back steps with a platter covered with rib-eyes and T-bone steaks, which she handed off to Sam—after giving him a smile and a quick kiss on the cheek. Bill released a sigh as he watched the look of love that swept over his friend's face at the sight of his wife. God had blessed two of his best friends with a great marriage. Bill was saddened at times that he hadn't been given that same blessing, but he had still been blessed with good friends, so he guessed he couldn't complain.

Julie patted Bill's arm as she walked by on her way back to the house.

"There are two platters there, Bill. When Sam gets the meat off the one, could you please bring it back into the house? He's likely to get talking shop with his father and forget all about it."

Bill gave her a grin. "Consider it done."

Once Sam had the steaks slapped onto the grill, Bill grabbed the platter and headed into the house with it as Julie had requested. He dropped it off in the kitchen, taking the time to say hello to Lottie Morgan and receiving a hug in return, and she too scolded him for not coming around often enough.

Still feeling the love, Bill had just left the kitchen when the sound of running feet echoed through the house, and he was soon attacked by Sam's and Julie's two children.

"Uncle Bill!"

Six-year-old C.J. Morgan looked up at Bill with a look of adoration which immediately melted Bill's heart—all the while trying to keep his balance as the youngster hugged his left leg.

"C.J., my man. I think you've grown a foot since I last saw you!"

While the little boy hugging his leg giggled, Bill turned his attention to the long-legged girl in front of him. Samantha Morgan had also grown—and was fast becoming a young lady. She had her mother's wavy brown hair and smile, but her father's gray eyes looked out at the world around her.

"Miss Samantha, how's that basketball working out for you?"

"Oh, Uncle Bill! I've been working on my free-throw, just like you taught me." The girl gave him a broad grin. "I think I'm getting lots better!"

Bill gave her a smile, feeling thankful for the opportunity to have a part—albeit a small role—in raising Sam's and Julie's children. They were great kids, and their parents could be very proud of them both.

He'd just extricated himself from C.J.'s grasp around his leg when the backdoor opened, and Zeke and Jessica Mosher and their two youngsters arrived. Again, Bill's hand was shaken, and hugs were given, his former partner's dark brown eyes studying him carefully.

"You've been avoiding us, Billy-Boy."

He shook his head. "Not at all, Jess. I've just been swamped with my job and working on the house."

The twins quickly demanded his attention, calling him 'Unca Bill,' which again melted Bill's heart. The two little guys were also growing fast. There must be something about the Montana air that made kids grow so quickly as Bill sometimes thought you could actually see them grow while you watched them.

Bill also noted Jess's spreading front, feeling awe at the knowledge that she and Zeke were going to be parents again. When Jess had called and told him their big news several months earlier, Bill had congratulated her, yet felt a pang of sorrow that he would more than likely never have a family of his own. He did note that Jess looked good tonight, though, and her smile as she watched her two youngsters run around after C.J. couldn't have been any wider.

After a few more minutes had passed, Bill was corralled into helping the women carry the plates and platters and bowls of food from the kitchen and putting them on the long table. It seemed as if every place was set at the table, and even then, if it weren't for a smaller table set up for the youngsters, Bill wasn't sure there would have been room for everyone.

He'd just carried a bowl of salad to the table when he heard the back door open again and turned, expecting to see Clay or Sam coming in with the grilled meat. Instead, it was Jack and Mary Byrd, and Bill's heart almost stopped when he saw who was with them.

Joy.

CHAPTER 28

Joy followed her aunt and uncle through the back door of the Morgan house, worried again that she should have just stayed back at their cabin. When her Aunt Mary had told her they were invited to dinner at the main house, Joy had been unsure whether she should go or not. As of yet, she'd avoided coming to the Morgan house—not knowing what her reception would be. Oh, she knew Sam and Julie would welcome her. They were always cordial to everyone who crossed their threshold. But in some ways, she felt as if she'd let Sam down somehow by her change of plans, and was still feeling a little guilty about it—even though Sam had assured her more than once that was not the case.

As they crossed the threshold, there seemed to be a lot of noise coming from inside the house. The sound of adults talking and children laughing filled the great room. And as her aunt and uncle stepped from in front of her so Joy could get a clear view of the place, her eyes immediately fell on the tall man standing next to the table with a shocked look on his face.

A look she was sure matched hers.

She hadn't known Bill Parker was going to be at tonight's dinner, although she guessed she shouldn't be surprised. He was one of Sam's friends, and the Morgan family and Bill had always been very close.

But the sight of Bill standing there, straight and tall and handsome, tied her stomach up in knots just like it had seven months earlier when she'd left Montana. She'd never forgotten the man and the way he'd always treated her—like she was a precious treasure, not someone who had been defiled and tainted by what had happened to her.

And evidently, by the butterflies fluttering away in her stomach, just seeing the man again was making her feel the same way it had before she'd left Montana. Which probably wasn't a good thing.

She was sure Bill Parker had forgotten all about the gal he'd helped out when she'd been insecure and scared. Surely he had a girlfriend by now. For all she knew, he was married. She glanced around the room to see if there was another woman present—someone she didn't recognize, and almost released a sigh of relief when there was no one else there.

Dropping her eyes from his, Joy tried to calm her nerves. Because the problem was, even though she'd put miles and miles between them, she was still head over heels in love with the man.

And he didn't have a clue.

♪ ♪ ♪

Bill watched Joy follow her aunt and uncle into the room, his eyes never leaving her face. She looked good. Gorgeous, actually. Tonight she wore a dark blue denim skirt that hung below her knees, her feet encased in leather sandals, along with a white peasant blouse with what looked like embroidery on it. Her raven black hair was braided in one long braid which hung down her back. She looked beautiful and utterly unaware of the effect seeing her again was having on him. He could barely breathe.

And she didn't have a clue he was in love with her—had been in love with her when she'd left Montana. And would, more than likely, be in love with her for the rest of his life.

Julie came into the room from the kitchen and noticed the new arrivals, and hurried over to greet them. When she came to Joy, Bill watched and listened, hoping to discern how long Joy was in town visiting. He'd never heard a word about her coming home for a visit, so her appearance had been a complete surprise to him.

"Joy, dear, how good to see you again. Are you all settled into your new job?"

Bill watched as Julie enveloped the small woman in a gentle hug, then Julie pulled back and looked Joy in the face as she waited for the younger woman's answer. Bill waited too, his heart beating faster than normal.

New job?

"Yes, thank you. I think I'm really going to like it."

Sam and Clay chose that time to bring in the platter filled with grilled steaks, and the next few moments were spent in utter chaos as everyone found a place to sit. Bill found himself seated between Jess and Julie, directly across the table from Joy, which was okay with him as he couldn't seem to see her enough.

It finally quieted as everyone bowed their heads while Clay Morgan stood from his seat at the end of the table to bless the food. As happened every time he was seated around the Morgan table, Bill was enveloped with a sense of love and family and felt the familiar longing in his heart to someday have a family too.

As the prayer ended and Bill raised his head, his eyes immediately fell on Joy Whitefox's face. The familiar draw to her was almost overwhelming, and he yearned for time to talk to her somewhere alone. He had questions. Lots of questions.

Why was she in Montana? Maybe just to visit her aunt and uncle, but she hadn't been in Missouri all that long, so he was surprised she had vacation time coming to her already. And this new job of hers—what was she doing now? How long was she staying, and how was she really doing? Did she have a boyfriend back in Missouri?

Did she miss Bill as much as he missed her? He didn't see there was any way possible the last thing could be true…

"How's the work on the house going, Bill?"

At Sam's question, Bill turned his attention to the man seated at the other end of the table, all the time feeling Joy's eyes on him as his eyes were on her when she wasn't paying attention.

"Good." Bill finished chewing and swallowing the bite of food in his mouth. "I got the last of the shingles on the garage roof, so that's one more thing I can cross off the list."

"You need any help?"

He turned his attention to Zeke. "I'm good, man, but thanks for the offer. Once I get the outside stuff done, I figure I have the whole winter to work on re-painting some of the rooms and cleaning up the woodwork and doing some of the other touch-up jobs on the inside. It should keep me busy when the weather turns too cold to work outside."

Bill noticed Julie look across the table toward Joy as if wanting to be sure to include her in the discussion.

"Bill's bought a house in Denning, Joy. It's really a cute place, although it needed a little work."

He chuckled as he watched Joy's eyes lock on his, an indecipherable look on her face.

"Yeah, a little work." He gave Joy a smile. "It will be a great place when I get everything the way I want."

Joy gave him a smile in return, but never said anything, which disappointed Bill. He had hoped she'd ask questions about the house, or his job, or something. But then again, maybe she really wasn't that interested in the monotonous life of one Bill Parker.

Dessert was served, and before Bill knew it, the meal was done, and the women stood to start carrying everything back into the kitchen, so Bill picked up a stack of dirty plates and followed Joy into the kitchen, her hands also full. Once he'd deposited the dishes on the counter, Bill reached out and lightly touched Joy's elbow to get her attention.

"Hey, can we go someplace and talk?"

Her dark eyes were huge as she turned her head and looked at him, then she gave him a small smile. "I'd like that."

Then she grinned and tilted her head in that cute way she had.

"Say, are you up for a ride, Cowboy?"

Bill chuckled, relishing the sound of her old nickname for him.

"I think I could manage it."

Her smile grew broader before she turned toward her aunt.

"Aunt Mary, Bill and I are going for a ride. Is that okay?"

Bill watched Mary as she looked from Bill to Joy. Her dark eyes sparkled, and Bill thought it looked as if she was struggling to keep from grinning.

"I don't see where that's a problem, sweetie. We have plenty of hands available to help clean up."

Joy turned back toward Bill. "Let me run over to the cabin and change into jeans, and I'll meet you in the barn. Okay?"

Bill nodded, his eyes following Joy as she hurried from the room. After watching her departure, he turned back around to see everyone watching him watch her. Clay, Lottie, Sam, Julie, Mary, Jack, and Zeke all stood around the messy kitchen with silly-looking smiles on their faces. The only ones who weren't there to give Bill googly-eyes were Jess and the children, and he knew Jess would have been if not for the fact that she was in the other room with all the kids.

Finally, Bill took a deep breath and released it, then gave the watching crowd a little smile.

"It appears I'm needed in the barn."

He turned to Mary and Julie. "If I don't get a chance to thank you later before I leave, thank you for a most delicious meal, ladies."

With that, he gave them all a little salute and scurried from the room, heading for the back door before someone made a comment that would embarrass him more than he already was. What was it about women that made you feel like you were an awkward high-schooler again?

Regardless, he was more than anxious to get to the barn and get the horses saddled and ready so that as soon as Joy got there, they'd be prepared to go. He chuckled when he thought about how clumsy he'd been around the horses when he'd first arrived in Montana. He'd sure come a long way.

In more ways than one.

CHAPTER 29

Joy rushed down the familiar path to the cabin, ran through the door, and up the ladder to the loft as quickly as her feet could carry her. As she pulled off her skirt and tugged on a pair of jeans, then a pair of socks and her boots, her mind raced. Her heart had just about jumped out of her chest when Bill had told her he wanted to talk with her someplace...alone.

She hadn't known he was going to be at the Morgan's for dinner, and when she had walked in and seen him there, it had almost overwhelmed her. All the time she'd been in Missouri, Joy hadn't been able to get the tall FBI Agent out of her head. There were so many times she'd wished she'd been able to keep in touch with the man who had filled her thoughts and her heart for so long. But Bill had never phoned her. He'd never sent her an email, or a text, or even an old-fashioned snail-mail letter or card. She'd never heard a word from him. So, Joy had come to the conclusion Bill hadn't felt the same affection for her that she felt for him, so she'd tried her best to forget the man.

But when Joy had seen the emotion on his face this evening when he'd asked her to go with him someplace and talk…alone…well, after seeing that brief look of longing on his face, Joy once again had hope.

Once she changed her clothes, Joy jogged across the yard toward the barn, then slowed to a more ladylike walk as she grew near. Just outside the door, she stopped and tried to catch her breath and settle her nerves, blaming it all on hurrying when she knew it was really caused by the excitement and nervousness of spending time with Bill again.

She'd missed him. She'd missed their talks. She'd missed the way his beautiful blue eyes lit up when he looked at her.

Praying for strength to face whatever Bill had to say to her, Joy timidly entered the barn. Standing at the far end, she was surprised to see Bill, holding the leads to both her horse Spirit and another horse that wasn't Bess. Both horses were saddled, and Bill was casually leaning against the door jamb as he waited for her. She couldn't hold back a smile at the look of him, wearing his cowboy boots and his Stetson. Somewhere along the way, the man had actually turned into a cowboy.

He must have heard her enter because he pushed away from the door and stood straight before looking her way. Her cheeks felt warm as she saw his eyes quickly rove over her before he smiled.

"There. That's the Joy I remember. None of this skirt stuff for my cowgirl."

Joy couldn't hold back the giggle at his words, although she was sure he was just turning a phrase. But how she would love to be his cowgirl.

"You already saddled the horses?"

He nodded, pushing his hat back on his head a little, so she was better able to see his face. "Yes, ma'am, I did."

Then he gave her another one of his toothy grins. "You spend enough time with Jackson Byrd, and I guarantee you're gonna learn all there is to know about horses."

She accepted the lead for Spirit from Bill, then spent a few seconds checking to make sure the saddle's girth was tight. She saw Bill watching her, then looked at the horse he'd saddled to ride.

"You're not riding Bess anymore?"

He laughed loudly, his eyes sparkling with mirth.

"Nope. I've graduated to Buttercup here." He patted the neck of the palomino, who Joy knew was a good horse for an intermediate rider. Not as slow and old as Bess was, but still calm enough to not get a rider into trouble.

"Well then, let's go."

They both mounted their horses and rode through the back pasture. As if they'd discussed it beforehand, Joy realized they were headed in the direction of the river. It was one of her most favorite places on the ranch, and Bill was well aware of that fact.

The two of them rode their horses across the open land, neither trying for conversation. But every now and then, Joy noticed Bill glance over at her and give her a smile. That was enough for her right then. Just being able to go for a ride with the man was more than she had ever expected.

When they came to the river, they both dismounted and led their horses over near the river's edge, tying the reins to a branch so the animals wouldn't wander, although Joy didn't think any of the horses on the ranch would do so. Jack Byrd was adamant about making sure every horse was trained to ground tie—merely dropping the reins to the ground should make most of them stay put. But there was no sense taking a chance when there was a branch to tie them to. It would be a long walk back to the barn.

Joy followed Bill over to a fallen log near the river's edge and sat down next to him. There was a moment of what felt like awkwardness between them as Joy wondered if she should talk first. But then again, Bill was the one who had asked *her* to come.

When she finally couldn't stand it any longer, she started to ask, "So you bought a house?" at the same time he asked, "So, you got a new job?"

They looked at each other and laughed, and suddenly, the awkward moment was gone.

"You first," she said quietly, her eyes locked on his beautiful blue ones.

He took a deep breath and released it, looking away for a moment before turning back to face her.

"Yeah, I bought a house in Denning. Now that I'm teaching there, I decided it was time I put down roots. It's the first real home I've ever had."

She smiled. It was easy to tell how much it meant to a man who, as a boy, had been shuffled from one foster home to another to finally have a place to call his own.

"That's great. I'm very happy for you." Then she added, feeling unsure about doing so, "I'd love to see it sometime."

That brought a big smile to his face. "I'd love to show it to you."

It was quiet again for a few seconds, then he spoke again, his eyes even bluer than she remembered as he looked over at her.

"How about you? What's this I hear about a new job?"

Joy chuckled. She couldn't believe he hadn't already known about her job. Surely Julie or Sam or someone would have mentioned it to him by now.

"I'm the new administrative aide to the superintendent of the Denning School System."

She saw the surprise cross his face. Bill really hadn't known.

"Here? You're working *here*? In Denning? At the school?" His eyes grew large, and she thought for a moment there was moisture there, then he smiled.

"How did I not know this? I can't believe the Denning school grapevine has so badly failed me!"

Laughing a little, Joy reached out and tentatively touched his bare arm, relishing the feel of his muscles under her fingertips. She knew she was being bold but suddenly didn't care. She needed to touch the man, to know for sure that he was real.

"I've only been back home for about two weeks."

His eyes dropped to her hand on his arm, then raised again, the smile evaporating as a more serious look crossed his face.

"I thought your dream was to get away from here—to go to the big city and make a life for yourself someplace else. So why did you come back to Montana, Joy? "

She gulped when she saw the disappointment in his face as he threw the words back at her that she'd said to him all those months ago. He was correct, of course. She had told him all those things.

"I was wrong, Bill."

Pulling her hand away from his arm, she sighed and turned to look out over the river flowing by them. Right then, she couldn't stand to look at his eyes and see the pain there. She hadn't known she was hurting him when she'd left. How selfish she'd been.

"The job in St. Louis was a good job, but one day, as I sat at my desk in a little office with no window and no fresh air, I realized how homesick I was."

She looked out over the land toward the mountains in the distance. She tipped her head back to gaze at the vast sky above her and closed her eyes for a moment before opening them and turning back to look at him.

"I missed the open sky, the fresh air, the sunshine, the freedom of riding on the back of a horse whenever I wanted to across an open prairie." She paused for a second before she added. "And I missed you, Bill."

She heard the intake of breath from Bill and saw his eyes widen, then he was holding both her hands in his large ones.

"I've missed you more than I can tell you, Joy."

She saw the muscles in his jaw work as he clenched and unclenched his jaw. It was easy to tell his emotions were as high as hers were.

"I knew I had to let you go chase your dream, just like I'd gone after mine, but it was the hardest thing I've ever done to not beg you to stay. It just about killed me to say goodbye to you."

Joy sniffed a little as she felt the tears building behind her eyes. This man had come to mean so much to her.

"So, where do we go from here, Joy?"

His words surprised her as she'd just been wondering the same thing herself. She didn't want to be just a friend to Bill Parker anymore. She wanted so much more.

Before she even thought about what she was doing, she pulled her hands from his and reached out and put them on both sides of his face, feeling the scratchiness of a day's worth of beard there. Then she pulled him toward her, placing her lips lightly on his, relishing the taste and the smell of him. And losing herself in the feeling of finally knowing what it was to love a man and knowing he loved her back.

♬ ♬ ♬

Bill was afraid to move as he felt Joy's soft lips land on his. He closed his eyes as a cascade of emotions rushed through him, then opened them as she pulled away, her dark eyes studying his face for his reaction. Without a moment's thought, Bill put his arms around her waist and dragged her to him, and this time the kiss wasn't the brief touch of a butterfly's wings but that of a man in love. When they eventually pulled apart, he was left breathless, knowing this was what he'd been searching for in a relationship.

"Well," Joy's voice was quiet, but he caught the note of teasing in it. "Guess that answers your question, doesn't it, Cowboy?"

He chuckled, the sound releasing him from all the worries and cares of his life. Now that Joy was back, that was all that mattered.

"I believe it does. So, to use an old-fashioned term, Miss Whitefox, I would like to court you."

Bill grinned, feeling at least ten years younger as he looked over at the love of his life. "I want to get to know you better and give you a chance to get to know me." He frowned as another thought crossed his mind. "Although, if you get to know me better, you might change your mind about wanting to have anything further to do with me."

The tip of her index finger was suddenly on his lips as if to silence him.

"I know plenty about you, Mr. Parker. I know you're a man of faith, a man of bravery, and a man of integrity."

Bill felt a measure of pride at the three words that made up the letters of the F.B.I. Those words had always meant so much to him.

"I also know you care about people—about family—about your students." She grinned. "I've been hearing good things about this Mr. Parker, who is a history teacher, and this Coach Parker, who is training young men about the importance of teamwork."

Her smile grew gentle. "And I know you are a man who I can envision spending the rest of my life with."

He had to grin when she dropped her eyes as if she suddenly felt shy about having shared that with him. What a graceful, lovely, humble woman she was.

"Well, then." He lifted her chin. "I think we need to spend a great deal more time together, Ms. Whitefox."

Then he added as an afterthought, "And I think I need to meet your father."

At those words, he saw her eyes widen and turn dark.

"It will not change my opinion of his daughter. But I want him to know who I am, and that you are the most important thing in my life."

Feeling brave, Bill added, "I want him to know the man his daughter is going to marry someday soon."

Joy's eyes widened even further, but they sparkled with happiness this time instead of fear as she gave him a little nod.

"I think that can be arranged."

He dropped his hand from her chin and smiled. "Good."

Then he pulled her closer to his side and kissed the top of her sun-warmed head.

"Do you think the folks back at the ranch have any idea what we're talking about out here?"

He could feel her body vibrate with laughter before he heard her chuckle.

"What do you think, Cowboy? They're the ones that invited us both tonight."

Bill grinned as he gazed out over the river. Yes, they had. And sometime soon, he needed to thank each and every one of them.

CHAPTER 30

Joy walked up the two steps that took her to the stage area at the front of the church and accepted the mic from the pastor, trying to calm her shaking hands.

She couldn't believe how nervous she was. It wasn't like this was the first time she'd ever sung in front of the congregation. But every time, it felt like the first.

Finally, she closed her eyes and listened as the first few notes of the music came through the speakers. She sent up a silent prayer that God would use her voice and the words of the song to reach someone listening—to bring them closer to Him than ever before.

When she finally opened her eyes, they fell on a handsome man sitting in the audience. A man who had touched her heart and her life in ways she never would have expected. Joy had been so sure after being attacked that no man would ever want her, but God had proved her wrong.

She and Bill Parker had dated for almost a year before he'd asked her to marry him, but Joy had known from the start that he was the man for her. Then one Saturday afternoon, she'd walked up this very aisle to become his wife.

The wedding had been a simple affair—just the way Joy had wanted it. She'd worn a simple ankle-length white dress and carried a bouquet of wildflowers she'd picked near Bluecreek River earlier that morning. Even though the ceremony had been simple, the wedding had been attended by practically everyone in Denning as both she and Bill were well-known by so many because of their involvement in the school.

The day of their wedding had been beautiful, soon followed by a fantastic trip to Arizona. They spent a week visiting the Grand Canyon and several other places before returning to Denning and the beautiful house that Bill had worked so hard on. Now, Joy was spending her days making it into a real home for them. And hopefully, someday soon, they would be filling the old house with their children.

But the best part of the wedding had been her father's attendance. Not only had Clarke Whitefox come to the wedding, but he had agreed to walk her down the aisle. And it hadn't happened yet, but Joy was praying that one day soon, her father would come to the saving knowledge of Christ. He was so close to making a decision to surrender his life to God; she just knew it was going to happen. When that day came, there would certainly be cause for praise and singing.

As the lead-in to the song finished, Joy began to sing the familiar words.

"...*Through many dangers, toils and snares, I have already come; 'Tis grace hath brought me safe thus far, and grace will lead me home...*"

Joy poured her heart out through the words, knowing that for her, they were true. God had brought her through so much and had given her so much more than she'd ever expected. And she and Bill both knew that whatever they faced in the future, His hands would continue to comfort and guide them every step of the way.

She closed her eyes as she sang the old hymn, all the time feeling the Spirit of God descend on her like a whisper, almost as if giving her a blessing.

During the final stanza, when Joy finally opened her eyes and her eyes locked on Bill's, she felt the smile on her face grow broader. She continued to sing her song of praise, thankfulness, and joy to the God of her life.

And Joy couldn't think of a more beautiful song to sing.

OTHER BOOKS BY RUTH KYSER

Mattie's Heart
(Book 1 in *The Morgan Family Saga* series)

Clara's Heart
(Book 2 in *The Morgan Family Saga* series)

Laurie's Heart
(Book 3 in *The Morgan Family Saga* series)

The Dove & The Raven –
A Christian Historical Romance

Endless Season

True Cover (Book 1 in the *True Cover* series)
Bluecreek Ranch (Book 2 in the *True Cover* series)
Second Chances (Book 3 in the *True Cover* series)

The Whispering Sentinel

The Healing Hills

Without Regrets

A Place Called Hart's Desire

September Skies – A Christian Romance

The Town Named Christmas

One Last Christmas

Oatcakes, Tea, and Me

Marcie's Mountains

If you've enjoyed reading *Joy's Song*,
please go to Amazon.com and/or Goodreads and leave a review.
You can contact me directly at ruth.kyser@gmail.com
I LOVE hearing from my readers!

Thank you in advance, and God bless you!